I0658464

DANGEROUS DECEPTION

AN UNBRIDLED ADVENTURE

by

CINDY MCDONALD

DANGEROUS DECEPTION

For information call: 304-285-8205
or Email: cindys.mcdonald@gmail.com

This book is a work of fiction. Names, characters, places, and incidents are products of the author's imagination or are used fictitiously. Any resemblance to actual events or locales or persons, living or dead, is entirely coincidental.

Designed by Acorn Book Services

Publication Managed by Acorn Book Services
www.acornbookservices.com
info@acornbookservices.com
304-285-8205

ISBN-10: 0985726741
ISBN-13: 978-0-9857267-4-4

Printed in the United States of America

For Shane

Yes the character in the Unbridled Series is named for my grandson.
People have asked me if he is anything like the character, and I tell them,
"I don't know yet. The real Shane is ten years younger than the
character, Shane."

Acknowledgements

There are many people I wish to thank that had a hand in the publishing and pre-publishing process of *Dangerous Deception*.

My dear friend and confidant, Linda Taylor, who always reads my manuscripts before they go to my editor—thank you for all of those wonderful "suggestions" of yours—I don't know what I'd do without them!

I wish to thank my wonderful publishing manager and fellow author, Lauren Carr, for her constant support and insightful editing; and the creative genius behind this fabulous cover, Todd Aune. Thank you to those at Acorn Book Services that worked behind-the-scenes on my behalf.

Last but certainly never least; I want to thank my husband, Saint Bill, your love and support always takes my breath away. Thank you.

TABLE OF CONTENTS

Prologue.. 13-16

Part One: *Severance Pay*
   Chapter 1 through Chapter 6 .... 17- 70

Part Two: *No Escape Clause*
   Chapter 7 through Chapter 12 .... 71- 132

Part Three: *Iron Horse Warriors*
   Chapter 13 through Chapter 20 133-196

Epilogue.. 197-203

Special Bonus: *Against the Ropes* (excerpt) 204

About the Author...211

"Grudges are like hand grenades—it's best to release them before they destroy you."—Barbara Johnson

"Old age takes away from us what we have inherited and gives us what we have earned."—Gerald Branan

DANGEROUS
DECEPTION

~ Prologue ~

As usual on Wednesday night, Barney's Bar and Grille was quiet. Barney's was a small hometown bar that sat along the highway between Lanzville, and the larger town of Rosemount. There was nothing fancy about the place, but it was always busy on Friday and Saturday nights. The square block building was painted a pale yellow with the words, "Barney's Bar and Grille" scrawled in black across the front. Barney was a huge Steelers fan.

Scanning the bar, Captain Patrick Lutz of the Rosemount Police Department pressed through the doors. His eyes fell upon Jack, a tall, muscular biker sitting in a dark corner booth. Lifting the corners of his mouth into a slim smile, he nodded casually at the bartender on his way past the long bar.

The only customers in the joint were a dark-haired man and a tiny sable-haired girl. Stretched toward each other on the bar stools, they nuzzled and whispered over their drinks.

Lutz slid into the booth. Glancing around the bar, he passed a brown paper package across the table to Jack Haliday.

Jack was good—damned good. An ex-Navy SEAL, Jack knew how to run a covert undercover operation. His military-style haircut had grown out to sweep against his collar. His clean cut face now sported a bristly beard that almost touched his chest.

"You've been keeping a close eye on Laura, I trust." Jack stuffed the package into the inside pocket of his black leather jacket.

"I stop in every night on my way home from the station. She misses you. She's hoping you blow this gang wide open before that baby comes." Lutz settled back against the booth.

Casually, Jack dropped his face into his chest when the bartender approached to deliver two beers. Wishing for a razor, he scrubbed his beard with his fingers. He also longed for the warmth of his wife's body against his.

He waited for the bartender to walk away before replying, "Six months is one hell of a long haul. I'd love to see her, but I can't risk going by the house."

"You've made a lot of progress," the police captain said. "Gunner must trust you enough to let you leave the pack to get drugs. When do you rendezvous?"

Gunner was the leader of the Nomads. A ruthless killer, he was on the top of their most wanted list. He was careful about whom he allowed into his pack, but Jack had broken through the barriers.

They were close to making a bust—very close.

Jack downed the beer in one long guzzle. "Couple days at the mansion. I'm picking up some guns for him from a friend. I'll be checking that operation out real close while I'm there."

"Where? We've got to know your location, Jack." Lutz's brows were pinched in concern.

"Don't know yet, I'll be in touch." Jack stood to leave.

The door of the bar opened.

The abrupt entrance kicked-in their cop-alert. Both Jack and Lutz glanced over to see a small crowd spilling through the door with Lieutenant Carl Lugowski amongst them.

"I'm outta here," Jack said.

"I'm having a beer with Lugowski." Lutz gestured to the police lieutenant strolling toward the booth. "See if he recognizes you." An ornery grin crossed his face.

With a snort, Jack parked his dark glasses onto his nose, stuffed his hands into his pockets, and strolled across the bar to shoulder his broad six-foot-one physique into Lugowski.

"Excuse me, dude," Jack said in a low tone while continuing toward the door.

Annoyed, Lugowski shot him a glance. Saying nothing, he hesitated to watch the cocky biker strut out of the bar. He took note of the artwork on the back of his jacket—a skull with scorpions scurrying from the dark haunting eyes sockets.

Nomads.

He flinched when a hand clapped onto his shoulder.

"Did you see the bike that guy was riding, Lugowski?" Shane West asked in total awe. "Harley Fat Boy—sharp. By-the-way, I wouldn't have messed with him either," he needled on his way to the pool table in the middle of the lounge. Shane's buddies were chalking-up their pool sticks and waving at the bartender for a round of beers.

The rumble of the Fat Boy's engine roaring to a start in the background drowned out Travis Tritt's voice filtering from the jukebox.

At the bar, Martin Krebs became annoyed when he noticed his sable-haired sweetie preoccupied with the young man at the pool table. Perched on the bar stool, her spine had stiffened and her eyes scanned him with a sultry smile on her lips.

With his sandy hair and crystal blue eyes, Shane West was dangerously handsome. His broad shoulders eased into lean hips. His defined jaw accentuated his rugged good-looks. The youngest West, he was a study in chewy charming man candy. At twenty-three, he was already notorious for his playboy antics.

A new jockey at Keystone Downs Racetrack, Ginger LaFond was interested in the handsome young man for more than his good-looks. His father, Eric West, owned a huge Thoroughbred operation, and that meant high quality mounts.

The sandy-haired chunk of hunk didn't look like a bad mount either.

Yum.

Unable to steal her gaze away from him, she leaned in toward Krebs for confirmation of the young man's identity. "I've seen that guy at the racetrack. Isn't he one of the Wests?"

Krebs' face wrinkled in distaste. "Oh yes, that's Shane West. He's—"

"That's what I thought." She hopped from the stool and adjusted her sweater while strutting toward the pool table to cozy-up next to Shane. "Can I buy you a drink?" She purred.

Shane glanced down at the five-foot-two, attractive, shapely girl. A thin frock of her hair brushed across her deep brown eyes. "Isn't that usually the other way around?" From out of the corner of his eye, he caught a glimpse of his friends' lifted brows.

Ginger agreed. "Uh-huh. Do you want to buy *me* a drink?"

Rolling their eyes, his buddies groaned. They figured Shane would be out of the pool game for the evening. They were right.

"You're not here with anyone?" Shane took note of the fierce stare that Krebs was shooting at them from the bar.

"Nope, just little ol' me," she insisted with a lift of her shoulder. She latched onto his arm and guided him toward a booth at the far end of the bar while ignoring his friends' disgruntled moans, and Krebs' loathsome gape.

PART ONE:

SEVERENCE PAY

~ ONE ~

The early morning sunshine trickled through the tangle of branches of the grand oaks that lined the driveway of Westwood Thoroughbred Farm. An ashen mist climbed from the valley below the long, white barns with blue tin roofs, surrounded by pristine white fences. A soft breeze wisped through the trees to drizzle dew from the lush green leaves.

Shane meandered down the driveway from the Victorian farmhouse that seemed to keep a vigilant watch over Westwood from a knoll above him. Munching on a piece of toast, he made his way toward the barn to embark on his daily ritual with the Thoroughbreds.

He showed up at the barn around seven every morning. Well, he tried to get there by seven. Sometimes, he tapped the snooze button three or four—Okay, six times before rolling out of his cozy bed.

His mornings consisted of saddling and leading horses to the training track to clock their workout; followed by saddling another Thoroughbred and leading it to the training track and clocking that one's workout.

Yada, yada, yada.

A long yawn escaped while he stretched his back and glanced down at his watch with a melancholy sigh. It wasn't that he was lazy or uncaring. Shane loved Westwood as much as his close-knit family—Siblings

Mike and Kate, and his father, Eric. His demeanor was more casual than the rest.

"It's what comes of being the youngest," his father always surmised.

Shane was never quite sure if his father was hinting that the youngest child was the most spoiled of the lot. If he were being honest, his father may very well have a valid point.

He hesitated in his walk toward the barn when his gaze fell upon Martin Krebs.

Sipping a cup of coffee, the stable hand was lounging under a tree. Hiked up on one elbow, his legs stretched out with his left leg crossed over his right, he could have easily been Webster's definition of "contentment."

Martin Krebs had the easy-going smile and a smooth voice of a motivational speaker. His brown eyes screamed "sneaky," and his smile was as devious as a snake. Everyone seemed to be sucked into his game of charming manipulation, but Shane wasn't convinced. He didn't trust Krebs anymore than a "friendly" pit-bull.

For the stable hand's benefit, Shane checked his watch again.

Krebs' relaxed gaze met Shane's. He nodded at him as he approached. Shane's purposeful gesture had not been lost on him. Indifferent to young West's intolerance, he continued to enjoy his coffee and the gentle breeze on his face.

"Kind of early for a coffee break, ain't it, Krebs?" Shane said with a set jaw.

The left side of Krebs' mouth lifted. "I was simply enjoying the beautiful morning, and the stunning view of your impressive farm."

"How about you enjoy it from the end of a pitchfork?" Shane suggested. *Wow, how about that? I'm sounding just like my old man. Eh, not such a bad thing—especially right now.*

Krebs didn't like being ordered around by someone at least ten years his junior. *The kid thinks he's the shit. He's a West, and that makes him damned important.* He kept his eyes locked with Shane West, whom he considered to be nothing more than a pesky little mosquito in need of squashing. *Not today. Today, the little punk is my boss.*

He lifted his body from the cool grass beneath the comforting shade of the oak tree. With a thin sigh, he shuffled to the barn while taking the last gulp of his coffee.

Knowing that this would not be his last run-in with Krebs, Shane watched his retreat. Oh no, it was plain to see that Martin Krebs was the proverbial thorn in his side. He wondered if the stable hand would soon graduate into his cross to bear.

Lagging a few feet behind, Shane followed him into the barn and took a right into the office. Behind the desk, Mike was dialing the phone.

To a stranger's eyes, these two West boys were nothing alike. With dark shaggy locks and hazel eyes that could cut you in half when he was agitated, Mike was strikingly handsome. They shared the same square jaw and broad shoulders. However, Mike possessed a no-nonsense demeanor, while his younger brother was a liberated spirit. Oh how Shane loved to goad his sibling. He was so damned easy to get a rise out of.

"Getting a haircut anytime soon?" Shane asked with a smirk. Mike's locks would skiff his collar when his schedule became tight and the Thoroughbreds were demanding.

Continuing to dial, he glanced up at the clock above the desk with an arched eyebrow. "Ahhh, look who's here. You made it by seven-thirty. Congratulations. By the way, Ginger LaFond called for you about fifteen minutes ago."

Shane's eyes brightened. "She's a good rider."

"I've heard."

Shane noted the sarcasm in his tone. "I'll be checking that out."

While listening to the phone ring on the other end, Mike cocked his head. "No surprise there."

More sarcasm. "Aren't you ripe this morning?"

"I've got to make a deal with old Wolfgang Whitmore right now," Mike said.

"Sucks to be you."

Shane watched his brother's uneasy expression as Mike tapped his fingers on the desk while waiting for the phone on the other end to pick up. Leaving Mike to his suffering, he snatched a bridle from the tack rack on the wall opposite to the office and made his way through the barn.

Scuttling about, stable hands toted fresh buckets of water, led horses from their stalls to the equi-cizer, and returned them to their freshly cleaned stall.

Once again, Shane spotted Krebs at the end of the long aisle. His foot propped up on an empty wheelbarrow, the stable hand was sipping yet another cup of coffee while leaning against the wall.

Oh yeah, he's up to his usual no-work-for-me-today policy. Agitation skittered up the nape of his neck. *Firing Krebs is gonna be the highlight of my week.* Gritting his teeth, he flung the bridle over his shoulder and marched toward him.

"Buenos dias, Shane." Carlos Rivera's voice broke his stride and intentions. Lugging two buckets of water, the pudgy Mexican stable hand stepped into his path. When he grinned at him, his chubby cheeks, sporting stubble from the day before, swelled over his ears. "Punch saddled that horse in stall ten for you," he said in his heavy accent.

Shane kept his eye on Krebs, who was sipping that coffee while smooth-talking a stable hand into mucking the next stall for him as well. Damn if it wasn't working. *Sonofabitch.*

"You did want the horse saddled, did you not, Shane?" Rivera asked.

"Yeah, yeah, thanks, Riv," Shane said. "Have you seen Vic this morning?"

Rivera hitched his chin toward a stack of hay bales at the end of the aisle, beyond where Krebs was schmoozing. Shane followed the stable hand's gesture before returning to scrutinize Krebs, who was still loitering instead of working. With no effort, he was conning the stable hand into pitching manure into the wheelbarrow that he had his foot resting on.

Walking past Krebs toward the bales, Shane hesitated, but did not turn to face him. "Hey Krebs, will this coffee break be over anytime soon?" he asked in a loud, irritated tone, while continuing down the aisle.

Scowling, Krebs pushed off the wall. He flicked Shane off behind his back.

Rivera sat the buckets down next to him. "I brought this bucket for your stall, Krebs."

"He's an arrogant little bastard." Krebs leaned in close to Rivera. "He struts around like he's lord and master. Do this! Do that! I know what I'd like to do to him." He shoved his hand to Rivera's temple as if it were a gun. Using his finger to pull an imaginary trigger, he imitated an exuberant explosion into the Mexican stable hand's ear.

Rivera chuckled. "Not in this lifetime, mi amigo. Are you dumping this bucket or what?"

"And spoil your fun? No way, dude." He stepped out of the way and swept his arms toward the stall. "Please, be my guest, good man." Snorting and shaking his head at Krebs' dramatic grand gesture, Rivera willingly dumped the fresh water into the horse's stall.

✽ ✽ ✽ ✽

Slightly built and all of one-hundred-and-ten pounds, Victor Deveaux was a staple at Westwood Thoroughbred Farm. He was an old codger of sixty-one, but he possessed the heart and spirit of a young, intrepid man. Vic wasn't in the habit of mincing words with anyone. Nosiree, he spoke his mind in a brusque manner. His thin hair was dirty grey. His old blue eyes were narrow, and set close together. His dimples were deep when he smiled and his nose was crooked from a bad break. Bow-legged, he walked with a limp.

Shane could hear Vic snoring strong and steady when he rounded the hay bales. The bristly hay cradled his head and his mouth hung wide open.

Shane urged a half-smile at the old-timer. "Yo! Vic!"

His eyes jerked open and his hand shot to his face to rub his left eye. "Got a piece of hay in my eye." He pushed his stiff, rigid body from the bale that he was resting on.

"Uh-huh, you ready to work this mare? Or, is it too early for you?" Shane goaded the old man.

Vic wasn't having it. "Listen, smart ass, I was working horses at six a.m. long before you was born."

Shane waved his hand in surrender. "I know, I know, Vic."

"You see any of those young riders here, yet?" Vic demanded to know.

"They're out on the track already," Shane murmured.

"What?"

"I said … we're almost ready."

On Thursday mornings, the Wests trained their horses at the farm, rather than at their stables at Keystone Downs.

It was Eric West's favorite day of the week. He would throw his rough-out saddle on his old Quarter Horse, Ike, grab a travel mug of fresh hot coffee; and then sit at the far end of the training track in the outrider position to wait for a rider to lose control of a mount. Booting Ike in his sides, they would dash down the track until they were galloping alongside the Thoroughbred. Eric would grab the reins, and the team would slow the renegade horse to a stop.

Eric and Ike were affectionately referred to as Bert and Ernie more times than not, especially by Eric's daughter, Kate.

They weren't out on the training track this particular Thursday morning. Eric was committed to a meeting at Keystone Downs. So Punch McMinn, the West's farm manager, and his old chestnut gelding, Cody, were standing in for the dynamic duo.

Ike knew it was Thursday and he wasn't taking his benching in stride. He snorted and pawed in his stall when Punch led Cody went past. There was no fooling the wise old Quarter Horse. Poking his head into the aisle, he searched for Eric. He was most irritated that Cody was leaving the barn, and he was left behind with a lousy pile of hay in the corner of his stall.

"Sorry, old boy, no action for you today." Punch patted his neck while passing the stall. He felt sorry for the horse.

Compassion was part and parcel to Punch McMinn's demeanor. The size of a linebacker, he was a huge black man. He commanded the facade of a bully, but he was a soft-hearted, gentle soul.

He glanced over his shoulder at Ike, who looked sad. *I'll bring him an apple when I come back.*

Punch caught a glimpse of Mike in the barn office. With his elbow on the desk, his cheek propped up against his fist, Mike was still negotiating with Old Man Whitmore. Yes, he was looking worse for the wear. Punch chuckled to himself. *Mike has his hands full with that tough old bird.*

Punch threw his leg over Cody, settled into his saddle, and urged the gelding down the winding path beneath the canopy of trees toward the training track.

The air was fresh, the breeze was soft, and the early morning mist was starting to dissipate. The rumble of horse's hooves and the cadence of their snorting with each bound came into ear shot as they drew closer to the training track.

"*Thursday morning just won't be the same without Eric and Ike,*" Punch found himself thinking as the track came into view.

Ears perked, Cody broke into a trot toward the gate, where Shane was struggling to control a nervous, wide-eyed mare while Vic fidgeted in the exercise saddle.

Clutching a clipboard and a stopwatch to her chest, a young stable hand named Delaney leaned against the railing. A tomboy-type of girl, she wore her long brown hair in pig-tails.

Shane pulled back on the mare's reins while waiting for an opportune moment to lead her onto the track amongst the exercise riders galloping horses.

"Where's Mike?" he called to Punch.

"In Whitmore Hell. Is Delaney doing the timing this morning?"

Delaney turned with an ear-to-ear smile and a nod.

A grin swept across Vic's craggy lips. "You out-riding on that ol' nag? He'll never hold up. How old is he anyways?"

Punch smiled. His eyes narrowed. "Eighteen, and this old boy could catch that mare anytime, old man."

"Bah!"

The mare's agitation was piqued. She tossed her head and danced in place while pounding and pawing with her front hooves. Arching her neck, she pulled on the bit.

Like the mare, Vic's patience was all used up. He poked Shane hard in the shoulder with his crop. "C'mon, butercup, let's get this freaking party started."

Sucking his lips together hard, Shane pressed his shoulder into the hyped mare's chest to hold her back.

Punch snickered at Shane's frustration. He wasn't sure who he was agitated with more. Vic or the mare?

Shane's blue eyes hardened. He was biting down on his tolerance. "Okay, okay, Vic. Be careful. She can be a real bitch."

"Yeah, yeah, yeah!" Vic smooched to the anxious Thoroughbred.

Eyes wide and nostrils flared, the mare darted onto the track amid a half a dozen galloping horses. She clenched the bit between her teeth, yanked on the reins, and bolted down the track. She weaved through the crowd.

With his old arthritic hands, Vic tried to gather the reins in tighter. He pulled and tugged in an attempt to reel the mare into a controllable pace.

She flattened her neck, extended her nose, and kicked into a higher gear. Wildly, she whipped in and out of the horse traffic.

Stunned riders waved their arms at Vic while calling out in Spanish, "Lo que el infierno es el asunto con usted?" *What the hell is the matter with you?*

He couldn't answer. He had his own quandary to deal with. "Whoa! Whoa! You damned demon witch!" He pulled with all his used up might.

Shane's brows furrowed. "What the hell is he trying to prove?"

"I dunno." Punch was baffled at the old man's out-of-control riding.

Delaney whipped the binoculars to her face. "He's in trouble. You'd better go get him, Punch, before he causes a major pile-up!" She watched the riders trying to get their mounts out of the way of the runaway mare at the far end of the track.

Punch slapped the old chestnut gelding across the rump with his reins. Cody dug in with his hind quarters. He leapt forward, and darted down the track. Punch couldn't help but think how pissed-off Eric would be when he learned of the excitement he missed on this particular Thursday morning. Oh yeah, Eric and Ike enjoyed a good chase, but

Cody owned the chase this morning. The old boy was tearing it up like a young feisty colt.

Cody was breathing heavy when they caught up with the mare, but he was game. He galloped alongside her. Punch stretched from his saddle to reach for the reins.

"Get away!" Vic hollered, "I don't need no help!"

"C'mon, Vic!" Punch stretched farther out of his saddle to grapple for the reins.

Vic's pride was in jeopardy. He had been a jockey forever. *I'm a damned good rider, and I don't need some crazy, half-witted cowboy running my mount down for me.*

Snorting hard, Cody thundered forward to match the mare stride for stride. Snatching at the reins, Punch stretched. Each time he almost seized them, Vic pulled them from his reach. Abruptly, the mare lugged in to push Cody against the rail.

Vic's temper had reached crescendo. Grabbing his crop from his boot he swung it furiously at Punch. "Get away! I said, get!"

Punch raised his hand as the crop cracked down across his wrist.

Cody's eyes bulged at the sight of the thrashing whip. Ducking the threat, he jumped sideways, stumbled, and then slammed into the racing rail.

Punch tumbled from the saddle, flipped over the railing, crashed to the hard ground on the other side, and rolled over the embankment.

Cody slowed to a walk. The reins dragging in the dirt beneath him, he limped around the track on three legs.

Shane sprang into a dead run across the track and vaulted over the rail. Slightly dazed and gasping for the breath that had been knocked out of him, Punch rolled over. He tried to focus on Shane, until he caught a glimpse of his old horse hobbling toward the rail.

"Christ!" Shane grabbed Punch by the arm.

Seeing Delaney, with a somber droop on her lips, approach Cody to place a comforting hand on his shoulder; Punch waved Shane away. He managed to push to his knees to get a better view of his old friend receiving help from Delaney.

Vic finally managed to rein the tired mare down. Glancing over his shoulder, he took in the damages left in his wake. Immediately, he noticed Punch cradling his left arm while climbing over the railing with Shane's assistance toward the injured Quarter Horse. He could feel the burn of stares boring into his back from the other riders on the track. He could hear the malevolent tone in their Spanish chatter. Bowed and arthritic, his knees whined in pain when he jumped from the saddle to lead the mare toward the calamity.

"What the hell did ya think you was doing, ya damned fool?" Vic shouted when he approached them.

Punch glared at him. "Listen, you old—"

"Vic! Your freaking stubbornness is wearing thin. Delaney, take Punch to the hospital—" Shane said.

"I'll be all right." Punch wanted to take his horse to the barn and care for him personally—the way Cody deserved to be cared for—the way only *he* could care for him.

"Bullshit! That arm's busted. Just shut-up and go." Shane had the Eric West "tone" going full throttle.

He turned. "Vic..." The harsh words caught in his throat. He could see the sullen expression that absorbed Vic's eyes. The old man had caused a wreck. Vic knew who was to blame. Shane could see the re-morse leaching into the old man's stubborn brain. He softened his tone. "Get that mare back to the barn."

Eric West scrubbed his chin while watching the debacle on the training track from a hillside near the barn. He had arrived home early from the meeting in time to witness the wreck that his old friend, Vic, had caused. He drew in a deep rueful breath.

Vic had been a top rated jockey in his hey-day, but let's face it; glory days are as fleeting as youth.

It took some serious convincing, but Delaney managed to persuade Punch to remain at the emergency room until his arm was properly cared for. She assured him that Kate would do everything she could to make Cody comfortable, and that the Wests would be upset if he didn't have his arm tended to by a doctor.

Delany watched Punch fidget in his chair, expel long sighs, grumble under his breath, and attempt without success to read last year's swimsuit issue of *Sports Illustrated*.

Delaney feared that at any moment he was going to march out of the door, which would force her to tackle him. She wasn't real confident on how that would turn out.

Finally, a petite, pretty blonde nurse called them into an examination room. Punch's sheer size was most daunting, but as the little blondie nurse escorted him to the exam room, he was a true gentleman. He blew off his long wait as "not a problem, I understand," when she gushed with apologies. In the next breath, she inquired if Delaney were his wife.

Subtle.

After an X-ray, the doctor happily informed him that the arm was not broken, but merely cracked. He cradled Punch's arm in a sling and instructed him to take it easy on that arm for a couple weeks.

Delaney snickered when the little blondie nurse tossed Punch a smile while stuffing a note with her phone number into his sling before she let him exit. *Oh, brother, blondes. They think size has everything to do with size. Hmmm, actually I kinda wonder the same thing, myself.*

Noticing her looking at him oddly, Punch tossed her a bemused glance. Embarrassed by the notion, she shook the thought from her mind. Terrified that she was blushing, she shoved his truck into gear and sped out of the hospital parking lot. *Enough of that, already.*

Is it possible for the day to get any worse?

Shane strode through the door of the equine swimming facility at the far end of the barn.

Unable to strike a deal with Old Man Whitmore, Mike helped his sister, Kate, to bandage Cody's front left ankle. An assistant to veterinarian Doc Spears at the racetrack, she was very concerned over the swelling in the ankle. "It doesn't look too promising," Shane heard her tell Mike.

Cody is a good ol' boy. Punch will be broken hearted.

The afternoon sun gleamed through the arched windows that surrounded the perimeter of the equine swimming facility to spark and shimmer off the water in the pool. The hum of the pump and the cloying smell of chlorine greeted Shane when he entered the pool room. The sound of splashing and snorting caught his immediate attention.

Krebs was swimming a bay gelding. He walked along the rim of the curved-in pool holding onto the long guide pole attached to the horse's halter, while the gelding swam along below him in the water.

That was nothing unusual—until Shane noticed the wide-eyed panicked look in the horse's eyes. Krebs had not noticed his presence, so he paused to see what was really going on.

Wearing a sadistic grin on his face, Krebs poked the horse in the face with the end of the guide staff. He was teasing and torturing the gelding while it struggled to swim faster and faster in order to escape the prodding. He snickered at the animal's anxiety and discomfort.

Sonofabitch.

Rife with rage, Shane bolted across the room and seized the staff from Krebs' hand. Startled by Shane's sudden presence, he flinched.

"What the hell are you doing!" Shane yelled.

Krebs displayed a crooked smile. His eyes were blood-shot and half-lidded. "I was just trying to make him go faster," he explained with the lift of his shoulder.

Shane winced at the stiff smell of whiskey on his breath. This thorn had indeed graduated to a cross—a big one. "You're drunk."

"Inebriated."

"Fired!"

Krebs liked the sound of that. Shane West was officially no longer his boss, no longer the keeper of his paycheck, and no longer off limits to a good ass-kicking. Tossing the young man another apathetic shrug, he turned as if to walk toward the door. Then, without warning, he clenched his fists tightly together, spun on his heels, and slammed Shane in the back.

Shane arched and then hurled into the pool near the pumping hooves of the spooked Thoroughbred. Frantic, the horse pounced up and down in the water.

Through the chlorine sting and the bubbles, Shane could see the horse's sharp hooves thrashing in the water. Pushing away, he surfaced for a breath at the same time Krebs dove into the water on top of him. Holding Shane by the throat, the stable hand drove him back down into the water.

Shane wrapped his fingers around Krebs' wrists and ripped into his skin with his fingernails, but his grip was unyielding. Fighting against the choking, the lack of air in his lungs, and the nip of the chlorine in his eyes, he reached up and managed to force Krebs' head back by the chin.

Unexpectedly, Krebs let go to surface for a breath.

Shane pushed off the bottom of the pool to surface to suck air into his burning lungs, only to immediately be forced to dive under again to escape the fifteen-hundred pounds of harried horseflesh swimming right at him.

When Shane came up, Krebs clobbered him in the face before grabbing him by the hair to slam him back under. Unwavering and merciless, he held him there.

No air, and with no real opportunity to get any, Shane could feel his body giving-in to exhaustion and unconsciousness. His lungs burned like hell fire while begging for a breath.

Barely able to hold on, barely cognizant, Shane could hear a stifled voice above the water yelling, "Krebs! Let him up! Let him up!" Then he felt the splash, and submergence of another body in the water. After a struggle, Krebs' hands released their grip. Mustering the awareness to swim to the surface, he gasped, coughed, and searched desperately for the edge of the pool.

Two frenzied Thoroughbreds ran around the pool, one was dry, the other wet. Somehow the horse in the pool had broken through the bridge that lay over the opening to the ramp to climb out.

Shane clawed at the smooth edges of the curved-in pool until he finally found the bearings to hoist himself out. His soaked clothes and boots weighed him down. He worked to breathe and to focus his eyes on the two men wrestling in the pool. The water splashed violently.

Mike jacked Krebs against the far wall of the pool. His nose was bleeding down his lips and over his mouth from the jabs Mike had wielded. Krebs hiked his feet up, braced them against Mike's chest to shove him across the pool. Diving on top of him, Krebs pushed Mike toward the wall of the pool.

Still huffing for air, Shane scrambled to grasp a pole resting next to the edge of the pool. Krebs shoved Mike against the wall. Much to his surprise, Mike head buted him to knock him back into the water. When Krebs surfaced, he was dazed and greeted by the clip end of the pole pressed hard against his throat.

"Like I said, get the hell outta here," Shane managed to say in spite of his dry and raspy throat.

Krebs shot Mike abrasive glance before lifting his fatigued body from the pool. His dark hair clung to the sides of his face. He blinked the chlorine from his eyelashes, and glared at Shane through bloodshot eyes. Hesitating before he turned to go, he pointed his finger at Shane. Silently, he forewarned him with a malicious stare that he was tired and he was beaten, but he wasn't finished.

Finally, he jerked his gaze away, and staggered out of the door.

Shane reached his hand over the edge of the pool to his brother to clamp wrists and help him out. Water spattered over the floor when Mike collapsed on the rim next to him.

His chest rising and falling hard, Mike huffed and puffed from exertion. Water dripped from his hair, his chin, and off his chest and shoulders to form a puddle around him before trickling into the pool.

"Thanks bro," Shane muttered.

Breathless, Mike nodded.

~ TWO ~

Keystone Downs Thoroughbred Racetrack was the cornerstone of Victor Deveaux's life. The racetrack was his family, and the horses were his children. For over thirty years, he arrived in the early morning to exercise his mounts. Rain or shine or snow or sleet, Vic could be counted on to gallop the horses over the track, and report back on their progress. Over the years, Vic had ridden many mounts for various stables. He delivered those mounts into the winners' circle for some of the top name stables at Keystone. Westwood Stables was the only big name that he still mounted-up for, and he found that he was being utilized less and less.

Mike preferred Sebastian O'Terra, a young Italian rider with an excellent win percentage. Mike or Punch would still send Vic out on a few horses every morning, but they were mainly the older horses that O'Terra didn't have time for. Vic rarely ever rode in a race; he had become more of an exercise rider than a jockey these days. A hard pill to swallow, it was a demotion he was forced to accept.

"God, it sucks to get old," Vic often thought. It was catching up with him, and was rapidly becoming an undeniable reality.

Vic steered his Ford Ranger into the parking lot, heaved his tired body from the vehicle, and made his way through the shed rows toward

Westwood Stables on his stiff bowed legs. Enjoying his favorite time of the day, he breathed in the sights and smells of the back side of the racetrack. The stable hands were dumping buckets into the roadway and saddling wide eyed youngsters raring to explode onto the track to show their stuff. The pigeons warbled and wobbled about. Steam rose into the morning mist from the heaping manure bins in the roadways between the shed rows. Horse's hooves were *clip, clip, clop and clopping* against the pavement. The Thoroughbreds snorted and tossed their heads on their way to the track. Finally, there was the Spanish prattle of the exercise boys calling out to one and other.

This was the life pulse of Keystone Downs. Vic had been a part of it for so very long, and he couldn't imagine his life without it. A gentle breeze whisked through the shed rows to blow the smell of fresh manure from the bins into his nostrils. Even the smell of fresh horse shit gave him a sense of comfort and belonging.

He snatched his scarred and battered riding helmet from the tack rack inside the stable door. He was tightening the leather strap around his chin when a heaping, overloaded wheelbarrow rolled into the barn aisle to smack into his legs and flip onto its side. Its load dumped over the aisle way.

"Sorry buddy," he heard a voice call from inside the stall. The voice sounded old and decrepit.

Cursing under his breath, Vic leaned against the wall and tugged at his riding boots now filled with the very horse shit that he didn't mind smelling. He did mind it inside his boots.

"Vic, Victor Deveaux. How the hell have you been, man?" It was the same decrepit voice.

He looked up from his boots to find an old bent over man with weathered leathery skin and white hair smiling at him. Stymied, he studied the face for a moment. The old man looked to be about sixty-three, or so. Like Vic, he was small: five-foot-two and he looked to weigh-in at about one-hundred-and-twelve, maybe.

The man straightened a little and grabbed his hand.

Vic looked into the dark eyes of the Mexican-American man until recognition suddenly washed over him. "Jose Torres?" He glanced at the wheelbarrow. "What are you doing here?"

"Started yesterday. Came in a week ago from Saratoga. I'm living in a trailer, number twenty-three, at the park. I was working for Doug O'Conner, but he's such an asshole. Eric offered me a spot here, so I took it." He smiled from ear to ear.

"Why aren't cha riding?"

"Riding?" Jose chuckled and smacked him on the shoulder. "I quit riding years ago."

"But you was a good rider, Jose." Vic's mind drifted to younger days. "Remember when your saddle slipped during that race? You rode that damned filly's neck all the way to the finish line." Slapping Jose's shoulder, he burst into laughter.

Jose laughed right along. "I beat your ass."

"Sure did."

Jose shook his head at the memory, "Ahhh, that was a hundred years ago, mi amigo."

Gloom bled into Vic's tone. "But mucking stalls, Jose? Ain't there nothing else you could do?"

He threw his hands up. "Like what? All I know is horses. I was a good jock. But now …" Lifting a shoulder, the old man glanced down at the turned-over wheelbarrow. "I'm too old. Too slow, like you, old boy." He laughed.

"Bah!"

❧   ❧   ❧   ❧

Certain things don't work quite as well as they used to when you enter middle age—specifically your eyesight.

A broad shouldered man of fifty-five years of age with a spatter of grey through his dark hair, Eric West stood over his cherry desk while rummaging through the drawers. After peering under a pile of paperwork, he searched the floor around his desk.

Mike leaned against the wall with his arms folded over his chest. Finally, he picked up his father's glasses, which were resting next to the phone. He held them out to him. "Looking for these?"

Eric was stunned to discover they were right before his eyes. "Thanks." Ignoring his son's smirk, he snatched them from his hand.

Eric noticed Shane's edgy mood. He fidgeted in the wing-back chair, got up and paced, and then plopped back down into the chair. Firing Krebs the day before could have been poking at him, but Eric couldn't figure why.

The guy was a slug. He should have been fired weeks ago.

Then again, Shane had asked him to invite Vic Deveaux to the house for a discussion this afternoon, but he hadn't gotten around to explaining why. Concluding that the core of Shane's dour disposition had everything to do with his aged friend, Eric rubbed his hand across his chin.

He had been thinking about Vic a lot lately, especially after the accident he had witnessed the day before. He hadn't told anyone that he had seen it. Vic was an old friend, reliable and strong; but his age was getting in the way of his work. He needed to slow down. Perhaps he needed to take an easier position on the farm.

"Did you manage to cut a deal with Wolfgang?" Eric asked Mike.

Mike drew a deep breath. "Finally. He wants five-hundred grand, cash on the barrel, when the mares are delivered."

Shaking his head, Eric chuckled. "He's a product of the depression, Mike. Cash is the only thing he trusts when it comes to horse deals." He sank into the leather chair behind his desk. "Mmmm, that's a lot of money to have in the safe. We have to make sure the house is locked up at all times." He glanced up over the rim of his glasses to find Rivera standing in the doorway of the study.

Rivera wore an ill-at-ease expression. "Perdone me por favor, the front door was open."

Clearing his throat, Eric shot his sons an arched eyebrow. "It's okay, Riv. what do you need?"

He pulled a bottle from his pocket. "Doc Spears dropped off some medicine for Cody. I thought I should bring it in before I leave for the day."

Mike ducked his father's scolding glance. "Thanks, Riv." He took the medicine. "Please close the door on your way out."

Glancing around the spacious study, Rivera took note of the safe in the wall behind Eric's desk. He nodded at the group as he turned to leave.

The front door clicked closed. "Like I said," Eric ordered, "let's keep the front door locked, or—at the very least—*closed*."

The grandfather clock in the foyer chimed four times. Shane's jitters couldn't be contained any more. "Dad, I really need to discuss Vic with you before he gets here."

"Vic Deveaux has been with us for a very long time, young man, what's the problem?"

Shane exchanged glances with his older brother. Mike's expression seemed to be saying, "Go ahead, have at it, dude." What he was about to say wasn't going to go over well.

The history between his father and Vic went too far back. Vic had been more than a prize-winning jockey in the past. He was a good friend and confidant. That was the root of the problem. .

Eric leaned far back in his chair, crossed his arms over his chest, and waited with a steely look over the brim of his glasses.

Mike had taken a seat on the sofa for the show.

Hell, it's time to just come out with what needs saying. Shane drug in a braced breath. "Vic can't handle the young horses anymore."

At this point, Mike laced his fingers together behind his head and settled deeper into the sofa. Helping him handle Martin Krebs in the pool yesterday was one thing, but it seemed Shane was on his own when handling their father.

Thanks, bro. "Look at what happened to Punch," Shane said. "Vic's stubbornness caused that whole accident, and it could've been worse."

"That's true," Mike said.

"I'm just sayin' ... I think it's time to leave certain things to the younger riders." Shane expelled a heavy sigh. "My point is, there's got to be something else around here that he could do."

"Yeah, give him something cushy, like ... Shane's job," Mike said in a snarky tone with gleam in his eye.

Shane turned to his older brother. "Ba-ha-ha-ha-ha!"

Knowing that his son was right, Eric tossed his glasses to the desk. *It's definitely time to discuss the option of managing the new breeding program that I'm planning to initiate with Vic. The mares that I'm purchasing from Wolfgang will be fine candidates for the stallions that I have in mind. Hey, Vic may have a few suggestions as well.*

"All right, all right, you've made your point. I'll talk with him," Eric said.

Shane was relieved.

Mike wasn't too convinced that the outcome of that conversation would be pleasant.

The cell phone in his pocket rang as Rivera stepped out of the house onto the front porch.

The call ID read: *Maria Rivera*.

Rivera sighed. His ex-wife wanted her support money, her rent money, and probably money for groceries. She wanted money that he didn't have. Not anymore, anyway.

Carlos Rivera liked to play the slot machines at the Keystone Casinos, located next to Keystone Downs racetrack. Unfortunately, he didn't know when to call it a night, or cash-out when he was ahead, which was rare. He didn't even have the money for his own rent. That meant keeping one step ahead of his landlord.

He wasn't in the mood to listen to Maria yap at him about his irresponsible nature, or what a "slug" he was. She really liked throwing around the term "deadbeat dad". Maria wasn't wrong. He simply didn't feel like hearing about it.

Rivera pressed the *IGNORE* button and continued down the steps toward his ratty, rusted-out Impala, where Krebs hunkered down deep in the front seat, as he sucked on a beer while waiting for him.

"Took you long enough," Krebs said when Rivera slid into the driver's seat.

"I wish I had the problems that the West's have." Shaking his head, Rivera turned the key in the ignition.

Krebs chuckled. "What kind of problems could the West's possibly have?"

The old car sputtered and then jugged to a start. "Eh, they've got a shitload of money in the safe, and nobody knows how to close a freaking door."

Krebs sat up in his seat. "Define 'a shitload'."

"Five-hundred-grand, amigo, I could sure use that kind of coin."

Krebs leaned back against the headrest. "Mmmm, I hear that."

❧ ❧ ❧ ❧

Henry David Thoreau once said, "None are so old as those that have outlived enthusiasm."

The very sad part of that quote was that Vic Deveaux never outgrew or outlived his enthusiasm for life, or for what he did for a living. A young fearless man screamed and kicked and fought like hell to survive inside Vic's stiff, aching body.

Aging is not an option, not for anyone. It is how gracefully we handle the process and how lucky we are, as the process handles us.

Vic had run out of luck.

The study was quiet. The soft glow of the brass lamp on Eric's desk was the only light in the room. Eric rested his chin on his knuckles, where he had laced his fingers together with his elbows on his desk. Staring at the blank computer screen, he contemplated the conversation he would soon have with his old friend.

Thoreau's words would be of little comfort to Vic. Nor was Eric sure that Vic would easily accept his offer of managing the expanded breeding operation, if at all. Vic could be hard-headed, stubborn as an ass, and difficult to convince. He was a "my way or the highway" kind of guy.

Just this once, Eric was hoping that Vic would see things in reality's light. It was time to embrace some of those life changes that they'd been warned would be coming, sooner or later.

It was later, but it sure as hell felt like sooner.

There was a rap at the front door. Eric pushed away from the desk. *Showtime.*

When he opened the door, Vic stood on the front porch with an old weathered smile on his lips. "You wanted to see me, Eric?"

He offered his hand and Vic shook it with a solid grip.

That was Vic—solid.

"Come in, Vic, come in." Eric cupped his hand on his shoulder while gesturing with the other hand toward the study.

He weaved around the desk and opened the beveled glass door of the liquor cabinet to remove one of his best bottles of brandy. After pouring the golden liquid into glasses, he handed one to Vic, and then raised his up. "Here's to glory days ..." He winked at his friend. "... and glorious women."

They chuckled and, savoring the flavor, downed the brandy.

Vic was a man who didn't beat the bushes. He furrowed his brow and looked Eric square in the eye. "What did ya want to talk to me about, Eric?"

He searched Vic's face for the right words. Funny, he had hours to gather the words, but they were strangers to him now. He urged a half smile. "You know, Vic, we sure aren't getting any younger ..." He poured another brandy for both of them. "I'm going to be fifty-six next spring."

Vic tipped his glass. "Just turned sixty-one, myself," he said with pride before downing his drink, after which he let out a satisfied breath.

Eric leaned a hip against the desk. "You know ... there comes a time when we need to slow down. Maybe leave the harder stuff to that younger generation."

Vic's eyes narrowed. Eric's subtle paradigm wasn't lost on him. "Whoa, if this is about yesterday, Punch never gave me a chance to get that mare in hand."

"Those young horses are getting tougher nowadays with all the new-fangled supplements. I was thinking maybe—"

"I'm a jockey, Eric. Now, if you and your boys don't think I'm good enough anymore, just say so," Vic said loudly.

"It isn't that, Vic. You just don't have the strength—"

"Are you *firing* me?"

"Of course not, I have a different job for you."

Vic waved his hands in front of his chest. "Like Jose Torres? No, Eric, that's not how I roll. I'll move along. You owe me for twenty gallops. That's two hundred bucks."

"Damn it, Vic, stop being so bull-headed. Sit down. We can iron this out."

Vic turned for the door. "I don't need to sit, and there ain't nothin' to iron out. I'll stop by tomorrow for my money." He slammed his glass down on the desk and marched toward the foyer.

Shane stepped into his path. "Don't blame dad, Vic. I talked him into giving you a different position."

Vic's eyes seethed at the young man. His lip twitched with anger. "Let me tell you something, young thang. I didn't ask to get old. It just happened. Someday you're gonna look in the mirror, and that pretty boy face of yours is gonna be worn and wrinkled just like mine. It's damned hard to swallow."

Roughly, Vic shouldered past him. After stomping out the front door, he slammed it behind him.

Eric poured himself another brandy and threw it back—hard.

~ Three ~

Jack Haliday learned patience during his time as a Navy SEAL.

Impatience could get you nailed—or worse—killed.

Gunner's contact had called Jack several hours ago to instruct him to meet them behind an old abandoned warehouse with a black swan painted on the front. Jack had arrived to find a long line of warehouses. It was like a mini-mall of huge rusting monsters crumbling among the high weeds that surrounded them.

The huge black swan with the regally arched neck stood out among them.

The gentle *clack ... clack ... clack* of an old ventilation fan far above his head grabbed his attention. The fan slowly rotated seemingly on it own. There was no wind. No breeze at all. It was as if phantoms breathed onto its paddles.

The contact was an hour late.

Jack was hoping he hadn't been made. While waiting it out, he was forced to call upon his patience. He leaned against a tree that overlooked the wide, quick-running creek known as Reardon's Run.

Thinking about Laura, he peeled away the layers of leaves from a long weed. It had been six long months since he had seen or touched his lovely, pregnant wife. Last night, just before dusk, he parked his

Harley two blocks from his home. From behind a tree across the street, he watched for a glimpse of her.

Mr. Wabash, the next door neighbor, dragged his trash can to the curb around seven-thirty. He then retrieved their trash can from behind their house and dragged it to the curb, as well. Mr. Wabash was a good neighbor. Jack appreciated him helping Laura out in his absence.

Finally the wait paid off, and he saw her.

Laura opened the front door to wave at the kind man. "Thanks, Mr. Wabash," she called across the lawns.

"How many times do I have to tell you, girl? Call me Walter," he replied with a wink before going into his house.

Laura stepped onto the small front porch.

Lord, she's a sight. Seven and a half months pregnant, she's sticking so far out the front that it looks like she could burst at any moment. The sight of her urged a loving smile on Jack's lips.

After patting her pregnant belly, she picked the dead-heads off the impatiens overflowing from the hanging basket. Before she stepped into the house, she scanned the front yard.

It was almost as if she could sense that he was close by.

How he wished that he could call out to her to tell her how much he missed her. Of course he would also have to take the opportunity to needle her about that big belly. He knew exactly what would happen, what she would say. She would narrow her eyes, plant her hands on her hips, and say, "Don't make me hurt you, Haliday."

The rumbling sound of a vehicle approaching jerked Jack from his thoughts. As Laura's image faded from his mind's eye, he looked up. An old rusted white panel van squeaked and moaned over the bumps, and through the deep potholes along the rough dirt road behind the warehouse.

Jack straightened and pushed away from the tree. Wearing black ski masks, two men armed with semi-automatic handguns jumped from the van. "Hands up," one commanded.

Jack complied.

After relieving him of his gun, the man patted him down. "Where's the bag?"

"In my saddle bags." Jack nodded his head toward the motorcycle parked beyond the tree.

The man rifled through the saddle bags attached to the Fat Boy until he came up with the brown paper package that Lutz had provided. Tucking it into his jacket, he smiled and handed Jack a black sack. "Put this over your head, and get in the van."

Jack gauged him and the other man. His eyes rotated to the van. In the driver's seat, a bearded man smoked a cigarette. "What about my bike, dude?" Jack asked.

The man threw the sack over Jack's head, grabbed him by the arm, and shoved him to the van. He heard the back doors open. Both men grabbed him by the arms and tossed him in. He heard their heavy footsteps next to him when they climbed in. The doors squealed and then slammed shut. The van pulled forward to bounce and sway through the ruts and bumps.

Face down, Jack rested on the floor. He could feel the tip of a gun against his ribs. *Either these guys are super careful, or I'm a dead man.*

⚜ ⚜ ⚜ ⚜

They drove for about an hour before the van came to a stop. The doors opened.

Jack was yanked out, and then hurried into a building, where they pulled the sack from his head. The bright fluorescent lighting washed over his face.

Trying to adjust his eyes to the light, he blinked to focus on the huge room filled with weapons—all kinds of weapons. There were two long tables in the middle of the room. The table at the far end was piled with AK-47's, M16's, flash grenades, hand grenades, and flame throwing guns. The second table held the handguns: Glocks, Berettas, and Colts were lined up in a row like mighty warriors marching into battle.

Unsure of his success, Jack tried to subdue his amazement. He hadn't seen an arsenal such as this since his time as a SEAL. This operation needed to be stopped—a long time ago.

"Sorry about the sack, dude. Gunner knows the drill. Can't be too careful, ya know." A gray-haired man sitting at the table with the handguns said. His voice was as rough as sandpaper. His straggly hair hung wild and wiry to his wide waist. He wore a strikingly white wife-beater T-shirt, and his arms were covered in tattoos. Both wrists were clamped with black leather cuffs decorated with turquoise gems.

His pudgy hands worked with a tiny grinder in milling away serial numbers from the guns.

On the table next to him, a square glass ashtray was filled with cigarette butts. A single trail of smoke snaked upward from the ashen tip of a fresh cigarette dangling on the edge.

While speaking, he didn't turn to show his face to Jack, nor did he hesitate from his chore. Guarding his every move, the two gunmen flanked Jack's side while keeping their ski masks in place.

"Gunner must be tired of the drill. He usually comes himself." The gray-haired man paused for only a second to inspect his handiwork. "He must trust you. I'm not sure that I like that. Where's the final payment?" He extended his right hand out.

The masked man to Jack's right dug into his jacket and produced the brown paper package to slap it into the gray-haired man's hand.

He ripped the paper, dipped his chunky pinky into the white powdery substance, smelled it, and then licked it from his finger. "Prime. The case of guns is there." He picked up the cigarette from the tray, took a drag, and then flicked the ashes toward a large black case at the end of the table.

The same masked man took it up.

"He'll be happy with the product, as will his customers. Now get the F out of here."

Once again, the sack was tossed over Jack's head. The men clutched his arms to haul him back to the van. After tossing him in the back, they closed the doors and pulled away.

Well, that was productive. I didn't find out a freaking thing. They're a cool bunch of customers. Cracking this group was going to keep him away from Laura even longer than expected.

Patience.

~ FOUR ~

Kate West wasn't happy. She had hoped that after a night's rest the swelling in the old gelding's ankle would have gone down at least a little. But this morning she took in Cody's very swollen ankle with her hands planted on her hips. The old horse wouldn't put any weight on the leg. When she checked his feed bin, she found that he hadn't eaten a bite since yesterday.

Not a good sign.

She dug in the pocket of her jeans and pulled out a hair band. She gathered her long blonde hair back to twist it into a knot, and then wrapped the band around it. Pinching her lip between her teeth she dragged her gaze to Punch.

He patted Cody's neck while waiting for her diagnosis.

Eric stepped into the stall. "How's it looking?"

Kate drew a braced breath and let it out slowly. "I'm thinking he has a badly cracked sesamoid."

Punch's face and shoulders dropped.

"I also think we should ship him to the track to have Doc Spears X-ray him," she added.

Eric bent down to take a look at the ankle. When his knees cracked loudly, he hesitated at the sound. He was feeling very much like the old horse. Perhaps a little used-up, but not necessarily ready for the pasture.

Punch laid his head against Cody's jaw. "He's been such a good ol' horse. I hate to think I'd have to—"

"Let's not go there, just yet." Eric rose to a standing position. He would've rather gotten up faster, but his knees weren't having it. "We'll get him to the track immediately."

"I'll hook-up the trailer." Punch took a step toward the stall door.

Eric touched the shoulder of his sling. "*I'll* hook-up the trailer."

❦ ❧ ❦ ❧

Mike was glad to get home. After setting down the briefcase filled with five-hundred-thousand dollars he'd drawn from the bank; he locked the front door, and then proceeded to the safe in his father's study. He would be mighty relieved when the money was securely locked away.

This is a ridiculous situation. He stuffed the money from the briefcase into the safe. *Wolfgang Whitmore is a fool not to accept a cashier's check.* He slammed the door and twisted the latch to the lock position. *Now the old codger not only has to trust his driver to deliver the money to him, but he also has to hope that nothing goes wrong—like a robbery between Pennsylvania and Kentucky.*

In Mike's book, that was a shitload of trust and luck. Relief in the knowledge that the money was secure had just washed over him when there was a firm rap at the front door. He gave the lever to the safe one last tug to make sure it was closed tautly, and then jogged to the door.

Vic was surprised to hear the mahogany door unlock before Mike pulled it open. The front door of the farmhouse was never locked during the day.

"Good morning, Vic." Mike tried to sound upbeat. He felt bad about the circumstances with the old family friend. Vic had been at Westwood for so long that Mike couldn't remember the horse farm without him, and wondered how it would feel when he was gone.

Maybe now would be a good time for some damage control.

Vic was stiff. His old eyes were hard, "Mornin' Mike. Is Eric around?"

Leaning against the door jamb, he shoved his hands in the pockets of his Levis. "No, they took Cody to the track for X-rays."

A tug of remorse rolled through the old man. "How is he?"

"Not too good, I'm afraid. Kate thinks it might be a cracked sesamoid."

"I'm sorry." Squaring his shoulders, he drug in a deep breath. "I'm here for my money."

Stepping aside, Mike waved his hand to invite him inside.

Vic followed him into the study. He gauged Mike while he searched his father's papers to find an envelope on top of the payroll manifest in the middle of the desk.

Biting his lip, Mike tapped the envelope against his fingers for a moment. "Vic, we really don't want you to leave. Dad was thinking that you might—"

"Just give me my money. I'll collect my riding gear, and be out of your way."

"Vic, let's be reasonable—"

"My money." Glaring into Mike's eyes, he jerked his hand straight out with the palm up.

Stubborn as a damned mule. Extending the envelope out to him, Mike let out a long deep sigh.

Vic snatched it from his hand and then turned to leave.

"Where are you gonna go?" Mike asked out of concern and respect for this man that had always been there.

Vic turned back to him with a look in his eyes that Mike had never seen before. It was contempt. "You think you're the only stable at Keystone Downs?" With one last coarse glare, he stomped out of the house.

The view of Westwood caused him to pause on the porch that over-looked the lush green paddocks, and the long white barns with blue tin roofs. The branches of the old oaks danced gently in the breeze. He loved this farm—Westwood.

Eric's father, Matthew West, had hired Vic as an apprentice jockey when no one else would. Matthew was a risk-taker. That quality turned Westwood into a force to be reckoned with. But, as the years went by, his drinking became the force that destroyed the greatness that she had enjoyed. Westwood tumbled into ruin.

After Matthew's death, Eric picked up the pieces to put her back together.

His lovely wife, Barbara, worked with the young horses. She was gentle. It was almost as if she could communicate with them with a touch, a look, or a tender whisper.

Michael was only three when his parents took over the reins of Westwood after his grandfather's death. So serious, he was a feisty little cuss. He could always be found scurrying at his father's heels in the barn.

Then, Kate came along. With blonde piggy tails and dazzling blue eyes, she was the bright spot in her father's world.

It was Shane who was so attached to his mother. He loved to work the youngsters with her, and his love for the winners-to-be grew as strong as Westwood did.

The memories burned in Vic's gut like a wicked fire devouring his soul.

The yearlings bucked and raced and nipped at each other in the paddocks. Ready to be broke, they would be next year's two year olds. Shane would be busy. Vic would miss it all. But he wasn't pushing no freaking wheelbarrow.

No way in hell!

His memories were jogged by the sound of the front door locking behind him. He glanced over his shoulder. *What the hell's going on around here?*

He made his way toward the barn to take in his last look at his old friend, Westwood. His riding boots crunched along the gravel in the parking area behind the barn.

It was almost ten in the morning. The barn help would all be gone until evening, so he wouldn't have to explain or offer good-byes. He was feeling most relieved about that, when he heard raspy whispers and devious snickering.

Scanning the parking area, his gaze locked on Rivera leaning against his Impala to pass a bottle of whiskey through the driver's side window.

Asshole.

His eyes narrowed. Vic could see someone hunkered down deep in the car. He shrugged in disdain. Wanting to get away from Westwood and the memories that he had made there, He hurried to his Ford Ranger.

"Hey, Vic," Martin Krebs called from inside the Impala. "What's the rush?" His voice was smooth as a Sunday morning evangelist.

Vic stopped. "What the hell are you doing here, slacker?"

"Riv let me borrow his car for the day. I came back to pick him up." Krebs furtively looked about. Satisfied that no one was around; he sat up to lean out the window. "Ahhh c'mon, Vic, chill out. Have a little nip with us," he cajoled.

Vic searched the barn area, and shrugged a shoulder. "What do I care?" Battered, hurt, and torn in half, he flopped against the car next to Rivera to take the Jack from his hand. He sniffed the bottle.

The left side of Krebs' mouth turned up and his eyes twinkled. He tossed Rivera a stealthy wink.

"We heard how the Wests fired you yesterday. That's cold, man," Krebs said as if he really gave two shits.

Vic raised the bottle of Jack up. "That's horse racing, boys. There ain't no excuses, and there sure as hell ain't no severance pay." He took a gulp.

Rivera shook his head slowly while staring at the rocks beneath his feet. "After all those years—just don't seem fair."

"Mmmm," Krebs sympathized. His tone shifted to up-lifting and optimistic. "What if you could get some severance money? What would you think about that, Vic?"

"What the hell are you yakking about?"

Krebs glanced at Rivera with a gritty grin on his mouth, and a plan etched in his eyes. Rivera urged him to continue with a confident nod. "Old Man West's got five-hundred-grand stashed in his safe."

Vic looked at him like he'd grown another eye. "I don't think so ..." It became clear to him. Mike had to unlock the door to let him in, and then he relocked the door after he had left. Mike was being cautious. Now he knew why.

"He's expecting a shipment of prize broodmares from Kentucky. The owner is demanding cash." Krebs said with cool complacency. "Riv over-heard their conversation yesterday afternoon."

Oh yeah, it's all making sense now. Vic chuckled. "Old Wolfgang Whitmore. So what?"

This is where it got tricky. This is where Krebs had to seduce Vic. He licked his lips, leaned in close, and used his smooth as silk influence. "So … Riv and I pick up Shane. Then, you visit your old pal, Eric, and you tell him to open up that safe … or else."

Vic blinked back. He braced himself against the car. His jaw dropped. "Get outta here. I've done some things in my life that I ain't proud of, but kidnapping? No freaking way." He shoved the bottle into Rivera's chest, and pushed away from the Impala.

Krebs reached through the window, seized him by the arm, and yanked him hard against the car.

"Why the hell not? He kicked you to the curb. He said you weren't good enough anymore. No gold watch. No 401-K. Just pick up your pay and we'll see ya around the manure pit, old man."

Beads of sweat formed on Vic's forehead. There was truth in Krebs' words. He glanced around the farm with a bitter burn in his eyes. "Get your head out of your ass, girls. Five-hundred-grand ain't that much money."

"Seriously? Have you got that kind of cash lying around? I don't. It sure could come in handy with being unemployed, such as we are." He lowered his voice to a purr in Vic's ear. "It's right over there in that house. Easy money, Vic. C'mon, are you with us?"

Vic swallowed hard. His thoughts were jumbled. Just then, Jose Torres pushed a heaping overloaded wheelbarrow of horse shit from the barn toward the manure bin. Late morning, he should be done with stalls by now.

"I'm too old. Too slow, like you, old boy …" Jose's words from yesterday throbbed inside his head. They were frightening words, more frightening today than they were yesterday. Yesterday, they were merely words, today they were his reality. He watched, as Jose dumped the load, rubbed his lower back, and then slowly, stiffly dragged the wheelbarrow back inside the barn.

Laughter rose in the distance. Vic turned. Shane was leading the mare that he had been riding the other day. He was laughing and joking with a little sable-haired female jockey who had he'd seen hanging around the track like a piranha looking for mounts. Smiling and flirting with Shane, she was mounted on the mare while he led her toward the training track.

Scowling, Vic pulled a red bandana from his pocket to mop his brow. He reclaimed the bottle of Jack from Rivera's grip and took a quick swig.

Yessiree, it's all becoming crystal freaking clear.

"He won't get hurt, right?" he asked his motley conspirators.

Krebs' eyes gleamed. His lips curled. "As much as he needs a good ass kicking, we only want the money. We won't touch a hair on his head."

"Give me the details, crackerjack."

Frowning, Doctor Ben Spears studied the X-ray that they had taken of Cody's ankle. It wasn't unusual to see the old veterinarian to scowl. A crotchety old man in his mid-sixties, he had been the head veterinarian at Keystone Downs for almost forty years. His hair and his eyebrows were white. Slightly bent over, he moved painfully slow.

He leaned back in his chair and cupped his chin in his hands.

Seeing what he saw, Kate sighed.

"Well, Ben?" Eric asked.

"The sesamoid is cracked, sure enough," he said. "Time and stall rest. That's all you can do for him, I'm afraid."

"And then ..." Punch asked.

"Young horses have a tough time after an injury like this. I shouldn't have to tell you that, Punch." Doc Spears peered at him over his bifocals. "What can I say? He's old."

Kate's heart broke for the big man. She wrapped her arms around Punch, and gave him a consoling squeeze.

The hammering in his chest wouldn't let up. Sweat dripped down his temples. Vic continually mopped his brow with the damp bandana while he followed Rivera's old Impala along the back roads.

I'm really gonna do this. I'm in up to my ears now.

The thought of kidnapping Shane West was giving him a case of acute heartburn. Krebs assured him over and over that he wouldn't be harmed in any way. The plan was that Krebs and Rivera would follow Shane to where ever he went on Saturday night. When the opportunity presented itself, they would nab him and take him to a remote location that Krebs had scouted out.

We've been driving for over forty-five minutes. Surely this remote location is coming up soon.

The Impala was kicking up dust and gravel while Rivera whipped along Old Mine Road. The homes along this route had been torn down years ago, when Bolt Mining Company strip mined the entire area.

Vic hadn't been out this way in a very long time. There was no need. There was nothing on this road of any relevance at all, which was the point. Finally, in the distance he could see the old estate behind what was left of the stucco walls—the Valentine mansion.

Upon looming pedestals on either side of the wrought iron gates hanging from their rusted hinges, two huge cement lions kept a vigilant watch over the Spanish-style hacienda that was out of place in rural Pennsylvania. The dilapidated mansion that once stood proud now suffered in varying stages of decay. The walls surrounding the compound were crumbling. The shrubbery was overgrown with towering weeds devouring the once well-manicured, sprawling lawns.

Vic steered his truck past the lions' watchful gape, through the wrought iron gates, and into full view of the once magnificent manor. Poison ivy climbed up the thick masonry walls coated with pallid stucco to frame the arched windows. Some of the windows were broken with sharp wedges of glass remaining in the casing. Waves of red tile roofing buted against tall round turrets at each end of the mansion. An enclosed courtyard attached the two wings of the hacienda with three arched openings dressed in a wrought iron trellises. A glorious stone fountain stood amid a ramshackle flower bed that could be seen through the trellises. The home's hey day was long gone, but the remnants of its grandeur were undeniable.

Rivera's car came to a stop in front of the arches. Krebs slid from the passenger's seat to take in the mansion up close. Swabbing his forehead one more time, Vic got out of the truck to look at the strangely misplaced hacienda amongst its sad landscape.

Krebs spread his arms wide as if to embrace it all. "If you think this is cool, wait till you see what I found inside." A priggish chuckle exploding from his chest, he motioned for Vic and Rivera to follow him.

They made their way through the weeds and the overgrowth to a wrought iron gate leading into the courtyard. The gate swung open to give easy entry to the square courtyard, where the stone fountain was once the majestic embellishment.

Rivera crossed himself and kissed his thumb. "This place gives me the creeps." he glanced over his shoulder at the windows overlooking the courtyard. "Are you sure this place is empty?"

Krebs pitched him a dry look. "What's the matter, Riv? Afraid of ghosts? C'mon."

He led them across the courtyard into the turret on the east side of the manor. They stood on a landing inside the tall column. To the right, the winding staircase led to the second floor. To the left, it descended to a basement.

Krebs turned to Vic and Rivera with wide eyes, a grin on his lips, and pumping his eyebrows up and down for dramatic effect. Pulling a flashlight from his pocket, he imitated Dracula's famous rolling accent. "Follow me to the dungeon."

Vic and Rivera exchanged wary glances. In this for the long haul, they followed Krebs downward into the darkness.

Wooden and rickety, the stairs shook while they tromped further beneath the mansion. The air grew dank, cool, and stale. The block walls were covered with beads of moisture and mold. Seeming to cling to nothing, black cob webs dangled from every direction. Just existing, they grabbed and clung to their faces.

"Where the hell are you taking us, muck head?" Vic finally demanded.

Krebs came to an abrupt stop at the bottom of the staircase to flash the beams across a dark room. Rivera's jaw dropped. Vic was stunned.

Krebs was rapt in the candid suggestions that the room offered up. "It doesn't get any better than this, boys,"

It was murky and dirty. The block walls trickled with moisture. The black cob webs were thicker and longer. Torches hung along the walls leading to a caged-in area, where chunky chain shackles were bolted into the blocks. The floor was wet and filthy.

"You couldn't ask for a better place to hide a prisoner," Krebs said.

Fiercely, Vic grabbed him by the shoulder. "You ain't putting Shane in this hell hole."

Trepidation engulfed Rivera. His body language screamed to turn and run. He didn't want to put the prisoner in the old dungeon either. Not so much because he felt bad for Shane West. Oh, no. It was because he didn't want to have to come down to feed him, or fetch him. It was a dark and frightening place. Rivera didn't like dark places. They terrified him.

Krebs could see the angst in Vic's face, and Rivera's eyes. Running a little damage control, he snorted and clapped his hand on Vic's shoulder.

"Of course not, that would be inhumane. I promised you no harm would come to your friend."

"He ain't my friend!"

"Fair enough, no harm will come to Shane West." He lifted his chin toward a window above that was half-way along the upper corridor of the house. "There's a bedroom upstairs that we can accommodate him more ... comfortably."

His insincerity made Vic want to wretch.

Finding great relief in Krebs' empty guarantee, Rivera let go a deep breath, feeling the flush of his nerves start to cool.

After staring at Krebs for a moment, Vic stomped up the stairs, causing them to tremble under his frustrated cadence. The musty feel of the dungeon clung to his skin even after he emerged from the dark chasm and the sun kissed his cheeks. On so many levels, he felt grubby. He hurried his way through the disheveled courtyard surrounded by the corridors of the mansion.

"Vic!" Krebs called out.

Vic turned.

"You know the plan ... as soon as Riv gives you the signal, you drop-in on Eric West with our demands. Afterward, you meet us here. You've got that?"

Vic was liking the kidnapping scheme less and less, but he didn't know what to do about it. Opting out didn't seem possible at this point.

He was trapped by his obligation to the plot, and the life circumstances that had been wielded upon him. He would have to see it all through. At least, Shane would come out on the other end of things unscathed.

"I know the plan." Vic made his way to gate at the far end of the courtyard.

"Can we trust him?" Rivera whispered to Krebs.

"Oh yeah, he'll deliver the goods. He doesn't want anything to happen to Lord West."

Rivera was feeling a tug of cowardice. "Nothing's gonna. Right?"

Krebs winked. "*Riiiight.*"

~ Five ~

Peering out an arched window above the courtyard, she brushed a frock of her long white hair from her face. Intently, she gauged the three men below.

It wasn't unusual for people to wander into Luzetta Valentine's mansion. Sometimes, they were thrill-seeking teenagers who would chase ghosts or engage in senseless vandalism. They were young, stupid, and disrespectful. Yet, they were the least of Luzetta's problems.

These three men were different. They came in the daylight rather than concealed behind the dark drape of the night.

This was the tall dark-haired man's second visit to her mansion in as many days. He had come earlier with a flashlight to prod around the long corridors, investigate each room, and peep into closets before discovering the staircase in the round tower at the east side of the house, which led down to her father's dungeon.

Even though he didn't damage anything or loot the mansion, she sensed that his intentions were sinister.

The web of deep wrinkles around her eyes twitched while she tried to feel the karma permeating from these men. She could feel naught. Nothing seeped into her mind's eyes, except a ghastly sensation that they meant someone great harm.

After the agitated older man left, the other two re-entered the house.

As swiftly and as quietly as a phantom, Luzetta scurried down the corridor to the hidden passageway that led to her meager living quarters. She slid the concealed wall aside and then closed it behind her. She glided through the dim narrow hallway into the open room, where she had been secretly living since the county had seized the mansion for delinquent taxes many years before.

In the corner of the room was an old ornate brass bed. The brass was dull and pitted from years of neglect. The blankets were battered and the sheets were threadbare. Against the far wall was a small wood stove, a pile of twigs, and scrawny pieces of wood resting next to it. That was all the seventy-nine year old woman was able to carry.

A pot, a pan, and a shabby teapot sat on top of the stove. The hardwood floor was bare and cold against her feet. Old lanterns were lined up along the walls. Only one was lit to provide dim, but ample light for the room.

Her father would be ashamed to see her in such a state.

Salvador Valentine had been a cutting-edge director in 1939. He had filmed Dracula movies in the dungeon set beneath the mansion and had used many of the other rooms for scenes in his films, as well. The mansion was beloved by the actors who had visited.

Salvador hadn't always shot movies in the rural compound. He was admired in Hollywood. Luzetta's mother was an up-and-coming starlet. But, when Salvador refused to cast a big-time producer's nephew in his new horror film, he found himself shunned from the Hollywood bigboys. Unable to find backers for his films because no one wanted to get into the boat that he was rocking, Salvador broke away from tinsel town. He became an independent filmmaker, a maverick; he made his movies on his own terms.

Luzetta was fourteen years old when he decided to leave. Her mother refused to go—her career was more important than preserving the family. Salvador was heart broken by her decision to pursue her career rather than stick beside him. Her rejection became a driving force for him to get away—far away.

When her father passed away years ago at the age of eighty-five, Luzetta had been left with mounting bills from his poor health. She was eventually evicted from her home. That is when she took up residence in the hidden room that her father had specially built for them to hide in should there ever be a Russian invasion.

As it turned out, the Russian's were not the intruders that she needed to fear. Now she could sense that these three men had invaded the Valentine mansion for depraved purposes.

Her white hair draped to her waist. She pulled it around her shoulder so she wouldn't sit on it when she lowered her tiny body onto the bed, closed her eyes and breathed deeply to concentrate.

What is it? What do these men want, and why?

Lifting her face to the ceiling, breathing in, breathing out, concentrating—

A man.

Breathe in. Breathe out. Meditate.

He's young, twenty ... No. Maybe twenty-three or four.

Breathe in. Breathe out. Reflect deeper now.

Money.

Thoughts diminished. That was all she could derive from her perception. She opened her eyes to the flicker of the small flame in the lantern. Her mind was most unsettled.

Did the young man owe these men money? Would the young man give them drugs for money? Or would they hold him for money?

Worry consumed her essence.

Strangers came into the mansion often to perform vile acts of destruction and immorality. Yet, no one had ever killed inside the walls. She feared that Salvador Valentine's dungeon set would soon be used for an execution. What could she do?

She felt a rumble in her mind that caused her to tremble. She knew the rumble all to well. She scampered to the corner of the room where she scratched a make-shift calendar into the stucco on the walls.

The days were marked off with a large cross. It was early, too early, but now the warning rumble had become a true roar in the distance on the road outside the mansion. It drew closer and closer still, until she could make out the thunderous sound of the engine of a mighty motorcycle—an iron horse.

Listening diligently, she closed her eyes. It sounded like a lone rider passing. Tilting her head, she honed in on the grumble of the engine ... traveling ... north.

Usually the bikers advanced from the north, but this rider was coming from the south.

How peculiar.

Odd or not, the rumble of the motorcycle was a certain signal of only one thing: they would arrive soon. They did once a month.

The Nomads.

All hell would soon break loose.

"Hurry up, Riv," Krebs called out to the tubby Mexican man urinating on the stucco wall near the driveway. "It's getting late and I want to take a shower before we pick up West." He sniffed. "You should get one too. Who knows how long we'll be on the road after Vic gets the money, and we have to leave town."

"We need some gas before we go." Rivera peered over the wall while zipping his fly to watch a biker on a Harley Fat Boy breeze by. A black case was strapped on the back of the bike. His long wiry beard blew against his neck.

Nice ride, cool jacket, carefree life. Immediately, Rivera knew exactly what he was going to do with his share of the ransom. Oh yeah, as soon as he got that money in his pocket, his life would be all about black leather on his back, a sleek Harley between his legs, and the open road yawning before him. No stalls to muck, no buckets to lug, no ex-wife bitching about the late child support payments, and no fat Americano landlord demanding three hundred bucks a month for that shithole apartment. *Gracias, Senor West.*

His eyes narrowed to slits, he turned toward Krebs who was fidgeting in the front seat of the car. Krebs had no intention of giving Vic any of the ransom. Not to worry. Vic wouldn't be testifying against them. Vic would most certainly be unavailable for comment. Nice. Rivera's part of the ransom would increase from one-third to a whopping one-half. At least he hoped so.

"What if the old guy doesn't show with the money?" Riv was concerned about how many eggs he had in his tiny basket. Lusting after the bike and that carefree life had eluded him since forever.

"That would be most unfortunate for Lord West," Krebs said.

~ Six ~

"Park over there," Krebs told Rivera when he turned the Impala into the parking lot of Barney's Bar and Grille. Rivera stopped the car at the far edge of the lot, away from the cheap wrought iron lanterns and Shane's black Jeep Wrangler.

The dimly lit parking area contained ten cars spread out over the gravel lot. As it usually was on Saturday night, Barney's was busy.

Rivera turned off the ignition and settled back into his seat.

"What are you doing?" Krebs asked.

Rivera jerked up. "Aren't we gonna wait for him here?"

"Hell, no, I want a beer." Krebs slid out of his car seat and headed toward the bar.

Furtively looking about the parking area, Rivera followed close behind.

The juke box was playing a Kenny Chesney song, and the rectangular green and gold tiffany chandelier illuminated the pool table, where Shane was engaged in a game with several of his friends. They were laughing and goading him, as he leaned over the table to meticulously make his shot. While the others hooted and whooped to egg him on, a tall lanky guy held his beer over Shane's back as if he was going to pour it over him. Unconcerned about the threat, Shane was focused.

"Three ball in the side pocket," he said in a quiet tone. With a confident skilled push of the cue stick, the balls snapped into a scatter across the table to dunk the three ball into the side pocket—as promised.

Smiling, Shane straightened and snatched his beer from his friend to take a long swig and receive congratulatory pats on the back.

A short, rotund man, Barney wore a comb-over and a hearty smile. Like an old friend, he would greet each patron when they came through the door. Krebs and Rivera were no exception. "Whatta ya having, boys?" he called out to them from behind the bar.

Krebs cringed at the boisterous broadcast of his arrival. Scowling, he glanced over at the group still spurring Shane. They were unaware of Krebs or Rivera's presence in the bar. *Good.*

"Two beers," Krebs said while directing Rivera to a dark corner booth where they could keep a close eye on Shane's activities while unnoticed.

Shane's interest in the pool game dwindled when Ginger strolled into the bar. After hitching her tiny hiney onto a barstool, she leaned against the bar on her elbows with a sultry curl to her lips. She pushed-out the appetizing curves under her taut V-neck sweater.

Ginger LaFond wasn't Shane's usual attraction. Like his brother, Mike, he liked his women tall, leggy, lean, and mean. Ginger was short and sassy; but Whoa!, watching her walk away was a steamy stimulus. Her tight little buns swayed like a sweet symphony, especially at the racetrack, when she slapped her crop against her tall riding boot with every stride. She was kinda cute, kinda kinky, and despite her lack of long legs and height, she was his kind of Saturday night. Shoving his cue stick into his buddy's chest, he returned her smile and sauntering with flash and swagger toward her.

Krebs sat straight up in the bench seat. His eyes widened and his mouth formed a tight thin line across his face.

Rivera chuckled. "Dude, isn't that the chick you were with last week?"

"You know why she's interested in him, don't you?" Krebs asked.

"Better sex?"

Krebs reached across the table to seize the snickering Mexican stable hand by his shirt. "She's screwing him for Westwood mounts, that's what." He pushed Rivera hard against the seat. "Yeah, the little whore was at the farm yesterday exercising that mare Vic got into trouble with.

She probably figures if she screws Lord West, she's earned herself a tough mount for next week."

From then on the evening dragged. Krebs huddled far into the corner of the booth while watching with malevolence as Shane and Ginger leaned in close. Flirting and laughing, Shane raked his fingers through her silken hair with a "come on" look in his eyes.

Barney had delivered many rounds of beer to Krebs and Rivera's table. The hour was getting late and crowd was thinning out. The juke box dropped in an old LeAnn Rimes song. "Without you..." Rimes crooned.

Krebs looked across the booth at Rivera who was sound asleep with a cigarette dangling from his lip. The ashes dropped onto his stained shirt.

Ginger pulled Shane onto the dance floor. He folded her in close to cover her mouth with his. Searching with his tongue, he caressed her back while pressing his arousal against her tummy. They swayed back and forth to the song.

Her hands ran down his ribs around his lean hips and smoothed over his firm buttocks. Breathing in deep, she drew her tongue from his mouth while giving his left butt cheek a stiff squeeze.

"Time to go," she purred. Taking him by the hand she led him out the door.

Finally. Krebs jerked from the corner and swatted Rivera's arm that was balancing his head on the table.

Rivera's eyes blinked to half-lidded. The butt of the burned-out cigarette fell onto his pot belly.

"West is on the move. Let's go, Riv." Krebs said.

Rivera dragged his drunken body from the booth to take a stumbling step toward the door, but Krebs grabbed him by the arm. "We'll be using the back door." He tugged him past the men's room and out the delivery entrance that led to the rear of the building. They crept among the crates and cardboard boxes piled against the block walls until they reached the edge of the building. Peering around the corner, Krebs watched. His staying power was wearing thin.

Leaning against her car, Ginger drew Shane in close to feel the stiff column in his jeans against her. "Do you have a condom?" she whispered soft and sultry.

"Uh, huh." he kissed her neck. His hand wandered over her shoulders, down her chest to caress her firm breasts through the sweater.

Reaching behind her, she lifted the door latch and shimmied away from him. "In that case, I'll see you at my place in fifteen," she said in a teasing tone while slipping into the driver's seat. She tossed him a wink, and then drove slowly away.

Shane was primed. He spun around only to come face-to-face with a dark shadow leaning on his Jeep. Krebs stepped into the dim light of the lanterns with a cocky grin on his face, and his arms folded over his chest. "Hey, Shane, how about a lift?"

Shane's jaw locked. His eyes narrowed to scan the parking lot with apprehension skittering down his spine. He knew something was up, he wasn't sure from which direction it would come, and then Krebs pointed the business end of a forty-five to his chest.

Clearly, payback is gonna be a serious bitch. He yanked the door open.

"Hold on." Krebs said.

Shane reluctantly turned.

"Give me your right hand." Krebs produced a pair of handcuffs from his hip pocket.

Rolling his eyes, Shane expelled a long breath and extended his right arm toward Krebs. *Oh yeah, this is looking real bad.*

The handcuff slapped against his wrist hard, and then Krebs attached the left piece to the steering wheel. His cocky grin filled out to a gleeful sated smile. Once Shane climbed into the driver's seat, Krebs rifled through his pockets yanking out his cell phone. After pressing the OFF button, he pitched the phone into the tall weeds beyond the parking area.

Keeping the gun trained on him through the windshield, Krebs jogged around the front of the Jeep to the passenger's seat. "Not exactly the evening you had in mind, huh West?" he chuckled. "Too bad. Drive."

"Where to?" Shane asked in disgust while starting the engine and shoving it into first gear. While steering the Jeep toward the edge of the lot, a pair of headlights glinted off his rear view mirror to draw his attention to an old Impala that pulled out of the shadows deep in the parking area following them onto Lanzville Road.

Krebs retrieved a pre-paid cell phone from his shirt pocket and dialed. "We're all set," he informed someone on the other end in a steely tone.

❧ ❧ ❧ ❧

The grandfather's clock in the foyer cut through the stillness of the house when it struck the two o'clock hour. Reading a book, Eric was awake in his bed while listening for Kate or Shane to slip through the front door.

It was an old habit he couldn't quite kick. Maybe it was the fact that he was left to raise them alone after Barbara had died. Maybe it was the fact that there was so much money in the house. Or maybe it was the fact that no matter how old your kids get, you still worry about them.

Yeah, that's probably it. He shifted against the pillows for a more comfortable position.

At twelve-thirty, the door clicking closed interrupted the tenth chapter of his book. He listened to Kate stealthily climb the stairs after her date with Holden.

Eric thought Dr. Holden Reese seemed like a nice guy. Not only was he good-looking and courteous, but the young man was also gainfully employed. Holden was a new veterinarian at the racetrack. His business was growing as he picked up some of the stables that old Doc Spears couldn't handle any longer.

After Doc had introduced them, the couple had been dating for several months.

Eric wondered if their relationship would turn into something more permanent. Only time would tell.

Actually, he was quite surprised that Kate hadn't gone to work for the young vet, who had hung a sign on his office door the other day that read: VET ASSISTANT NEEDED, APPLY WITHIN.

Ironically, Kate hadn't made a move. She stuck with Doc Spears.

Perhaps she's exercising some of that good old common sense that I've tried to instill in all my children. Good girl.

Eric turned the page with a crooked curl to his lips.

Then there was Shane. Girls came in and out of his life like a revolving door. Eric couldn't keep track of their names. For that matter, he wasn't so sure that Shane could either. That was okay. The kid was only twenty-two. He should be out enjoying life, before life grabbed him by the back of the neck to force him to drive a minivan and warm bottles at two a.m. instead of whatever he was doing right now at two a.m.

Eric preferred not to fill in the blanks. He chuckled to himself. *Testosterone and common sense are like oil and water.*

John Grisham was unable to hold Eric's attention any longer. He marked his page, and placed the book on the night stand along with his glasses. After folding his hands behind his head, he leaned back against the pillow and stared at the ceiling. His thoughts drifted to his quiet evening at home with Jen Fleming.

Usually Eric took her to dinner on Friday nights. However, he wasn't feeling confident about going out and leaving the house empty even though the money was securely in the safe.

Jen didn't mind. She surprised him by showing up at his front door with Chinese take-out. Jen Fleming was a blessing that came into his life. She was the first woman he'd even considered having a relationship with since Barbara's death ten years ago. They had spent over a year flirting.

Jen Fleming was the nurse at the racetrack. Her pixie-like features caught his eye. The way her short brunette hair curved around her heart-shaped face and the gentle sprinkle of freckles over her nose—not to mention her pretty green eyes.

They spent the evening in front of a cozy fire in the fireplace. The only light in the room, the trembling flicker of the flames danced over them where they were wrapped in a fleece blanket while watching an old Dirty Harry flick.

Amazingly, Eric found a woman who actually liked Dirty Harry. Well, at least, she put-up with him.

Damn, if she didn't look so tasty under that blanket with that twinkle in her fairy-green eyes and sultry smirk on those perky plump lips of hers. Not so innocently or absently, she smoothed her shin up and down his thigh. Occasionally, her leg would brush over his crotch. She would pretend not to notice.

He noticed. Oh yeah, he noticed, big time. Things were starting to bulge and throb and ache for her. She tossed him an askance look, and that was the end for him.

It had been so long.

Dragging his fingers through her silky tresses, he pulled her to his chest and covered her mouth with his. God, how things had become unbridled between them these past few months. Surreptitiously, Jen's fingers unbuttoned his shirt, slipped inside, and caressed his chest while they made their way to his belt.

He wasted no time in tugging her blue cable-knit sweater over her head to reveal a dainty pink satin bra. After slipping the straps from her downy shoulders to bare her round breasts, he gently eased her to the floor onto the white sheepskin rug in front of the glowing snapping embers in the fireplace.

Somehow their clothes ended up in a scatter over the floor around them.

She was warm and soft and inviting. It had been so long since he let himself feel this way.

That sheep skin rug is never gonna be the same.

Usually the inconsiderate slam of the door closing, or the sound of Shane clomping up the stairs, would jerk Eric from his thoughts or sleep. Instead, the sound of fierce pounding on the front door brought him up onto his elbows to listen.

The knock grew harder.

He tossed the blankets out-of-the-way and swung his legs over the side of the bed to listen again.

Hard and insistent, the rapping continued.

Already wearing a pair of lounging pants, he snatched a T-shirt from the chair to shimmy over his head and down his torso. He hurried down the hallway, stairs, and across the dimly lit foyer to grasp the deadbolt.

Cautious, he hesitated. "Who's there?"

"It's me, Eric ...Vic Deveaux."

Yawning, Eric ran his fingers through his hair. He opened the door to find Vic standing on the porch. Washed-out from sweating, he wore an absent expression on his face.

Eric's eyes narrowed in concern. "Vic ... are you okay?"

Vic didn't respond. He stood there with hollow eyes staring at him. He resembled a dark phantom. Eric studied his old friend for a moment before stepping aside and gesturing for him to come into the house.

Vic stood statuesque in place.

"Did you want to talk, Vic?" Eric asked.

Vic blinked. "What?"

"Would you like to come in?"

Vic stepped through the door while perusing the foyer as if he'd never seen it before.

The thought came to Eric's mind that perhaps the heated discussion they had earlier caused Vic to suffer a mini-stroke, but he decided to go for a more pleasant scenario. "I hope this late visit means you've had a change of heart."

"No." Vic's answer was as disjointed as his presence. Sweat dripped down his face. He worked his jaw, except nothing came out. His shirt was saturated with perspiration.

Eric had never seen his friend so unraveled. "What's wrong, Vic?"

The old jockey lugged his gaze to meet Eric's. Pulling out of his funk, he swallowed hard. "Gimme the money in your safe, Eric, if you ever want to see Shane again."

Once again, his eyes narrowed. An uneasy chuckle escaped him. The right side of his mouth lifted. "It's kind of late at night for a joke, don't you think, Vic?"

His old blue eyes never wavered. "I'm not joking, Eric. Gimme the money or my friends are gonna kill Shane—just as sure as Sunday's coming."

Scrubbing his hand across his tightened jaw, Eric stepped back.

Vic slogged down a thick swallow of saliva while watching his long-time employer and friend measure him for exactly what he was—a Judas.

Eric couldn't believe what was happening. He didn't want to accept the bite of betrayal stabbing through his gut. Spinning on his heels, he dashed through the foyer, up the staircase, down the hallway, and burst into Shane's bedroom.

The room was still. Shane had left a window partially open. The curtains billowed out and then sucked back against the screen. Sure enough, his bed was undisturbed. His barn clothes lay in an untidy pile in the middle of the room.

Eric hadn't dozed off to miss Shane's return home. He never did. He was so damned worried about the money in the safe that he never considered a scheme like this. He certainly never thought his good friend, Vic Deveaux would be involved.

Stymied, he fell against the door jamb to gather his thoughts.

Vic leaned against the braided edge of Eric's cherry-wood desk. The hot embers in the stone fireplace across the room smoldered like orange, red, and amber sequins among the pasty ashes. The brass lamp on the desk cast a soft, homey glow throughout the room.

Vic had watched many Steelers game here, drank plenty of brandy, and discussed future races of many young horses within these very walls. His soul was filled with shame. Remorse washed over him like an ice cold waterfall. Yet, the sweat on his brow was inexorable. Tentative footsteps from behind caused him to turn. Eric's jaw was set and his eyes were seething.

"They're gonna kill him for sure, if I don't return with that five-hundred grand you've got in that safe," Vic said. "Don't call the police. That will get Shane killed for sure. You got that?"

Eric grabbed him by the front of his shirt. "Do you realize what you're doing, Vic?"

Angry, Vic swatted his hand away. "What choice did you give me, Eric? All I had was my career, my truck, and that shit-hole apartment near the track. What stable is gonna want me after the Wests' fired me 'cause I'm too freaking old?" It was a poor excuse when he heard it tumbling out of his own mouth, but it was all he had.

"I didn't fire you, Vic! You quit! You didn't even give me a chance to tell you what I had in mind!" Eric shot back in a fury.

"I'm no stable boy! Now, give me the money so I can get on with it." Eric's brusque stare filled him with a stinging urgency. He wanted the messy part of this job over with, promptly. "Now, Eric! Do. It. Now!" he yelled loudly.

Eric made his way around the desk toward the wall safe. Sorely vexed, he pitched Vic a glower, before kneeling in front of the safe, typing in the security code, jerking it open. Vic watched in silent compunction as he tossed the cash into a briefcase, slammed it closed, and slid it sharply across the top of the desk. The case crashed to the floor at his feet. All Vic could do was gawk down at it like it was a hissing, two-headed serpent.

"Pick it up," Eric said. "You're too proud to muck stables, but you're not too proud to commit a federal offence; or, better yet, betray an old friend."

Eric's words sliced him to the core. It was too late for regrets, and much too late to back out now.

Vic grabbed the briefcase and hobbled toward the foyer.

"Vic!" Eric bellowed.

Vic stopped.

"If Shane is harmed in any way ... there won't be a corner on this earth where I won't find you."

Vic didn't turn around. He couldn't. "Remember, no cops, Eric. Our plan is to drop him on one of those *Old Mine Roads*. By the time he walks home, we'll be gone. I promise you, he'll be in one piece."

Vic slammed the door behind him.

Flummoxed by Vic's treachery and betrayal, Eric stood breathless at the bottom of the staircase. A thin sigh and a shuffle above him drew his attention. He looked up.

Her expression filled with anguish, Kate, in her pajamas, clung to the stair railing.

"Oh my God..." she muttered.

PART TWO:

NO ESCAPE CLAUSE

~ SEVEN ~

The moonlight yawned over the fountain in the courtyard. The Valentine mansion rose from the shadows like a pallid menagerie in a desolate wasteland. The flicker of the flame in the lantern provided little light down the long narrow corridor through the passageway from Luzetta's room. The breeze through the broken windows flowed through her long white hair when she made her way to the front of the house.

The evening had been quiet.

The strangers had not returned, and she decided to investigate to see if they had left behind any clues about their intentions.

Her senses had grown dull with her old age. Perhaps it was the lack of practice. Anxious to hear their future, no one came to hold her hand anymore. That all died with Salvador Valentine and the days of filmmaking.

Her life was filled with isolation, loneliness, and fear. When strangers came to the mansion, they didn't come to hear their fortunes, they came to destroy the past with frivolous vandalism. She spent her time huddled in her room until after they left to collect any crumbs of food they might leave behind.

Hesitating at the scarred, heavy arched door spray painted with horrible words, Luzetta listened for footsteps or voices on the other side. Stealthily, she shouldered the door open while holding up the lantern.

She slipped into the living room. The walls were splashed with graffiti, cracks, and gouges. The ceiling wore brownish red stains from the rain and the snow leaking through the roof. The floor was heaved from water damage. Booze bottles, paper, and cans were strewn about and piled in the corners.

Luzetta picked her way through the rubbish toward the kitchen.

The cabinetry hung lopsided from the bulkhead. The counters were cracked and splintered and spray painted. Through the dim light cast by the lantern, Luzetta could see several plastic bags from the Stop-N-Shop Mart on the counter. Rummaging through the bags' contents, she found potato chips, tortilla chips, pretzels, and the mother-load: a box of Dolly Madison mini-doughnuts.

Hunger overtook her. Stuffing them into one bag, she snatched the doughnuts and bag of pretzels. It had been so long since anyone had left behind such treasure.

On the floor rested a battered dirty red cooler. Upon opening the lid a rush of excitement swept through her. Dipping her boney purple veined hands into the ice, she discovered cans of Coke and Mountain Dew and Budweiser beer.

The strangers had also left several folding chairs.

Sitting in one of the chairs, she closed her eyes in an attempt to connect with them. Breathing in deeply, trying to relax; she took in the vibrations, the sensations. All she could see was a birthday party.

Children batting at an odd-looking piñata ... a man with a red head and blue tights in a squatting position.

Not understanding that image, she was unsure if it were relevant to the situation at hand.

The lights from a vehicle flashed past the arched window that looked out over the overgrown lawn and rutted driveway.

Luzetta's eyes flew open to dismiss the vision. She leapt from the chair to gather several bags of goodies and several cans of soda. Her curiosity won over, she crept to the window to make sure it was the same men that had been there that afternoon.

❧ ❧ ❧ ❧

Shane slowed the Jeep to a stop in front of the mansion, with the Impala pulling up behind him.

Rivera jumped from his vehicle. "We can't leave these cars out front." He was breathless, panicked, and unsteady from the booze.

Gesturing with the gun for Shane to step out, Krebs unhooked the handcuff from the Jeep's steering wheel. "I'll take West inside. You hide the cars around back, stupid." he cuffed Shane's hands together.

Glancing around, Rivera nodded. "This place gives me the creeps, dude, especially in the dark."

"You're drunk out of you mind." Krebs slammed his fist into Shane's stomach. He crunched over with a grunt. Krebs' swift punch between his shoulder blades knocked him to the pavement.

Rivera's blood-shot eyes bulged. "What the hell are you doing, man?"

"Livin' large." Krebs delivered a hard kick to Shane's gut. He grunted and coughed.

"Vic's not gonna like this. We're not supposed to hurt him."

Krebs whirled toward him. "Do what you're told, amigo, if you know what's good for you!"

The glare in Krebs' eyes gripped Rivera with fear. He dragged his harried fingers through his hair while watching the young man's strong constitution as he struggled to get to his feet. He managed to his knees. Krebs greeted him by pressing the gun to his forehead.

Shane's defiant gaze was unyielding. The acrid taste of his own blood filled his mouth.

"I said move the cars!" Krebs roared over his shoulder to Rivera. "I'll meet you downstairs."

"No, wait for me, and we'll go together," Rivera said.

Krebs turned to him with a glower indicating that there would be no tolerance for his trepidation, only punishment, only persecution, perhaps worse.

Realizing that he'd climbed into the preverbal bed with the devil himself, Rivera breathed deep. His penance was Krebs' escalating temper and wicked mood. There would be no escape clause from this dirty deal.

Krebs shoved Shane toward the house while prodding him in the shoulder with the forty-five with every step.

Luzetta's stomach churned while she watched the dark-haired man beat the defenseless younger man.

Meanwhile, the chubby Mexican man stood by, shifting his weight from one foot to the other, and raking his fingers through his curly unkempt dark hair. The Mexican man's body language sent goose bumps up her arms. His fright ran deep into her senses. She could taste the trouble that he had become entangled in. He feared the tall, dark-haired man. He feared for his life. He was sorely compromised.

As for the younger man?

She held the grocery bag close to her chest. Breathing deep, she pressing her old gray eyes closed, and then blinked them open, when she heard the heavy door to the east turret open—the dungeon.

Good Lord in Heaven. They're taking the young man to the dungeon!

The small beam from the flashlight sliced the darkness of the wobbly spiraled wooden steps. The dank air was hard to breath and the footing was slick from the moisture as they descended around and around and lower and lower until they finally arrived at the bottom.

Shane took several blind steps forward until he bumped into a barred object. Krebs flashed the light in front of him to reveal a heavy metal gate covered in slimy mildew. At the edge of the light, he could see mice scampering across the floor.

After pushing the gate open, Krebs whacked Shane across the back to knock him through the gate to the soggy cement floor.

Slightly dazed, Shane watched the small flickering flame from a lighter jiggle in the darkness toward the wall. Krebs touched it against something. *Tsssss...* It crackled, and smoldered, and then *whoosh* a torch burst into flames to reveal the menacing dark prison. *Whoosh* another torch ignited, and then *whoosh* still another. The pungent odor of old igniter fluid was rank. Dark creeping arms of smoke slithered across the room.

Krebs coughed.

Shane pushed to a sitting position in awe of the horrid conditions that he was certain that he would be tolerating until whatever plans Krebs had were carried out. At this point in the game, he was having little trouble figuring what those plans were—Murder. His murder.

"Get up." Krebs delivered a brisk kick into Shane's thigh.

The thick dark smoke from the torches wove an ominous tapestry over their heads. The flames danced like unleashed demons gleefully spitting sparks against the filthy block walls to illuminate the dungeon more clearly now.

Garbage, old crinkled leaves, and cans were strewn across the floor and swept up in the corners where mice scampered amongst all of it.

Krebs shoved him toward the shackles hanging on the walls inside the caging. "Welcome to your final accommodations, Lord West. Not what you're accustomed to, but you should fit in comfortably among the rest of the vermin."

He attached the handcuffs to the shackles and then stood back to revel in the power that he held over his hostage. To his disappointment and disgust, he was most disconcerted with the young man's uncompromising demeanor. His obstinate glare scraped a fierce frustration down Krebs' spine.

He isn't afraid. He isn't bending to the ambiguity of his future. He should be. Shane West's future is non-existent. Doesn't he get it? What the hell's the matter with him? The cocky bastard is still too confident. Before this is all said and done, I'll have him begging for mercy. The five-hundred-thousand that Eric West is going to provide is a grand piece of cake, but killing this sonofabitch is the icing.

His own fluster and Shane's arrogance perturbed him. "I could kill you right now!"

Shane locked eyes with him. "You won't." he said with a thin smile.

The smile burned deep into Krebs' aggravation. It reminded him of his father's haughty smirk. The grin he would launch at him when he thought his father was proud—only to be slammed with his condemnation. He hated that smile—that look—and the denunciation that always followed.

It was as if Shane knew, and was using it to his advantage. Krebs could see it in his eyes.

What the hell? I'm coming unraveled. I never allow that to happen. Cool, collected, calm, I learned how to hold it together long ago. I'm in charge. I don't have to take this from this cocky punk. I evened the score with my father three years ago, and now it's time to even it with this over-confident smug sonofabitch.

A slight bead of sweat formed around Krebs' hairline. Breathing in a deep breath, he yanked a long stiff piece of fabric from his back pocket to wipe the bead away.

Shane's incensed stare never left Krebs' face.

No matter.

Krebs slapped the fabric around his eyes, fastening it tautly around his head.

Blindfolded, Shane's head moved about while listening attentively for movement. Tense, his body stiffened.

Now he isn't so sure. He isn't so full of himself. Now I have him right where I want him.

Nothing but darkness, the musty heavy air on his face, and his arms growing numb from the restrains over his head, Shane knew something bad was coming, but he didn't know what. He listened to Krebs' footsteps traveling across the cement floor. He heard him pick up an object in the corner of the room, and then his marked footsteps approaching until he could sense Krebs standing over him. Bitterly aware there was nothing he could do to stop any kind of assault, he braced for the worst.

"What the hell is that, Krebs?" Rivera's frantic voice echoed through the chamber.

He heard Krebs' feet grind against the grimy floor when he turned. "Get the hell out of here, you stupid piece of shit!"

With that Shane heard a hard bump, and then *Zzzzz...zzz.* Rivera screamed. Shane heard his body fall to the floor.

Badump!

He listened to Rivera's heavy panicked breaths, the sound of his hands milling over the damp grubby floor while scurrying to his feet and scampering to a far corner of the dungeon.

"I ain't going to prison for you, Krebs!" he cried out.

Shane could hear his feet hurry toward the gate and the metal clanging hard when he slammed it. His gasping breaths were panicked when the *bump, bump, bump*, of his feet pounded up the stairs in the turret.

Krebs' feet ground against the floor again when he turned toward him. Shane braced himself. Whatever he had just put Rivera through was coming his way.

Krebs chuckled quietly as he approached his footsteps deliberate and measured.

Shane curled his fingers into tight fists in anticipation.

"What was that sound, West?" he whispered, "What was it? Huh?" His voice was laced with a vindictive taunt, as he finally stood over him and shoved the hard bat-like object against his chest.

Zzz, zzz, zzz.

Shane's body jolted. He cried out when the burning electric shock tore through him. Pulling it away, Krebs hooted.

Shane stiffened. Gasping, he fell limp against the damp block wall.

He couldn't see it coming. He didn't know when it would happen or where it would strike, the only hint that it was coming was Krebs' sudden silence while meticulously picking his next spot. Then, under his left armpit…

Zzz, zzz, zzz.

His body shook. The shackles jangled. Krebs whooped like a drunken teenager at a pop concert.

"Damn! This thing was worth the thirty bucks I paid for it on e-bay. Don't you think, West?"

Zzzz…

"Don't you think?"

Zzzz…

"I can't hear you, West!"

Zzzz…

"Fuck you, Krebs!" Shane shrieked.

Though his body shook uncontrollably, he heard Krebs click the cattle prod off. "You're being a poor sport, West," he snickered softly. "Well as much fun as this has been, I'm hungry. But don't worry, I'll be back for more fun and games later, you just won't see me coming." He bent down close to Shane's ear. His whisper was deviously wicked. "But you'll know. Don't worry, you'll know."

He heard Krebs walk across the floor, place the prod in the corner, and then cross the dungeon. The metal gate creak open and clang shut.

Shane listened to his footsteps ascend around and around the staircase. The heavy oak door dropped closed at the top.

He was alone in the dank dark dungeon. The mice scuttled over the floor, several scampered across his legs and nibbled at the knee of his Levis. The sweat dribbled down his spine and his wrists were turning raw from the metal handcuffs. His fingers were turning cold, and his arms were stiffening with a bloodless ache.

He laid his head against the wall. He was certain that he heard Rivera mention Vic Deveaux's name when they were in the driveway.

Good God, I knew the old guy was pissed, but I can't believe that he would take up with the likes of Martin Krebs. And what's with Rivera? He's worked at Westwood for almost two years now. What the hell's his problem?

Shane gave a quick tug at his shackles, they didn't budge. His wrists sent a jab of pain down to his elbows. The Valentine mansion was out in the middle of nowhere, and no one that he knew ever come out this way. *Great.* Trying to keep a cool head, he took a deep breath. He would have to reserve his strength. His father and Mike weren't going to take this bullshit sitting down. They would come looking. He only hoped it wouldn't be too late.

Slowly, Vic drove along the winding gravel road that led away from Lanzville toward open country. The strip mines had bought up the prime property years ago to turn into a waste land. Salvador Valentine had refused to sell his beautiful Spanish-style hacienda to the big mining companies. As a result, the Valentine mansion remained standing among the dead trees, and a few vacant crumbling homes.

Arriving at a fork in the road, Vic stopped to stare at the divide. Not quite ready to deal with his new-found friends, he steered the Ranger onto Route 220 away from the waste land that the mining companies had created.

The usually busy road was quiet. At three-thirty in the morning, there wasn't even a big rig in sight. The moonlight splashed across his windshield.

Vic felt like shit. He had betrayed an old friend. Now there was no way out. He was in too deep. He had put Shane in harm's way. The only way to get him out was to see this cockamamie scheme through, as much as he hated it, and as much as he hated himself for getting involved. There was no one to turn to. He was alone with his guilt and self-loathing.

The briefcase filled with five-hundred-thousand dollars rested on the passenger's seat.

Sweet Jesus, I've stolen five-hundred-thousand dollars from a friend, and I've put his son in more danger than I know what to do about. I don't trust Krebs. Rivera ... shit, he's a bona-fide wussy.

Maneuvering a long bend in the road, Keystone Downs came into view along the highway at the very edge of Lanzville, before 220 crossed over into the larger more populated town of Rosemount. The lights on the track were dimmed, only the dusk-to-dawn lights over the stables lit up the area.

The silhouette of a lone man in the faintly lit guard shack reminded him of how much he would miss Keystone Downs. It was his life blood. That was all gone now. He was a fugitive, a thief, and, worst, a traitor.

Directly across from the racetrack was Keystone Kourt. Most of the stable help and a few low-level jockeys lived in the low-rent park. Its grounds were shabby. The trailers were old and in disrepair.

Remembering that Jose Torres had mentioned that he lived in the park, his foot pressed the brake. Slowing the Ranger to a crawl, he turned into the entrance. Turning his headlights down to the parking lights, he cruised through the park looking for Jose's trailer.

Trailer twenty-three was dark, except for the lantern at the end of the sidewalk. Well, it was kind of like a lantern. It had a pole and a light bulb. The decorative glass encasement was broken-off to leave only the light bulb.

Grabbing the briefcase full of money, Vic turned off the ignition, slid from the vehicle, and made his way toward the front door of Jose's trailer.

Looking over his shoulder, he drew the briefcase close to his chest while picking up the pace to climb the steps onto the small wooden landing, and rap on the door.

"Where've you been? Wrong trailer, silly, I'm over here," a female voice called out from next door.

Clutching the case even closer to his chest, Vic froze.

Ginger squinted to see who was there, and then sighed. "Oh, sorry Mr. Deveaux, I thought you were someone else." Pulling a silky robe tightly around her waist, she stomped up her steps and slammed her door.

Shit, that pushy girl saw me.

Panicked, he tapped harder on the door. Finally, a lamp turned on in the living room. The front door jerked open only to be stopped by the rusted security chain on the other side. Dazed, Jose peeked through the narrow gap. "Vic, what are you doing here?" he said in a groggy voice.

"I gotta talk to you, Jose, right away," he said in a hushed voice while watching over his shoulder.

The young woman peered at him through pinched back curtains from her window. Taking note of Vic's anxiety, Jose studied him through the opening. He closed the door. Vic heard the chain release and smack against the jamb. The door opened, and Jose waved for him to come in. Jose stepped onto the landing outside the door to look up and down the park before stepping back inside to close the door and reconnect the security chain.

Vic measured Jose's humble home. It reflected the life of an old bachelor who had made his living on the back of a horse. Now, he was cleaning up after them. Null and void of fancy furnishings, the trailer was barren—except for a small table and two wooden chairs in the kitchen, a nineteen-inch TV on a rickety stand, and a battered Lazy-boy recliner that looked to have been purchased around 1985.

Jose combed his twisted fingers through his bed-tousled hair. "What's up Vic? Ya look like death warmed over."

Not quite sure what he was searching for, Vic paced from window to window to pinch back the threadbare curtains. He was a renegade now, and he had to be on the constant look-out. Thankfully, the lights had gone out in the young woman's trailer next door. *She must've given up on whoever she was waiting for.*

Jose rubbed the back of his neck. "I heard ya quit at Westwood." He was trying to get anything out him.

Without warning, Vic slammed the briefcase on the kitchen table and opened it.

Jose was jolted from his lethargy. His eyes popped and his jaw dropped. "Holy shit, Vic! Did ya rob a bank?"

"Close," Vic muttered. "Listen, Jose, us old jocks gotta stick together. Look after each other, cuz nobody else is gonna, ya understand?"

Baffled, Jose fingered the money in awe. "What the hell are you talking about?"

"I'm gonna give you half of my cut," Vic said.

Jose's brows furrowed in bewilderment. "Your cut of what?"

"They tossed me out, Jose," Vic said, "like I was a worthless piece of garbage." He parked his hands on the table and leaned in toward Jose to look him in the eye. "So ... I let Martin Krebs talk me into a bad idea." The mere thought of it set his gut on fire. He sunk into the chair. "I guess I figured they owed it to me after all those years of wins I gave Eric."

Now it was Jose's turn to ease into a chair on the opposite side of the table. "You *stole* this money from the Wests?"

Vic could hear the shock and abhorrence in Jose's voice. He was ashamed. "Worse, much worse."

~ EIGHT ~

"Mike ... Mike..."

Someone was shaking him out of a deep, much-needed sleep by his shoulder. Mike's eyes blinked open and his body jerked upward onto his elbows.

Hovering over him, Eric had a look on his face that he rarely witnessed—angst mixed with panic. His father never came into the bungalow that he lived in on the far side of the farm without a phone call or knocking on the door. But there he was to summon him fiercely out of his sleep.

This has to be damned serious.

Hoping not to see flames shooting from the roofs, Mike's gaze darted to the bedroom window that faced the stables.

So far, so good. But something is definitely wrong.

Eric hurried to the bedroom door to swat the light switch and fill the room with a burst of intrusive radiance to blind him.

Blinking hard while trying to adjust his eyes, Mike fell back to the pillow. Without warning, a pair of his Levis jeans hit him in the chest.

"Get dressed," Eric said, "we've got trouble."

Mike was wrenched from his sluggish state when his father filled him in on Vic's visit in the wee hours of the morning. He found himself trying to decipher if he was really awake, or jumbled-up in a bad dream. Shane could be as annoying as poison ivy in the crotch, but he loved his kid brother more than anything. He couldn't imagine his life void of the ornery agitation that he wielded so effectively.

While shimmying into a black Henley shirt that his father had tossed him, Mike tried to figure how Vic could muster up the malice to deceive his father in such a way. Who could he have possibly conspired with so quickly to pull it all off? Vic was a loner. His abrasive personality put people off. Mike concluded the stubborn old codger preferred it that way.

Shoving his feet into his boots, Mike also questioned how Vic knew that the money was in the house. *No one knew about the money, right?*

"What's the plan?" Mike knew that his father would follow Vic's instructions not to involve the authorities, though he wasn't convinced that was the most viable option.

To be honest, Eric West was as stubborn as Vic Deveaux. When it came to the security of his family—it wasn't a wise idea to mess with the man. *Vic should know that.*

Eric reached back and pulled a Glock from the waistband of his jeans. He tossed it to Mike. "We're going to track them down."

Mike caught the gun, stood up, and shoved it into his Levis. "And if we find them?"

"*When* we find them." Eric was quick to correct. "There will be bridges to cross, and more-than-likely to burn."

∾ ∾ ∾ ∾

"Dulce madre Maria," *Sweet mother Mary*, Rivera muttered in disbelief to himself.

He searched the counter, the floor, and even the cabinets, but a bag of treats were missing. The doughnuts he had picked up for breakfast— gone. So was the bag of pretzels. He wasn't crazy. He had left the bags on the counter.

This could mean only one thing. The mansion was haunted. He knew it.

He couldn't do the math. He wasn't sure what his cut of the ransom would be, but it was starting to matter less and less.

Martin Krebs' noose was tightening around his neck. It was becoming all too apparent that he had no intention of letting Shane West go. He had his doubts that Vic would survive to receive his cut. Plus, he was growing more skeptical of Krebs' plans for him. The only thing he was certain of was that he wanted out of this creepy old house—the sooner, the better.

What the hell is taking Vic so long? They had picked Shane up hours ago. All the old man had to do was go to Westwood, get the money from Eric, and then shake-a-leg to this scary old shit-hole.

Rivera's sausage-like fingers scrubbed the thick dark stubble on his chin. He checked the time on his cell phone. It was almost six-thirty. Krebs had fallen asleep on the floor in the other room. He was afraid to disturb him, but he was becoming antsy.

Maybe the old codger doesn't care about Shane as much as we thought. Maybe he took-off with the money.

Anxiety rolled through him. He shuffled into the room where Krebs, wrapped in a sleeping bag, was snoring on the floor. The old warped floor creaked loudly as Rivera made his way to the dirty cracked windows to pinch back the threads of curtains that remained.

Wincing, Krebs lifted his head from the sleeping bag. "What time is it?" he asked around a yawn.

"Six-thirty," Rivera said. "Where is that *viejo bastardo?*"

"Don't worry, the *old bastard* will show. Go get West, I want to tell him our evil plan."

Rivera was annoyed at the request. "Why don't you go get him? I don't like that damned dungeon. It's creepy and there're rats, and you promised Vic that you wouldn't put him down there."

"Don't be a wuss. Go get West and make it quick." His eyes were tight and mean.

Rivera swallowed.

"And get me one of those doughnuts before you go," Krebs said.

Rivera was about to surrender to his demands when a sliver of defiance slithered up his spine. He hesitated at the threshold. "Do it yourself, *muchacho.*"

❦ ❦ ❦ ❦

"Boy ... hey, boy ..."

A feeble voice whispering in the darkness stirred Shane. He had slipped into unconsciousness. The thin female murmur and the light touch of her hand to his shoulder joggled him back.

Listening intently, he tilted his head. He wasn't sure that he really heard the voice, or if it were part and parcel to his funk, not to mention the fierce ringing in his ears that was the equivalent of John Bonham playing a bolstering solo on his ear drums.

"Boy... can you hear me?" she whispered again. The tone was raspy and aged. The boney fingers on his shoulder squeezed with little strength.

"I can hear you," his whisper was gravelly.

"I don't know what kind of trouble you've got yourself mixed up with, but I brought you something to drink." She pressed a can to his lips. Her grasp was unsteady and shaky, but she managed to pour the liquid into his mouth while dripping only a few drops onto his chin.

Coke.

His mouth and throat were dry, and he was grateful for the drink.

"Thanks." He licked his parched lips as she pulled it away and wiped his chin with a rough cloth.

"What's your name?" the little voice asked.

He lifted his blindfolded eyes toward the voice. "I'm Shane West." He didn't know who this could be, especially since she didn't know who he was. If she wasn't part of the kidnapping scheme, what the hell was she doing in the mansion? "Who are you?"

There was a long measured silence. He thought she may have gone, but then he heard her draw a ragged breath. "Don't you worry about that." Providing him with another swig, she pressed the quivering can to his lips again.

"Will you help me?" he asked when she pulled the can away.

"I don't know what I could do, other than what I am."

"Call the police."

There was no response.

He turned his head to the right, and then to the left while listening for her breathing or for movement.

There was nothing.

"Hey... hey..." he whispered into the dank air.

Nothing.

She was gone.

He plunked his throbbing head against the wall while listening to the deafening ringing in his ears staring into the blindfold, and fighting through the pain jabbing down his arms.

A gust of air swept down the stairs and through the cell as the heavy door at the top squealed open, and then dropped closed with a weighty bang.

Clomp, clomp, clomp. Footsteps descended the stairs. The metal gate moaned as if it were in grave agony when it was shoved open. His buttocks were sore and his hips were stiff, but his spine straightened. Bracing, he listened and waited.

The sounds of the footsteps were grittier now while making way across the filthy cement floor of the prison. Coming closer, they stopped and straddled him. He couldn't see him, but he could feel the presence of the figure hovering over him. His aching shoulders clenched.

Splash!

Ice cold water splattered hard over his face and down his chest. Shocked, he gasped.

Splash!

Another wave of the chilled water hit, hard cubes of ice bounced off his cheeks to pelt the blindfold before he could catch his breath.

He grunted when a firm kick jolted his gut.

"It's six-thirty in the morning and I haven't got my money," Krebs said, "Someone doesn't love you. I'm not sure who that is. Maybe you shouldn't have fired Vic Deveaux. Or maybe daddy doesn't think you're worth it. What do you think, Lord West?"

"What the hell are you talking about?"

Splash!

More icy water exploded over his face.

Splash!

Another before he could catch his breath.

"Deveaux was supposed to pick up that five-hundred-grand that dear-old dad had in his safe. He was supposed to bring it back here. That was hours ago, and he's never shown up. Where do you suppose that leaves you?"

His arms ached fiercely, he was dirty and wet and cold from the freezing water dripping from his face onto his chest. But he wasn't going to let this piece of shit get to him, break him down, like he intended.

He lifted his blind-folded face toward Krebs' voice.

"What are you waiting for? Kill me, Krebs, if you've got the balls."

Splash.

Splash.

"And ruin my fun? Not so fast, I'll bet this mother really shocks like hell when you're wet."

Zzzz.

Zzzz.

Zzzz...

❧   ❧   ❧   ❧

"Vic...Vic... Wake up, man" Jose shook his old friend's shoulder where he slept across the briefcase on the kitchen table.

Vic's eyes burst open. He blinked hard, and shook his head before glancing up to find Jose standing over him with a mug in one hand, and a coffee carafe in the other. "What time is it?" he asked in a tone mixed evenly with grogginess and panic.

"Almost seven." Jose poured the coffee into the mug and handed it to him. Vic scrubbed his fingers over his whiskers. He couldn't believe he had slept so late, or at all. The anxiety must have beaten him into a state of exhaustion that he couldn't fight. He took a big swig of the coffee.

"They're probably wondering where the hell you are," Jose said. "They're probably antsy as hell. What're you gonna do?"

"Let 'em wait. There ain't nobody looking for them."

"How do you know?"

"Cuz I know Eric. He's looking for me." His eyes narrowed. "Are you willing to help me, Jose?"

"Whoa, Vic, I ain't got much." He gestured at his humble dwelling. "I ain't interested in getting involved in any kidnapping. I don't much like jail."

"Neither of us is going to jail. C'mon, I've got a plan." Vic grabbed the briefcase and hobbled toward the door. He unlatched the security chain and glanced out the crack in the door to scan the quiet trailer park. The sable-haired girl's car was gone. He turned to his friend. Jose ran a hand through his white hair.

Vic could see the contemplation in his eyes. Jose wasn't sure if he could trust what he had in mind. Vic didn't blame Jose. One thing was for sure. Vic needed him.

"You coming?" Vic asked.

Jose let out a long deep sigh, shook his head in uncertainty, set the coffee carafe on the table, and then followed Vic out of the door.

A county map was spread across the dining room table.

Eric's mind was racing to figure out where Vic and his mystery partners could possibly have Shane stashed. He and Mike had spent the better part of the night giving Vic time and space while figuring a plan, pacing the floor, and mulling over suspects.

Feeling like she had to do something, Kate kept brewing pot after pot of coffee in hopes the caffeine would trigger some ideas of where to start searching.

The sun had crested the horizon over an hour ago. It was now time for action.

Squeezing the bridge of his nose with his forefinger and thumb, Eric pressed his eyes tightly shut.

His mind kept going back to Carlos Rivera's sudden appearance in the study. How much did he hear? Regardless, Eric couldn't picture Vic taking up with Rivera—it just didn't match. *Hell, nothing is matching. Rivera is as much a possibility as anyone else.*

He opened his eyes to stare at the map before tapping his finger on an area where he knew of an abandoned warehouse near the railroad. "The old Swan's Lumber Company warehouse could be a good place to start. It's abandoned, out of the way, and probably a good place to hold someone unnoticed."

Mike glanced down at his cell phone. "It's quarter to eight. Maybe they've let him go by now. They got the money hours ago. You'd think they'd want to get the hell out of town."

"Or they could lay low for a day or two to make sure I haven't got the police involved."

"If that's the case, we'll have to park a mile or so from the warehouse, hike along the creek bed below the warehouse, and go in from the back." Mike swept his finger along the lines of the map to indicate his strategy.

Kate's stomach was in a knot. She wasn't in love with any of the ideas. "Maybe we should call the police and let them handle it, Dad."

He turned to his apprehensive daughter to fold her into his chest. "Everything's going to be okay. We're going to be careful, but we're not going sit around waiting for them to release Shane, because they may decide not to."

"You don't really think Vic would let anything happen to him?" Kate asked.

Gently, he took her by the shoulders to look into her eyes. "I didn't think he would ever do something like this. I have to wonder how much I can really trust what Vic Deveaux is capable of now, don't I?"

"I suppose so," she muttered.

She was feeling betrayed by the man who used to bounce her on his knee, or lead her around on one of the horses. She couldn't figure out what happened.

Vic Deveaux's coarse attitude was a constant around Westwood, but not with her. He always smiled at her and called her by his pet names. When she was small, he used to call her "princess" or "Cindy-rellie." As she grew into a woman, those childish terms of endearment went by the wayside. Now, he called her Miss Katie.

Where did that Vic Deveaux disappear to?

"We could stop along the way and see if anyone has seen Vic. It would give us some idea of what direction he was heading, and maybe a timeline," Mike said.

"Good idea, the Stop-N-Shop is on the way. He likes their coffee," Eric noted on his way toward the kitchen door. Mike followed after hesitating at the threshold to glance back at his sister.

"Be careful," she pleaded.

With a thin, reassuring smile, he nodded and closed the door behind him.

They were silent during the drive down Route 220.

Mike could see the tension growing inside his father with every passing moment. The uncertainty of where Shane was or what was happening was eating a huge hole in his gut.

Eric stared out the passenger window. Vic's bitter bite of betrayal was scraping down his spine almost as much as his dire concern for Shane.

Searching his mind, Mike spent the drive tapping his fingers on the steering wheel.

How did Vic know about the money in the safe? Who was Vic close enough to form an alliance with, and plan a kidnapping in such a short period of time? The only people who were in the study discussing the money was Dad, Shane, and me ... until Riv came in with Cody's medicine.

He took in a braced breath. In all the panic he'd forgotten all about Rivera's brief appearance. Until now...*How much did he overhear?*

The thought that Rivera could possibly be involved started to marinate in Mike's brain as he pulled into the Stop-N-Shop. They jumped from the Denali. Mike yanked down on the back of his shirt to make sure that the gun that was tucked in his jeans was securely concealed. Eric made a beeline for the cashier, while Mike hung back scanning the store.

"Mike West..." a voice called out from near the dairy cooler.

He turned to find Ginger LaFond standing behind him, with her hands planted on her tiny hips. She was wearing a pair of riding breeches and her tall riding boots, with a crop stuck in the right boot. She had a tight pout on her lips and a glower in her eyes that he couldn't decipher.

"Hey, Ginger. How are you?"

"Not happy," she replied. "Where's that brother of yours?"

"I'm not sure," he said. "When did you see him last?"

"Last night at Barney's, he was supposed to—We were supposed to meet somewhere, but he stood me up and never showed." She grabbed the crop from her boot to slap it hard against the leather.

Mike flinched.

The not-so-quiet conversation drew Eric's attention. "What time was that, Ginger?" he asked.

She softened her tone for the older West. "I dunno, about one. I waited for him until three in the morning. Then, I just went to bed."

"Have you seen Vic Deveaux?" Eric asked.

"Not today," she said. "I saw him last night."

"At Barney's?"

"No, at the trailer park, he was going into the trailer next to mine, twenty-three, some old stable hand lives there. I think his name's Jose, I'm not sure. His truck was still there this morning when I left."

"Did you happen to see Carlos Rivera?" Mike inquired.

"He was at Barney's last night, too. But he was passed-out in a corner booth. Why?"

Mike displayed a cool front with a shrug of his shoulder. "Just wondering. Was anyone with him?"

Agitated, the left side of Ginger's lip sucked in. "I don't pay a lot of attention to stable hands." she snapped.

"What was I thinking?" Mike replied, wryly.

Eric felt as though they retrieved as much information from her as they were going to. They were now wasting time. "Thanks, Ginger," he said as he rushed out of the door.

Before Mike could escape, she stabbed him in the chest with the crop to bring him to a dead halt. "Tell your brother that I'm pissed. I'm going to un-friend him on Facebook."

"He'll be crushed." Mike sidestepped past her out the door.

"Those old guys are more ambitious that you gave them credit for," Mike called to Eric while climbing into the driver's seat.

"More ambitious than *Shane* gave them credit for. Let's get to that trailer park fast."

∾ ∾ ∾ ∾

The aching in Shane's arms was almost unbearable. His hips and buttocks throbbed, and the ringing in his ears had grown to an unbearable ruckus. He wasn't sure how long he'd been shackled with his arms over his head while seated on the hard damp cement floor. He'd lost all track of time, in and out of consciousness while trapped in total darkness behind the blindfold. The dungeon's dank air clung to his face and the cloying stench of mold and mildew was sickening. Wet and cold and sore, he was beginning to think that maybe Krebs would ultimately kill him before help arrived.

He was worried that he may never see his family again. His mind began to drift.

Shane loved them.

Mike is a total workaholic with a little OCD thrown into the mix. He takes himself way too seriously. But hey, maybe that's what I love about him the most. That is the very reason I tease him as often as possible. We don't always see things eye-to-eye, and many times those discrepancies bring us to task, but we are brothers. It is a bond that can never be broken—no matter what the disagreement.

Although Mike possessed a "must win" attitude, he did what was best for the horses at all costs. For that he had Shane's respect and admiration.

Kate was the big sister and the little sister and the daughter, that always knew what was best for the West men, whether they liked it or not. She wanted them to be happy and looked after them like an old mother hen—especially her father.

If he concentrated hard enough, he could smell the sweet aroma of honeysuckle, lilac, and apple-cinnamon. She always had candles burning throughout the house to fill the rooms with comforting warmth. He teased her mercilessly about the candles. The truth was, he loved the soothing fragrances. The thought of it helped to soothe him at this moment.

She reminds me so much of Mom. She would've been proud of the woman Kate has become—strong, reliable, good-hearted. She deserves a good man. Holden Reese seems like a good man. He's lucky to have a woman like Kate—and he better treat her right.

It was his father that Shane really looked up to. The man was rock solid, unyielding in his convictions, and inexorably fair to everyone.

He would never ask anyone to do anything that he would not be willing to do himself. God, I can only hope to turn out to be half the man that he is. There's no doubt that Mike will. Disappointing that man is not an option.

I'm not sure that I haven't already been a grave disappointment. It was a regretful thought. *If I make it out of this jam, I will have to work harder to make the grade. Amen to that.*

He drew in a long calming breath, his sore ribs and spine screamed with ache. *Reserve your strength, asshole. Don't let Krebs get into your head. Don't let him get the upper hand, or it will be all over. I'll never see my family again, and I can't let Krebs rob me of that. Stay resolute, strong, unyielding, like Dad would, like Mike would.*

"Shane ... Shane ..." Luzetta's ragged whisper jerked him from his thoughts.

He opened his eyes against the wet blindfold. His body shook and throbbed. Her tiny feeble fingers wrapped around the black cloth to tug the blindfold down around his neck.

He blinked his eyes. The view was fuzzy and blurred. He could make-out her long white hair draped over her shoulders. Her wrinkled face and grayish-blue eyes came into focus. She was frail and gaunt, but there were remnants of a once lovely woman.

He looked around the dungeon at the mice scurrying amongst the garbage, the flames dancing atop the torches on the walls, and the metal gate that led into the turret.

The old woman pulled a doughnut from her tattered apron. She held it between her fingers, ripping off a piece, and placing it in his mouth. Ravenous, he chewed it up. He was thankful to get something in his stomach.

"This is much worse than my senses told me." She fed him another piece of the doughnut. "I knew they meant you harm, that they would use the dungeon for wicked things, but I didn't realize how bad."

"Who are you?" he asked around the mouthful.

"I'm Luzetta Valentine, and you are in my father's dungeon."

Hokay, that's freaky. "Mind if I ask ... why does your father have a dungeon?"

Realizing how utterly disturbing that must have sounded, she chuckled lightly. "My father was Salvatore Valentine. He filmed Dracula movies in this very dungeon in the 1930's and for a good part of the 40's." She gave him more of the doughnut. "That was the golden age of film, young man, in case you're wondering."

"Don't you mean the golden age of Hollywood?"

"There's nothing golden about that place, I'm afraid." Luzetta's voice had a somber tone.

Shane studied her for a moment. "Did you call the police?"

"I don't have a telephone, but I do have this." She dug deeper in the pocket of the apron and produced a tiny screwdriver.

Shane smiled. "It's better than nothing."

She stuffed the rest of the doughnut into his mouth. While he chewed it up, her unsteady hands gripped the screwdriver to poke at the lock of the handcuffs. "You're going to need to get out of here as soon as possible. I can feel the rumbling inside me that the others will be coming very soon."

"Do you mean Krebs or Rivera?"

"No young man, the ones that ride the motorcycles. I can feel their approach. They won't want anyone else at the mansion for their ... meetings."

"You let a motorcycle gang have meetings here?" He was quite shocked by the old woman.

"No—" The heavy door at the top of the turret opened to toss its squealing echo down the staircase.

Luzetta froze.

Sucking in a long breath, Rivera peeked through the doorway.

Luzetta dashed into a dark corner at the far side of the dungeon and tucked herself deep into the shadows.

Furtively looking over his shoulder while rubbing his hands up and down his arms, Rivera slowly made his way to the top of the stairs. He had been able to convince Krebs to come to the dungeon himself earlier, however, the second time he commanded Rivera to make the trip. He felt it was in his best interest to do as he was told.

The thin beam of a flashlight searched the staircase before he began his decent. Filled with angst, he stopped halfway down the stairs to slice the darkness with the tiny beam before continuing.

Shane could hear his heavy anxious breaths. Mumbling curses in Spanish, he approached the gate. He cringed at the mice scrambling over the floor. Disgusted by the vermin and filth, he shoved the gate open and made his way across the floor.

He searched Shane's face for shades of fear as he approached. Shane didn't give him any.

"Comfy?" he asked while keeping a wary eye on the mice.

"Gee, Riv, where'd you come up with this bright idea? Google?"

His eyes narrowed in disdain. His voice flattened. "It is a good thing that the blindfold came off, compadre. You wouldn't want to miss your own death."

He pulled a gun from the back of his waistband, and the keys to the cuffs from his pocket. Shane was certain that he could easily overpower Rivera, if his arms weren't so numb and stiff and sore. He wasn't even sure that he'd be able to bring them down to his sides right away.

Rivera was careful to keep the gun trained on him when he opened the cuffs.

Shane's shoulders cracked and his muscles screamed in agony as he lowered his arms. Slowly, he rubbed them, to get his swollen fingers moving, and the blood flowing through his arms once again.

Rivera kicked him in the leg. "Get up."

Everything ached. Everything seemed locked-up tight while he struggled to a standing position.

Rivera nudged him hard with the barrel of the gun. "Let's go."

Luzetta shivered with fright as she watched from the shadows. Wrapping her arms around her body, she pressed her eyes closed and rocked back and forth while searching her mind for anything that her psyche would give her.

The others were approaching, in groups. The rumble of the engines roared through the vision. The motorcycles were on their way. If the mansion wasn't empty there would be more hell to pay than she could begin to imagine.

~ NINE ~

The door crashed open to split the safety chain in half. Mike stumbled into Jose's trailer. Scanning the living room, Eric followed with his gun drawn.

Mike led with his Glock. Stealthily, he made his way down the long narrow hallway to peer into a small bedroom, a tiny bathroom, and the master bedroom at the end of the hallway. All the rooms were unoccupied.

Lowering his gun, Mike crossed through the living room and into the kitchen, where Eric had his hands wrapped around the coffee carafe on the table. "The coffee is still a little warm. They haven't been gone long." Eric sank into a chair.

"Do you still want to go to the warehouse?" Mike was surprised that his father was sitting.

"No," Eric muttered. His eyes were filled with contemplation. "Vic was so rattled last night, and the more I think about it, the more I'm starting to believe he doesn't trust whoever he's involved with."

"Rivera?"

Eric bit his lip and nodded, "I think he overheard us talking about the money in safe. I'm not sure how Jose got involved, but obviously, he did. " Eric shook his head. "Vic was so private, a loner. In all the years

I knew him, he never went out drinking with the guys or mentioned a woman that he may have been involved with, or even dated." He rubbed his fingers over his bristly, unshaven face. *Vic Deveaux—introvert—big time.*

Mike picked up a pile of mail on the counter. "He was probably rattled because he was feeling guilty about betraying you. Funny, I've never heard him say more than good morning to Rivera, and now they're partners in a kidnapping? It's hard to wrap my head around it." He shook his head, bemused.

Resting his mouth against his fist, Eric leaned an elbow on the table. He replayed the conversation in the foyer over in his mind when Vic was leaving with the briefcase full of money...

"Vic! If Shane is harmed in any way... there won't be a corner on this earth where I won't find you."

"Remember, no cops, Eric. Our plan is to drop him on one of those Old Mine Roads. By the time he walks home, we'll be gone. I promise you, he'll be in one piece."

He slammed his fist against the wooden tabletop. The coffee splattered from the mug over the scarred surface. His eyes and nostrils widened.

Eric's eureka moment didn't escape Mike, who pitched the mail aside. "What is it, Dad?"

"Old Mine Road. Isn't that where the strip mines are?"

"Yeah ..."

"There's an abandoned mansion out that way too." He snapped his fingers in the air. "The ... the ... Valentine Mansion, I think it's called."

"Do you think they're holding him there? Why?"

"Because Vic said they'd drop him off on Old Mine Road, but I think he may have been giving me a clue as to where Shane is ... in case his partners got greedy. Who knows why? Let's go." He jerked from the chair making haste for the door.

Mike was at his heels. "That's a forty-five minute drive, at least."

"Step on it."

"Good morning." A deep friendly, familiar voice shook Kate from her heavy thoughts while she made her way through the quiet barn.

Seeing her twitch, Punch chuckled. "Didn't mean to scare you. I was beginning to think no one was gonna show this morning. Where is everyone?"

Swallowing the thick knot of tension in her throat, she noticed that the skeleton crew for Saturday morning was absent. Rivera and Torres were supposed to be on duty. It didn't matter—the horses would have to manage with the bare minimum this morning.

"Oh, we had some problems this morning." She tried to put on a cool front, but was failing.

"Anything I can help you with?" Punch asked.

She urged a gentle smile. "I don't think so. Hey, how's that arm?" She touched his injured arm that was still cradled in the sling. Now it seemed like weeks ago.

"I'm just about ready to yank this damned sling off. It gets in the way."

"You do as the doctor says, or I'll slap you across the head," she said.

A little bit of sass, that's better. "Yes ma'am. Have you got time to take a look at Cody?"

"You know I do."

They walked in silence toward the old Quarter Horse's stall. Punch could see the tension in her stride, in her shoulders, and in her eyes. *Oh yeah, the Wests have problems. Whatever they are, they're eating at Kate from the inside out.*

He wanted her to confide in him like she used to when she was younger. Kate had always shared her deepest secrets with him. Who her latest crush was, how she and a friend had skipped school one Friday, and the biggie: when she lost her virginity. Back then things were simpler. As the West children grew older and the pressures of life got in the way, there was less and less time for those talks. Punch deeply regretted that.

Cody met them at the stall door by nuzzling at Punch's chest. His big hand stroked the gelding's forelock.

Kate ran her hand down Cody's chest and down his leg over his ankle. It was still swollen and hot. She frowned. "Are you painting the ankle with DMSO?"

"Everyday—it seems like the pain is less. I've still got him on bute," Punch told her.

"Mmmm, we don't want to keep him on that for terribly long. It's bad for his stomach. Let's cut back on the bute. Keep him in the stall and quiet. It's like the Doc said, time and rest." She patted Cody's head. "Isn't that right, buddy?"

She expelled a long, heavy sigh as if to cleanse her lungs of the trouble she was holding back. Running her hand through her blond locks, she turned to exit the stall.

Hesitating, she turned to her old confidant. "Punch ..."

"What is it, girl? You know you can tell me."

She knew that really wasn't true. What could he do? She didn't know where Shane was. She didn't know where her father and Mike were. In the hours that had past, they had plenty of time to get into plenty of trouble. She was at the very edge of her sanity. At this point, with each hour that slugged by, the risk of losing all three of them was getting higher.

She swallowed hard. "If someone you knew was in trouble, would you go against the rules to help them?"

Punch's eyes narrowed, he cocked his head to one side. "What rules?"

She pinched her lip between her teeth. "Oh, I dunno, like maybe calling the police. As an example, I mean."

An example, yeah, sure. Something was more than wrong. Something was drastically wrong. She was sworn to keep the police out of it. It was tearing her apart. For some reason, Kate felt that they needed the police.

Punch recalled seeing Mike and Eric tear out of the driveway several hours ago—no Shane.

By the process of elimination, he bet that the dire situation had everything to do with the youngest West. Was Shane missing? He didn't know what to tell her. He was pretty sure that what information she had given him was all he was going to get. He hoped to eek-out a little more. "Is this person in trouble with the police? Or do they need help from the police?"

Averting her eyes, she bit her lip again. She had gone too far. She couldn't involve Punch. He was injured and this wasn't his problem. Punch was like a member of the family, but if she told him the situation he would put himself in harm's way. She couldn't bear the thought of being responsible for that. "I think I know what I'm going to do. Thanks, Punch." After kissing him on the cheek, she darted from the barn without a clue of what to do next.

Watching her panicked retreat, Punch decided to keep a vigilant watch over Kate.

Worry consuming her, Kate flopped down into a chair in the dining room. She considered calling Holden to see if he could use some help at the track. Keeping busy might soothe her troubled mind.

Reaching into her pocket, she fumbled for her cell phone until her teary eyes were drawn to the map of the county still lying across the table. She raked her fingers through her hair while her mind raced back to the moment that she had crept down the staircase after harsh voices from the study woke her.

The voices belonged to her father and to Vic Deveaux. She was used to hearing Vic speak harshly to most everyone at the farm, never to her father. That was what drew her from her bed into the hallway. When she reached the top of the stairs, she witnessed Vic, her father's briefcase clutched in his hand, stomping from the study into the foyer. She heard her father call to him from the study ...

"Vic!" He marched into the foyer after him. The look on his face was one that she'd never seen before—panic and rage in a malevolent mix.

"If Shane is harmed in any way ... there won't be a corner on this earth where I won't find you."

She recalled that Vic didn't turn around. It was as if he couldn't face him. She remembered taking two more steps down the stairs while wondering what they could be talking about.

"Remember, no cops, Eric. Our plan is to drop him on one of those Old Mine Roads. By the time he walks home, we'll be gone. I promise you, he'll be in one piece."

She came to a dead stop halfway down the staircase. Her heart gripped inside her chest, she couldn't believe her ears or her eyes.

The memory was forever burned into her brain. It was a morbid recollection of the shame that was etched into Vic's expression when he walked out the door. It was that look that had her clinging to the hope that he wouldn't let anything happen to Shane. Dropping her elbows onto the table, she buried her face in her hands peeking at the map through her fingers. There is was, a thin red line on the far end of the county with the tiny black words slithering along the line: *Old Mine Road.*

Her head spun. She snatched a black *Sharpie* pen resting on the table and dropped it to the map. Fingers clenched tightly around the pen she drew a thin black line along the area that Old Mine Road wound through along the old strip mines.

Some of the kids she went to school with used to go there to party and make-out. They used to talk about an old abandoned mansion along that road. It had a wonderfully romantic name, but she couldn't recall it. She marked the guesstimated spot with an X.

She dialed her father's cell phone. It rang and rang until his voice mail picked up. *Damn it.*

With shaking fingers, she dialed Mike's phone with the same result. Dread cut deep while she imagined why neither one of them would answer. They were either in a dead zone; or, God forbid, they couldn't answer.

Panic ripped through her body to steal her breath away. She needed to get to Old Mine Road. It would be foolhardy to go alone.

She rushed into the study to toss back the curtains to peer out the bay window. Punch's red pickup was still parked outside of the barn. At any other time Punch would be her first choice. He wouldn't hesitate to help, except she didn't know what she would be walking into. With his arm out-of-commission, she couldn't risk it.

Biting her lip, she slipped her cell phone from her hip pocket to stare at it. She was swamped with indecision. Perhaps Holden—no, there was someone else who she could trust—who she could call. It was simply a matter of mustering the nerve to dial.

Vic rolled his truck to a stop in front of the mansion. This was it. He had arrived with the ransom.

He had dropped Jose off about a half-mile out and waited for him to walk to the back of the mansion, and climb in through the bedroom window where Krebs swore that he would hold Shane. Vic had promised Eric that his son wouldn't be harmed. He was going to keep that promise. Jose would release Shane, and they would escape the same way he had come in. Krebs had promised that Shane would be secured in that upstairs bedroom rather than the dungeon below the mansion—he didn't trust Krebs. Maybe Shane would be in the bedroom, and maybe he wouldn't. He had to show up with the money in case Krebs double crossed him. The money gave him a cheap insurance policy—very cheap. It was all he had to work with.

As for the rest? Vic hadn't thought that far ahead—just yet.

Grabbing the briefcase from the passenger seat, he slid from the truck, and made his way into the mansion. He was late. He knew Krebs would be agitated. *Screw Krebs.* He could only hope that things would go as smoothly as he and Jose had planned.

Jose crept around to the side of the mansion where Vic had directed him. There was a statue of three naked cupids dancing in a circle in the side yard. Two of the little imps were missing their heads. The one that still had his head was missing both arms. The shrubs were overgrown and prickly. The weeds were as high as his hips.

Jose waded through the Spanish thistles and fought his way past the overgrown bristly ewes next to the wall hiding a wrought iron trellis that climbed to a second story window. Wrapping his arthritic fingers around the rusted trellis that shook from years of neglect, he hoisted his body upward and shoving his foot in the first wrung of the trellis.

After climbing several latches up, he stopped to look up and then down.

I'm too old for this shit.

He took note of the many feet yet to scale to reach the window, *if* he reached the window, and *if* he would be able to get the damned thing open once he got to it. Iffy situations weren't his strong suit.

❧　❧　❧　❧

Krebs heard the truck pull up to the house. He peered out the window to scan up and down Old Mine Road to make sure the old man hadn't been followed. Only weeds, scrub brush, and stubby broken trunks of dead trees were scattered over the land that was stripped of all nutrients. This made it easy to see up and down the roadway for quite a distance.

He looked down on Vic hobbling toward the house with the briefcase full of prosperous future plans that he couldn't wait to employ. He could hear the old codger's steps echoing as he traveled along the corridor that led to the living room. Rubbing his hands together, the tinge of greedy friction burning on his palms; he anticipated opening the case and relishing in the piles of neatly banded bills.

A grim glower filled Vic's expression when he stepped through the threshold of the room with a white-knuckle grip on the briefcase.

A greasy grin snaked across Krebs' sated lips. "How did it go?"

"Just Jim freakin' dandy," Vic bitterly bit out.

Rivera interrupted the conversation to shake Vic's rehearsed calm when he shoved Shane into the room.

Vic met Shane's cold as steel gaze. He couldn't help but swallow hard around the knot of shame in his throat. It was as if he were looking into Eric West's eyes. *Damned if the man hadn't passed that unyielding West constitution on to his sons.* It made the pang of guilt flow through him like a raging river.

Shane's silent reprimand and the thick remorse rushing through him were suddenly interrupted by the sound of a loud thud.

Krebs' and Rivera's brows furrowed. Exchanging suspicious glances, their heads jerked toward the noise. "Better go check that, Riv," Krebs said.

Rivera turned to leave.

Knowing exactly what the sound was, Vic moved swiftly. He opened the case to exhibit the cash before slamming it shut when his fellow desperados stepped toward him.

Rivera's eyes widened. He had never seen that much money in all his life. He was practically foaming at the mouth.

Krebs was cool, unimpressed, but attentive none-the-less.

Vic had their undivided attention. "Okay," he said, "I did my part. Where do we go from here, buckwheat?"

Krebs' grin grew wide. He locked eyes with Shane. His expression did not twitch with a second thought, rather it dazzled with an uncompromised plan in place. "We drive to a remote location, somewhere in the mountains, and we kill him."

Vic's palms were sweating. Tightening his grip on the case, he swallowed a thick slog of saliva. "Just like that?"

"Just like that," Krebs said.

"I've screwed an old friend, but I sure as hell ain't gonna murder his son."

Krebs' poker-face never wavered. He was holding all the cards. "I'm sorry you feel that way, Vic. I'm not surprised. Therefore, I'm afraid that you're going to go down with him."

Vic glanced at Rivera, whose eyes were like daggers.

Thirsting for the money, greed oozing from his pores, Rivera flashed him a look that said "more for me".

Vic measured Shane's battered and bruised appearance, and yet still holding solid to his uncompromising West gape.

Vic wasn't at all surprised.

Without glancing about, without pause, Vic swung the briefcase around to smack Krebs across the face. The blast knocked him backward to the floor. Shocked by the old man's attack, Rivera flinched.

Still stiff and numb, Shane could see that this was his only opportunity to act. He tackled Rivera at the waist and crashed him to the floor to knock his gun free.

It went spinning across the floor.

Vic stood paralyzed, not sure what his next move should be. Rage brought Krebs to his feet to snatch at the briefcase. Vic held tight to the case even after Krebs cuffed him hard in the jaw to send him stumbling backward to slam against the wall. Dazed, he relentlessly clung to the briefcase.

Shane's arms and hands were not cooperating. His grip was weak and pain stabbed down his forearm to his elbows. He succeeded to push away from Rivera and get to his feet, but the stable hand grabbed him from behind to wrap his arms around Shane's torso squeezing with all his might to rob him of air.

Krebs smacked Vic hard across the face to seize the briefcase from him before ripping his gun from the back of his waistband. When Vic lunged for the gun, Krebs kicked him in the gut to send him to the floor.

His arms still wrapped around Shane, Rivera swung him around to face Krebs. "Shoot him, Krebs! Shoot him!" Rivera screamed. The rolling struggle between Rivera and Shane made his aim shaky.

Panic shot through Vic. He had promised Eric that no harm would come to his son. He had to keep that promise if it was the last thing he ever did with his miserable life. Crawling to his knees, he reached for Krebs' wrist before he pulled the trigger. Shane whipped his head backward to head butt Rivera, hard. The impact shocked Rivera sending a burning throb from his nose through his eyes into his brain. Blood spewed from his twisted nose. He released Shane turning toward Krebs grabbing his face with an angry scream, "Fuck! Shoot him now!"

Out of nowhere a two-by-four struck Krebs' arm as he squeezed off one round. The gun exploded.

There was a silence. Nothing seemed to move, the world seemed to tilt on its axis, the room was frozen in time.

Rivera's eyes bulged in the horrific reality that Krebs had shot him. He collapsed to his knees with a grunt and a groan. Blood seeped into his shirt to saturate the fabric in crimson that slithered across his chest.

Krebs looked up to see who had struck him to find Jose clutching an old rotted board.

Shane knelt down next to Rivera. The blood began to pump from his chest.

Krebs gestured with his gun for Jose and Vic to move near Shane and Rivera.

Krebs drew in a deep, gathering breath. "You picked the wrong team, old man," he told Jose.

Rivera quivered next to Shane. His shaking hand grabbed the hem of Krebs' jeans. "You gotta help me, Krebs," he begged around a desperate agonized groan.

"Your friend needs an ambulance," Shane said.

Krebs studied the pleading man. He was unmoved. Dropping his gun low, he squeezed the trigger to shoot Rivera in the face. Shane fell backward, in shock when Rivera's brain matter and blood splattering over his pants.

"I'm all about problem solving, gentlemen," Krebs said.

~ TEN ~

The grave was shallow—only deep enough to cradle and cover Rivera's body. Krebs had his ransom money and now he wanted out of the mansion fast. He wasn't willing to invest a lot of time on the pomp and circumstance of a proper burial.

Sweat moistened Shane's clothes stained with Rivera's blood and grayish brain matter. Revolted, he tossed the last shovelful of dirt over Rivera's trivial grave. Krebs made Vic help him carry his body into the courtyard to be buried under the fountain.

Wincing, Shane tried not to look at Rivera's shattered bloody face while they carried him through the walkway adorned with old wrought iron trellis' leading into the courtyard. The sound of their footsteps echoed through the corridor as Vic grunted laboriously with each step. Rivera's blood dripped from his body to leave a path like soggy bread crumbs along the way.

The throbbing in Shane's arms and hands had lessened, his back and hips were starting to loosen-up, and the ringing in his ears had quieted to a dull headache. In his mind, he had beaten Krebs to death, or at least to a bloody pulp, with the shovel a dozen times over. Not happening. In one hand he gripped the briefcase, while in the other he held the gun firmly trained on Vic and Jose. He never shifted his hard gaze from Shane's gruesome task.

Defeated, Vic and Jose looked whiplashed. Although Shane appreciated Vic bringing Jose along as some sort of back up plan to get them all out alive, it was too little, much too late. He considered Vic an asshole for getting involved with the hot mess in first place.

Now that he wasn't wearing handcuffs, his fingers, hands, and arms were starting to come back to life. Shane was working overtime trying to hatch a plan. Concentrating, he tried to draw from his brother's cool head and cunning demeanor, as well as his father's imposing strength and repose.

Fighting back his hot-headed impatience, he had to wait for the right moment. *It will come. Sooner or later, it has to come.*

Thankful that the grisly chore was done, Shane stabbed the shovel into the disheveled ground next to the meager mound that was Rivera's grave.

"It's nice to watch the big boss do a little hard labor for a change."

Krebs' quip was greeted by Shane's disgusted sneer filling his dirty exhausted face. "Aren't you gonna say any words over him?"

Stepping forward placing his hand over his heart, Krebs chuckled. "Riv was a good man. He wasn't too bright, but he did what he was told. He just got in the way … literally." He met Shane's seething stare with a smile. "Ahhh, sheer poetry. I should've been a preacher."

"You're a sick sonofabitch," Shane said.

"On many levels. Did you know that I attended Harvard?" Krebs reveled in Shane's "no way in hell" expression. "Oh yes, it's true. My father, one of the great defense attorney's in Boston, was so proud, until he caught me screwing his new young bride. He cut me out of everything. His life. His parties. And his money. Now that's the one that really hurt."

"I'll bet he'd be real proud right about now." Shane ground out—his jaw was so sharp that you could've cut a steel beam with it.

"Hmmm." Krebs scrubbed his chin. Playfully, he contemplated Shane's retort. "You'll get a chance to ask him." A wicked smile filled his face. "I killed him, too. Got off on a technicality, mentally diseased. Imagine my relief." Krebs enjoyed a hearty snicker at Shane's dazed expression. He stepped on Rivera's pitiful grave as if he were the king of the mountain. "The funeral is over ... or not. By the way, none of you will be granted a grave. It looks too much like work. It's time to go, gentlemen."

He gestured toward the Jeep with the gun. When he noticed Shane's quick glance at the shovel, he raised the gun a little higher. "Not a wise choice, Lord West."

Pitching Krebs a malicious glower, Shane fell in line behind Jose and Vic, their heads hanging in disgrace, to walk toward the Jeep. They were beaten.

Every several weeks the groan of many engines in the distance would grow to a frightening roar. The windows that weren't broken would rattle before the motorcycles mounted with hoodlums would surround the mansion.

Luzetta could feel them coming. Her senses would alert her to their approach hours before they arrived. Her senses were screaming their alarm right now. She couldn't stop them. She was old and alone. All she could do was hide in the shadows and wait for them to go away, while listening to their laughter, drinking, and oftentimes drug-induced erotic orgies.

She would watch the men dressed in leather jackets baring a horrible picture of a skull with scorpions crawling from its empty dark sockets trade guns and drugs. The rough, well-used women that accompanied them would swap partners among the men.

She was shaken to the core by the events of the past days. There was no time to calm her old frazzled nerves before the motorcycles would converge upon her home.

She was jerked from her hiding place when the first gun shot rang through the house.

A vision flashed through her mind's eyes. The strange looking piñata she saw in a vision earlier fell from the tree to the ground. The children screamed in horror as hundreds of scorpions scuttled from the broken piñata.

When the second gunshot exploded, she could feel death closing in all around her. Hands shaking, she made her way through the secret passageways. Through the window, she watched the tall dark-haired man make Shane bury the nervous Mexican man at the foot of the fountain in the courtyard. The once graceful beautiful garden was now marred by murder.

Helplessly, she observed while he forced Shane and the two older men into a Jeep and pull out of the drive.

Her heart felt heavy that she couldn't help the young man more than she did. What could she do? Everyday was a new challenge in survival for her. As the days, weeks, and years past, that challenge became harder and harder. Pressing her eyes closed, breathing in deeply, she searched her mind for the young man's future ... nothing.

Her heart sank as she slowly opened her eyes to see the Jeep disappear in the distance.

The hazy sunlight seeped through the curtains to shimmer over Stella, the silky white Persian cat sleeping on the window sill. The flickering candles carelessly left to burn sent a waft of vanilla throughout the room to camouflage the smell of sex.

Ava West's auburn hair cascaded across her shoulders. Her breathing was shallow and steady against Carl Lugowski's chiseled chest.

Lieutenant Carl Lugowski worked homicide for the Rosemount Police Department. Like most cops, he was normally a light sleeper. Subconsciously, they had to be prepared for that emergency phone call jolting them from their beds because a body had been found in some dark alley, or a domestic argument had gone awry to result in a murder.

This morning his sleep was deep and his gentle snore was restful while holding Ava's beautiful naked body against his after their night of abandoned love-making.

God, she knew how to get to him.

Carl had taken the day off to spend with his girl. When he arrived at her apartment last evening to take her to dinner and a movie, Ava had other plans. Not a problem. Nosiree, Bob. She answered the door in a dark blue lace teddy that accentuated the swell of her round breasts and her stiff nipples peeking through the sheer delicate fabric. Her sultry green eyes had a "come on" look. Her plump lips begged to be kissed hard.

Ava didn't flirt. When she wanted sex, she was shameless. She opened the door and pressed her lips to his. Running her hands over his chest, she unbuttoned his shirt. There was no fumbling. The buttons slipped open with unerring precision.

He slipped the strap of the teddy from her shoulder to bare one of her beautiful breasts. Running his tongue over the pebbled nipple, he felt the undeniable pressure of his erection.

Pushing him away, her smile turned devious. Ava was like that. She teased.

He knew what she was about.

As gracefully as a dancer, she swooped up two glasses of wine from the hall table and strutted toward the bedroom. Her long silky hair lightly caressed her back as she moved.

Lord, have mercy. How he loved to watch her walk toward that bedroom where pleasure would rule the night, where once would never be enough to satisfy her desire. Ava was a demanding lover, and he aimed to please and please and freaking please.

Who needs a movie? We'll pickup a matinee tomorrow—maybe.

Now their clothes lie on the floor. They were spent. The sheets lightly covered their warm, moist, naked bodies, until the surreal quiet was broken by Lugowski's cell phone buzzing and vibrating against the lamp on the nightstand.

Dragging slowly, his eyes rotated toward the meddling reverberation and the clock—whoa, he'd slept later than usual. He let out a low grouse reaching for the phone.

Ava tugged at his arm. "Let it go to voice mail," she murmured.

Not a bad idea. He was seriously considering it, when he caught the name on the screen: *Kate West.*

Game changer.

His relationship with Ava meant the world to him. He had wanted this woman since well, forever. He wanted her when they were in high school. He wanted her while he was away at the academy. He still wanted her when he returned to find that she was Mike West's wife. Now, she was exactly where he always wanted her to be, in his life, and in his bed.

Wrangled and rocked beyond his control, his heart skipped a beat when Kate West was around. Hell, when Kate West's name was merely mentioned. She stirred something inside him that he couldn't explain. He couldn't wrap his head around it. She confused and, quite frankly, scared the hell out of him.

Kate wasn't the clichéd blue-eyed, blonde-haired, "girl next door". She was definitely a woman any man would want to come home to, wrap his arms around, and make love to night after night. Kate West was what Lugowski would define as "a keeper".

C'mon, he was in bed with the woman of his dreams. *I should really let the call go. Yeah, really, that's what I should do.* He was totally baffled by the call. *Why would she be calling? We don't have anything but a professional relationship. So...*

"I need to take this. Sorry, baby." Sitting up, he pressed the phone as tightly and as covertly as possible to his ear. "Lugowski..." He made sure he sounded authoritative and official.

"Carl, I'm so sorry to bother you. This is Kate West."

Running her fingers through her hair, Ava perked her ears when she detected a slightly familiar female voice filtering through the receiver. It made her brows pinch together and her lips purse. Suspicion was mixing it up with jealousy. Lugowski had successfully muffled the voice, but she tilted her head against the pillow. Engaged, she narrowed her eyes.

The voice sounded like Kate's. That was definitely an unacceptable intrusion on her plans of morning sex, afternoon delight, and evening erotica.

"What's going on?" Lugowski recognized the disquiet in her voice.

"I don't want to talk about it over the phone, but it's really important, Carl. Can we meet at McDonald's?"

Coffee. He had had coffee with the lovely blonde at McDonald's several times. Usually it was at his request. It had become almost a code between them—never anything sexual.

Carl wasn't sure what he would do if it ever did. *Shit, what am I thinking? Kate is Mike West's little sister and Ava's ex-sister-in-law. It's too complicated, too weird, too out-of-control.*

"I'm on my way." The words spilled right out of his mouth.

Ending the call, he pitched the sheets aside, swung his legs over the bed, and reached for his boxer briefs.

Briskly sitting up, Ava grabbed his arm. The black satin sheets slipped to her waist. Her breasts bobbed into glorious view. "What? Wait a minute, where are you going?" Her tone was high-pitched, a sign of her annoyance. It only took a nanosecond for her green bedroom eyes to morph into a jaded glower.

It was a justifiable question that Carl knew he couldn't give an honest answer to; unless he was absolutely sure that he wanted to endure the repercussions. To say the least, Ava would be furious, if she knew he was leaving her bed to go to Kate's aid, or whatever it was that he was going to, he wasn't sure. He only knew that he had to go.

"There's a problem with a case I'm working on. I'll be back as soon as I can," He shoved his left leg into his pants pulling them onto his lean hips with a jerk before zipping the fly.

Appalled, Ava fell back onto her elbows. Her full perfect breasts to remain exposed. Her auburn hair sprayed across the pillows.

She tilted her head against her shoulder. "There's a problem right here in my bed." She tossed the sheet away and spread her long legs to entice him to resume their extracurricular sexual activities. Not-so-subtly promising erotic bliss, she licked her curled lips.

Lugowski eddied into his shirt, quickly flipping the tie around the collar. With nervous fingers, he buttoned his shirt. He shoved his feet into his shoes. *Screw the socks.*

He didn't dare look in her direction. He knew what the instant reaction would be. Perhaps that would be the smarter option. He didn't have a relationship with Kate. He couldn't afford a relationship with Kate, who possessed the most captivating pair of crystal blue eyes he'd ever gazed into. Nope, he didn't want a relationship with Kate. Right? *Damned to hell.*

He snatched his suit jacket that was flung over the leopard print vanity chair. Feeling the inside pocket, he found his emergency pack of cigarettes. *Yeah, I'll be needing those, badly.*

He turned toward the bedroom door to find Ava blocking his path. A daunting glare in her eyes, she was tying a dark blue silk robe around her.

If looks could kill, Kate West would be dead. He sucked in his lips at the almost humorous situation—almost.

"I'm sorry, baby. I've gotta go." He gave her a slight peck on the cheek, scuttled past her, and darted down the hallway.

The apartment door slammed.

Ava swept the cat into her arms. Purring, Stella nuzzled against her shoulder. Pinching back the curtain, she gazed down to the parking area below. Gauging Lugowski with a lifted brow and a pout on her lips, she watched him jog across the lot and hop into the unmarked police SUV.

⚬ ⚬ ⚬ ⚬

Mike slowed the Denali to a crawl past the Valentine Mansion to survey the grounds as best as they could from the road. The dilapidated mansion rose portentously from behind the stucco walls and the wrought iron gates. The overgrown shrubbery and brush made it impossible to get a good view of the estate.

"We'll park down the road and come in on the east side of the walls," Eric said.

They drove a half-mile beyond the estate to park the SUV in heavy brush. Ducking low, they jogged toward the house. Sucked against the outer wall, they hesitated to catch their breath while Mike glanced around the area.

"That's a lot of house to cover," he said. "Have you got a plan?"

"Once we find an entrance, I'll go upstairs, you go down," Eric said. "Be careful, we don't know how many might be in there."

They inched their way toward the lions perched on the pedestals at the entrance. Eric ducked under the first lion, while Mike dashed across the driveway to hide under the other. Peering around the lions, Vic's Ford Ranger came into view. Eric and Mike exchanged telling glances. Using the overgrown ewes, rhododendrons, and brush as camouflage, they made their way to the truck. From behind it, they surveyed the mansion for any sign of movement.

All was quiet.

They scurried to the turret on the east side of the mansion. Gingerly opening the metal gate, they slid along the wall to the doorway that led inside the tower. Slipping through the door, they each sucked against the wall on either side of the threshold in the dark dank turret.

They noticed the stairs that led upward, and the steps that went down.

Eric yanked his Glock from his waistband. With a nod, he gestured to Mike that he was going up.

Holding his gun close to his chest, Mike began his decent down the stairs. The stale air and the thick cobwebs greeted him. He could see the flicker of light at the bottom of the turret. Though he heard no sound, no voices, his apprehension was on high alert.

Reaching the bottom, his eyes widened at the sight of the dungeon beyond the heavy metal gate. Meager flames danced atop the torches; still they provided enough light to display the dungeon's despicable conditions and the chunky chain shackles hanging from the wall inside the cell. The cloying smell of mildew, garbage, rats, and filth was overpowering.

The room was eerily empty, as if the prisoners had been cleared out while waiting for new to torment.

Breathing through his mouth, Mike, in total disgusted awe, forced himself to press forward toward the shackles with measured steps. He found only the open cuffs dangling from the shackles, but it was the sight of the cattle prod leaning in the corner that overwhelmed him. With tentative hands, he lifted it from its resting place.

Remembering a time that he himself had been strapped down and tortured like an animal at the hands of a maniac, Mike broke into a cold sweat. The thought that they may have very well had used the cattle prod on his brother made his stomach wrench and his anger boil.

Vic made a promise to his father. Had he no honor left?

"Holy shit," he muttered to himself.

Keeping alert for sounds, for movement, and for voices Eric crept along the wall of the corridor. The house echoed with menacing emptiness.

He came upon the first threshold to peer around the corner into the empty living room. At once, his eyes were drawn to the huge crimson pool of blood slowly seeping into the floor in the middle of the room. Fear like he'd never experienced before gripped him. It gripped him yet tighter, when he noticed the drops that led from the room back into the corridor that he had just come from. Trying to catch his breath, he dashed to the center of the room. His hand shaking, he dipped his finger in the blood.

It was still wet and fresh.

Panic coiled through his gut while his eyes retraced the droplets back to the corridor. Slowly he rose to his feet. Swallowing a thick knot of dread, he followed the stains leading him back to the turret, and down through the dark staircase.

He stepped into the corridor as Mike stepped out of the doorway of the turret. He didn't want to tell his father what he had found. If Shane was here, he didn't want his father to see the grisly conditions those sonofabitches had held him under.

When Eric turned to him, the look on his face boldly revealed that he had seen something much worse.

Saying nothing, Eric pointed at the trail of blood that continued down the corridor. His glance lifted through the tangled branches of the dead wisteria drooping on the trellis into the courtyard.

Immediately, they saw the low-lying mound of dirt beneath the fountain, and the shovel nearby.

"Christ Jesus." Abandoning all caution, Eric broke into a dead run down the corridor and burst into the courtyard with Mike at his heels. They slid to a stop at the gravesite only to stare at it. They were unable to move or even to breathe.

Eric dropped to his knees. Frantically, he pawed at the dirt.

Mike couldn't stand the sight. He grabbed the shovel and his father's shoulder. "Dad, let me." He was barely able to muster the words. With shaking hands, he stabbed the shovel into the loose, moist dirt.

"That's not your son's grave," a feeble voice spoke-out from behind them.

Meeting his father's eyes, Mike froze. They turned to see a tiny white-haired woman peering at them from behind the trellis.

Eric slowly rose to his feet.

"Who the hell is that?" Mike murmured.

"No idea." With an uncertain stride, Eric made his way to the trellis. He could see the distrust in the old woman's eyes. Slowly, he grasped the rusted metal, his nerves and frustration won out with a white knuckle grip. "What do you know about my son?" he asked in a raspy, desperate whisper.

Luzetta studied his face. She never showed herself to intruders of her mansion, but she strongly sensed that these two men were on a mission—a mission for someone they cared for and loved. She could see the rugged strength in this man's eyes. The same strength she had observed in Shane's. It matched the square determined jaw and broad shoulders wide enough to carry many a burden. There was no doubt in her mind that this man was Shane's father. She prayed that he had not arrived too late to help his son.

"They left not long ago. Traveling north," she said quietly through the dead wisteria branches.

"Who's in the grave?"

Luzetta drew her face yet closer to the trellis to lace her frail fingers over the metal next to Eric's. Her gaze lugged to the heap of dirt at Mike's feet beneath the fountain where colorful flowers used to grow and the crystal clear water trickled delicately, rhythmically from its curled basins.

"A Mexican man. I believe they called him Rivera. The dark-haired man killed him."

"Krebs," Mike said. "Rivera was kind of cozy with Martin Krebs."

Swallowing hard, thankful that there still might be time, Eric gently touched her fingers, while urging a grateful smile. "Thank you." With that, Eric spun on his heels to rush toward the gate.

Dialing Kate's number again, Mike was right behind him. *Where the hell could she be?* It didn't matter ... the call wasn't going through.

~ ELEVEN ~

Managing to keep a country block between them, Punch followed Kate into Rosemount. He was careful to maintain at least four cars apart during the drive down the main drag of the town. She didn't seem to notice his red, Dodge Ram pickup tailing her. Traffic slowed and cars bunched up when they approached a construction site half-way through town. Kate was waved through by the flagman as were the two cars and the SUV between them, but Punch was forced to stop.

Damn! He was certain he would lose her in the construction zone. Luckily, she pulled into the McDonald's restaurant right beyond the work area. When he was waved through the zone, he parked across the four-lane at the Arby's. He watched her go into the restaurant. Not too long after, Lugowski's white, unmarked SUV pulled in and parked next to her Mustang.

While stuffing an unlit cigarette behind his left ear, Lugowski appraised the parking lot before going into the restaurant.

Evidently, Kate had decided to break the rules for her "friend" and felt comfortable consulting with Lugowski. *Mike would be pissed to hell if he knew.*

That wasn't an assumption on Punch's part. It was a fact.

❧   ❧   ❧   ❧

Lugowski pressed through the glass doors of the fast food restaurant. Instantly, he spotted Kate sitting away from the other patrons in a corner booth at the far end of the restaurant with her back to him.

Mechanically, he took note of the crowd: a young woman coaxing her toddler to eat his apple slices while wiping something sticky from her baby's face. There was a beer-gutted man wearing a faded John Deere T-shirt and a Redskins ball cap wolfing down a Big Mac next to the windows that looked out over the parking area. He was keeping a vigilant eye on the big-rig parked across the lot. As always, several teenaged girls sat dead center. Giggling like a pack of hyenas, they passed a cell phone while taking turns reading a text message.

Bullying at its finest. He approached the booth where Kate waited with two cups of coffee on the table in front of her.

Her rapping fingers on the tabletop and tapping foot provided clues to her nervousness. Her blonde hair was swept across her shoulders. The red tank top that she was wearing defined every curve of her delicious body.

Carl breathed in deep. *Yeah, those are the kind of details that I need to get out of my freaking head.* He was cursing the no-smoking regulations in restaurants. He could've used a nicotine fix right about then.

He slid into the booth across from her. She jerked in surprise causing him to half-smile and utter a low chuckle. "Didn't mean to spook you. Is this coffee for me?"

The left side of her mouth turned upward. She pushed the coffee cup toward him, "Cream, no sugar. Thanks for coming, Carl. I hope I didn't drag you away from anything terribly important."

Important? No, nothing terribly important, just a horny snarling tiger abandoned in her bed. Nevertheless, this was Kate. For some strange reason that he couldn't figure, that made it okay.

"You said it was urgent," he said. "By the look on your face, you weren't kidding. So here I am." He took a sip of the coffee while noticing her odd stare. *Do I have bed-head? Am I buttoned all cock-eyed?* He dragged his fingers through his hair to find the cigarette perched behind his ear. He swiped the cigarette away to tuck into his suit jacket. "Nasty habit," he mumbled.

"I thought you quit." She surveyed his mussed hair; the disarray of his tie, which was dangling low on his chest; and the fact that the top four buttons on his shirt were open. It was a very curious look for Lieutenant Carl Lugowski, indeed. Slightly amused, and unable to take her eyes off his tousled appearance, she took a sip of her coffee.

"Always." He tried to stay focused on her problem, rather than the subtle swell of her breasts at the neckline of that clingy tank top or the way her juicy lips caressed the coffee cup. "What brings us to McDonald's for coffee, Miss West?"

Kate's gaze dropped to her lap. Her shoulders tensed. A slice of betrayal scraped through her gut. Her fleeting amusement was set aside.

She hated involving Carl. Her father would be outraged. Vic had specifically instructed him to keep the police away, but she hadn't heard from her father or Mike. She didn't know what was going on. Were they okay, or were they in as much trouble as Shane, God forbid?

It was time for action. At least that's what she kept telling herself over and over again while driving from Lanzville into Rosemount.

She dragged her gaze to meet Lugowski's. It had taken over an hour for her to find the nerve to call him. He could sense her fear, see her trepidation. He was waiting for an explanation.

Okay, I called him here. It's time to quit lollygagging. Out with it.

"Shane's been kidnapped," she blurted out.

Lugowski's spine spiked to attention—mid-gulp of his coffee, "What? When? Didn't you talk to the police?" He shot the questions at her like bullets from a semi-automatic rifle.

"I'm talking to them now." She looked him square in the eye.

"That's not how it works, Kate—"

"That's how it *has* to work. Please, Carl." Her tone was half insistent-half plea.

He studied the desperation in her lovely, gentle face. Her stunning sapphire eyes were glassed-over with worry. *Christ, how this woman gets to me.* He sighed. "No promises." He firmly began, "Give me the details, and don't leave anything out."

Trying to convince herself that she was definitely doing the right thing, she emptied her lungs of the breath that she'd been holding in since overhearing her father and Vic Deveaux arguing in the study. She explained how angry Vic was at her father because he wanted him to take an easier post at the farm, and how he returned demanding the money in the safe in exchange for Shane. She also explained that Vic had partners. She didn't know how many, and they couldn't figure who these partners might be.

Lugowski flipped the unlit cigarette through his fingers while listening to her story. When she reiterated Vic's mention of Old Mine Road, apprehension tightened his face.

"You're talking about the Valentine Mansion," he said.

"Yes, that's it, the Valentine Mansion. I couldn't recall the name." Her worry was punched up a level when she saw his gaze drop to the coffee cup in front of him. "What? Do you know something about the mansion?"

Jutting his lower lip, he dragged his gaze to hers.

This isn't good.

"Our gang unit has been watching the mansion for quite some time. The Nomads have been using it for drug deals and other extra curricular activities."

"Who are the Nomads?"

"A bad-ass biker gang that the department has been trying to infiltrate for ages." He watched her rake a harried hand through her hair, and bite down on her lip so hard that he expected blood to squirt across the table at any moment. *Oh yeah, she's holding something back, and I have a very bad feeling what that something is.* "Is there anything else that you haven't told me?" Her eyes met his. She subtracted nothing and added even less. "Kate..."

She looked away to watch the young woman take the toddler's hand, hoist the baby onto her hip, and walk out of the restaurant. He watched as her eyes rotate to the high school hyenas huddled together. Cackling, they composed yet another text. *Yeah someone on the other end was either having a good day, or a very, very bad one.* At last she focused on the clouds that were darkening outside. Darkening, like her beautiful, grief-stricken eyes.

"Kate... what are you leaving out? I can't help you if you aren't completely honest with me."

She cupped her forehead in her hand. Tears welled in her eyes. "Oh, God, Dad and Mike went looking for them. I haven't heard from them for hours. No—I haven't heard from them at all." Sobbing, she reached across the table. Her fingers clenched around Lugowski's wrist so tightly that her fingernails turned from pink to white. "Please, Carl, we have to go to that mansion. If I've figured it out, certainly Dad has, too."

Shit. "Too dangerous, Kate, I need to call in a team," Lugowski said. "We can surround the mansion and force them to release Shane ... and anyone else that may have gotten in too deep. Seriously, what the hell were they thinking?"

"No," she replied. "Let's drive out to the mansion and check it out. I could be wrong. We'll see if anyone is there. If so, then you can call in back-up." Now she was pleading.

Whoa! She got to him in ways that was so freaking ridiculous.

She got to him in ways that Ava didn't. With Ava it was wickedly simple. This is what I want. Give it to me or else.

With Kate it was always deep—knee deep. She turned to him because she was in trouble. For some crazy reason, the girl trusted him. Mike West's head would explode if he knew the intricate relationship that he had with his little sister. The man's jaw was always set, and his glare was always buzz saw tight when he saw him with his ex-wife, Ava. *Oh yeah, Mike West would want to take me to task if he knew about Kate, as well.*

"And if we don't find anyone there? What then, Kate?"

She wrung her hands in her lap. Lugowski was a cop. She called him here for his help, and that's exactly what he was offering—cop help. *What did I expect, for Christ's sake?* Again, he was waiting for an answer, and again, it was time for action. "Okay, we check out the mansion and then we call for back-up. We're wasting time, can we please go, Carl?" She slid from the seat and made a bee-line for the door.

Four dusty construction workers were on their way in, they stepped aside to admire her as she past. Lugowski couldn't blame them. She was a sight. The way her jeans clung to her tight little derriere, and that tank top showed off the lush curve of her breasts. *Oh yeah, she's a study in "oh, ba-by".*

Still, Carl didn't like their eyes undressing her. He knew what they were thinking. He wanted to clobber them, except for the fact was that they weren't doing or thinking anything that he didn't every time he was with her.

   ❧   ❧   ❧   ❧

Taking the last slurp of his chocolate shake, Punch jerked to attention when he spotted Kate and Lugowski jumping into the SUV and pulling out of the McDonald's parking lot. After starting his truck, he pulled into traffic to fall in five cars behind them.

Following Kate without being noticed was easy. Tailing Lugowski undetected would be another ball game. Punch breathed a sigh of relief when the detective pulled out of the restaurant and turned left—away from the construction zone.

~ TWELVE ~

The road was straight. The land that yawned before them was barren and ugly through the vast strip mined region. The view was monochromatic and monotonous and depressing.

Almost in a hypnotic state, Shane had to blink hard to stay alert while trying to avoid looking down the barrel of Krebs' gun, which was pointed in his direction at all times.

Krebs' severe stare was unrelenting. Slowly, as they traveled farther away from the strip mines, the trees grew taller, wider, and greener. The thick brush and grasses were alive. The gravel road beneath the Jeep's tires became winding and tempting to awaken his mind in order to simulate the plan in his head.

Shane thrust the Jeep into a higher gear and pressed down on the accelerator. As he rounded the bend a motorcycle whizzed past, followed soon after by small groups of motorcycles of all makes, styles, and sizes. The groups wore black leather. Some of the men wore long bristly beards and dark sunglasses, while others wore do-rags, or helmets with spears bolting out from the top. Many of the riders had women clinging to their waists. The cycles whipped along by the dozens.

Krebs barely noticed the acceleration in the Jeep. He was too busy gawking at the menagerie of motorcycles parading by. Shane glanced into the rear view mirror to make eye contact with Vic. Narrowing his eyes, he raised his hand to his seatbelt to caress the harness and gave a subtle nod to his head.

Vic understood. He tapped Jose's hand, and buckled his seatbelt while silently urging Jose to do the same. Stealthily, his friend complied.

The last group of iron horses rode by, and Krebs fidgeted in his seat.

"What's the hurry?" Krebs jerked Shane's attention back to the road.

Saying nothing, Shane kicked the vehicle into a higher gear and picked up momentum.

Krebs raised the forty-five toward his temple. "Slow down, asshole."

Remaining silent, Shane steered the Jeep fiercely around a sharp bend to almost smack into a Harley Fat Boy dallying farther behind the groups.

The cyclist cursed and threw him the finger.

Sorry, buddy.

Shane focused on the twist and turns in front of him while still picking up speed and praying for a good straightaway and a shitload of nerve.

Krebs pressed the gun hard against his temple.

Vic and Jose shot anxious glances at each other while bracing themselves against the back seat.

Shane could feel the cold steel against his head. With his jaw clenched and a white-knuckled grip on the steering wheel, he willed himself not to give-in, show no fear, not to look, or even think about looking at the gun or Krebs.

Drive, damn it, just drive.

"Stop or I swear I'll blow your fucking head off!" Krebs screamed. Sweat beaded on his brow.

In the short distance ahead, Shane spotted a large oak tree. It was time to cooperate. "You want me to stop?" He kept his eyes trained on the tree.

"Stop!"

Swinging the steering wheel dead straight for the tree, he pressed his eyes closed, and smashed his foot hard against the brake. The seatbelt jerked Shane roughly against his seat as the Jeep bucked and slid to catapult Krebs through the windshield. Glass shattered and recoiled across the dash and the hood. Krebs was like a rag doll slamming and bouncing over the Jeep's hood. The airbags exploded from their encasements to punch Shane in the face, and force his head against the headrest. A piece of glass bounced off the dash to hit him above the eye when the Jeep smashed against the tree with a deafening, jolting crash.

Everything went black.

Steam rose in thick billows of ashen mist from the crumpled hood to form a murky pillow around the wreck.

Dazed, Shane pushed his totally deflated airbag away from his body and glanced at the empty passenger's seat. It was empty but the air-bag was still inflated. Krebs departure was so quick and violent, that he missed the safety feature.

Shane wasn't sure how long he'd been unconscious. He wasn't sure if he had been. He wasn't sure how much time had past, but his head was thumping like John Bonham was playing a boisterous encore on his ear drums. Blinking his eyes and trying to shake away his funk, he felt thick warmth dripping over his right eye. He lifted his hand to find it filled with blood. His forehead burned and his body was stiff.

Painstakingly, he reached to his side to unbuckle the shoulder harness, when he heard a groan. Lugging his gaze to the rearview mirror, he met Vic's pallid deer-in-the-headlights expression.

"Where the hell did you learn to drive like that, boy?" Vic said. It was soft, and it was weak, but it still qualified as a bellow.

Shane surrendered against the headrest. "Mario Cart. You guys okay?"

Vic glanced across the seat at Jose, who was rubbing the nape of his neck and down his shoulder. His face was pale but he was in one piece.

"Yeah, we made it. I'm too damned old for this shit," Vic said.

"Really, Vic, really?" Shane realized that like it or not, he had to see if Krebs was dead, or if he needed an ambulance. It was most unlikely, but even if he did, no one had a cell phone to call for one.

Stiff and sore, he pulled and yanked to free his legs from under the crunched dashboard. For a moment, he thought his legs might be crushed. Soon, with a little tight painful maneuvering, he was able to free his legs, and crawl out of the door.

Vic met him outside of the vehicle. He touched Shane's shoulder lightly. "I'll look with you, son."

Shane studied him for a long moment. This was the Vic that he remembered. Rock solid. With tentative steps, they walked the dreaded short distance to the front of the Jeep. Wincing at the thought, Shane could only imagine what they would surely see. Krebs' badly mangled body wedged between the tree and the Jeep. His dead, glassy eyes would stare stoically up at them. Blood would be spewing like red waves of nausea from his mouth, and dripping from his ears and nose to form dark crimson beads on top of the dry dirt.

Exhausted, used up, and completely freaked-out at what he was about to witness, Shane leaned against the Jeep.

It had all been too much. Krebs had tortured him physically. He had tortured Rivera mentally and verbally before finally killing him in cold blood—without hesitation or remorse.

Shane wondered if he had murdered his own father in the same way.

From Shane's assessment of Krebs' wicked character, it was most probable indeed. If he had had his opportunity, Krebs would have killed them without pause. *I should be glad that Krebs is dead. But seriously, no one should die the way that he just did. I did what I had to do, period.*

The rationalization didn't make him feel any better about it. The emotional overload shuddered through him, and he swallowed hard against the rigid knot in his throat when they finally arrived at the front of the Jeep. They froze in place as if someone had tossed a bucket of ice water in their faces.

Krebs' body was not at the base of the tree.

Shocked, Shane dashed to the other side of the vehicle. Perhaps he was lying there, except again his corpse was eerily absent. Shane and Vic exchanged frenzied glances while their heads twisted and turned to scan the area in search of someone who absolutely, without-a-doubt, had to be dead! But there was no body in sight.

Shane yanked the passenger's door open. He punched at the airbag until it deflated, and searched the floor for the briefcase and the forty-five that Krebs was toting. He came up empty-handed.

"How long were we out?" he asked Vic. Confusion bleeding like a sieve through his voice.

Searching his mind, Vic shook his head.

Shane was in total awe. "I saw him go through the windshield! I saw him—"

The epiphany that he did not see Krebs physically hit the tree punched him in the face. The airbags had inflated to skew his view of what happened once Krebs went through the windshield. After that? It was a total blank.

Shane could see Vic searching his mind with the exact same thoughts as he was having: *He had to be dead! How could he have survived such a bad crash? And if he did, surely he was injured, but how bad? Surely, he would've taken the opportunity to kill all three of us while we were out.*

Shane ran his harried fingers through his hair. He was in a tailspin. Baffled and concerned that Martin Krebs was still out there somewhere, he fell back against the Jeep. Where and how?

The crunch of gravel in the distance caught his attention. He glanced up to see a black Denali coming over the horizon while kicking up dust in its wake.

His shoulders dropped in relief. He knew that black Denali. He knew that the very people that he was afraid that he would never see again were coming over the hill, and he couldn't wait to embrace them.

The SUV slid to a stop next to the jumbled Jeep.

Eric leapt from the passenger's side. "Shane!" He darted for his son to wrap his arms around him. "Are you okay?" He brushed Shane's tousled hair from his face to examine the bruises and the severe slash over his right eye.

"I'm good." He held on tight to the man he loved, missed, and respected above all.

Keeping his son close to his chest, Eric surveyed those who were present.

With his head hung low, Vic turned his back to lean with both arms against the Jeep.

Still trying to catch his breath, Jose sat inside the vehicle.

"Where's Martin Krebs?" Eric asked Shane.

"We don't know, Dad. He went through the windshield during the wreck. I thought for sure he'd be dead, but he's gone." Shane couldn't believe the words as they were spilling from his lips. *It isn't over. Damn, it isn't over.*

Eric scoured the area. Shane knew that his father would search every inch of the county to bring Martin Krebs down.

Stuffing his cell phone back into his jeans, Mike approached the wreck. "The police are on their way, but it's going to take a while. I still can't get a hold of Kate." He turned to Shane. "Are you okay, buddy?" he mussed his kid brother's hair. He was glad and relieved as hell to see him, battered, beaten, and bruised; but alive.

It wasn't enough for Shane. He grabbed Mike to fold his arms around his torso tightly and hug him with all his might.

Mike let out the breath he'd been holding in since his father woke him from a deep sleep that morning. At the same time, he couldn't let his moment to goad Shane pass. Lord knew he was way behind in the constant pissing match that his brother kept alive and active. "What? Are you goin' all soft on me?"

Shane looked up at him, the left side of his lip lifted. "Still no haircut, Mike? Really?"

Jeez, if the little pain in the ass doesn't land on his feet.

Vic turned to the man who he always had the utmost of respect for, had been his friend, and the man he had betrayed. "Eric..." He sucked in a braced breath while searching for the right words. There simply were none. "I'm sorry. That's all I got."

Eric gauged Vic's tormented, guilt-ridden face. *Not good enough.* Shaking his head, he walked toward his Denali.

There was a tight grip on his arm. Eric turned to find his younger son's face filled with desperate compassion. "Dad, Vic tried to stop Krebs. He brought help." Shane tried to oddly enough defend Vic Deveaux.

"You call Jose help?" Eric asked. "Why didn't he call the police, Shane? Hey, why didn't he walk away from the whole scheme to begin with?"

"We can't send him to prison." Shane looked to his older brother for back-up.

Locking his eyes with his father's, Mike scrubbed his hand across his bristly unshaven face. He searched his face for a trace of empathy. There wasn't any.

Eric glanced at Vic. The urge to beat him to a bloody pulp was unnerving. He took in a long calming breath before looking sternly into Shane's pleading eyes. "He knew when he walked into our home last night that he had crossed a line, and there was no going back. One person is dead, Shane. From the looks of you, there could have been two. Krebs is still out there, and who knows what the hell he's capable of. Vic was a part of that."

Every muscle in his body screamed with ache. The blood ran down his slashed face. The acrid taste trickled into his mouth. Krebs could feel his cheeks swelling and his left eye was swollen closed. Managing to bounce and roll off the right side of the Jeep he missed hitting the tree, but his hips and legs were sore and wrenched. He landed hard on his right arm and it broke, but he survived the crash and when he woke, he seriously considered shooting the three men still unconscious in the vehicle.

Too easy for West. Let him sweat. Let him look over his shoulder while wondering where I am and when I will come for him .. .or maybe his family.

Through it all, he managed to hold tight to the briefcase. The money was all his now. There would be no three-way cut. It was his to spend as he pleased. But the burn for West blood was like acid scorching through his veins.

He had dropped the forty-five during the wreck, but he found it on the floor of the Jeep, when he opened the door to see if Shane was still alive. Shane's head was rolled toward him against the headrest—out cold.

He had picked up the gun from the floor with his left hand and aimed it at him. Caressing the trigger lightly, his eyes narrowed. Oh how he wanted to press it. How he wanted to watch Shane West's head explode, and his brains bathe the interior of that freaking Jeep. Drawing a deep gathered breath, he favored torment instead. Shane West would get his soon, very soon.

Careful to stay in the grassy areas, he forced himself to walk until he could find a hiding place. He needed to rest, to think, and to plan. His vision was blurred from the severe bruising and swelling. He was exhausted and weak, when he came upon a huge tree that had been blown over. Its roots had hundred of arms, like a Medusa. They curled around to form a deep cave. He crawled inside to lie down. He laid his head on the briefcase and then set his broken arm across his stomach. His ribs stabbed with pain and his breathing was labored, but his malevolent ambition would drive him forward.

The dirt rained down around him from the intrusion of his body, and the creepy crawlies scampered around him and over him. Closing his eyes, he was certain that it was a good camouflage, until he could get some rest and hatch a vengeful plan.

PART THREE:

IRON HORSE WARRIORS

~ THIRTEEN ~

Lugowski was well aware that the Valentine Mansion was being watched closely by the Rosemount gang squad, but he didn't know the particulars—only that they suspected the Nomads, a notorious biker gang, were using the mansion for drug deals and possibly illegal gun trading.

There was no way in hell he was going to let Kate within five feet of danger. So, during the drive to the middle of nowhere, he kept reminding her that if there was any activity at all at the mansion, they were steering clear.

Dutifully, she would nod. Ahhh, but she was a West, and he didn't trust what was going on inside that pretty little head of hers—nor could he ignore her alluring scent. It was sweet and flowery and sensual. When she would turn to speak to him, he had to jerk his eyes back to the road. Those gorgeous eyes drove him wild in ways that he could barely keep under wraps.

When he turned the SUV onto Old Mine Road, a drape of thunderheads was beginning to fill the sky. By the time he pulled the vehicle into a patch of high bristly brush, the wind swept against the skeletons of the dead twisted trees.

"We're walking from here." Studying the turbulent skies hoping that it would hold off a bit longer, he turned off the ignition.

"How far away is it?" Kate asked.

"Maybe a half a mile. We'll approach from the back of the mansion." He gently grabbed her hand when she went to get out of the vehicle. "Remember—"

"I know. Any sign of trouble, and we call for back-up." She repeated the terms of his cooperation.

God, ya have to hand it to her. The girl's got moxie, and she looks freaking sexy with wind-tossed hair, to boot. He blinked back. *Okay, those are the kind of thoughts that could get us both killed.*

Uneasy about what they might be walking into, Lugowski patted the Glock in his shoulder holster under his jacket and started across the coarse deadwood toward the old estate. Kate followed behind him. The thunder moaned a distant warning to hurry about their business.

"Stick close," he said over his shoulder.

It was getting harder and harder to see and to keep pace with Lugowski's SUV. Punch drove along the dark back roads while keeping a half a mile between his truck and the SUV. The deeper into the outskirts of nowhere they traveled, the deeper his concern grew that not only was something up, but that something was worse than he had imagined. There was trouble—big trouble. When Lugowski finally turned onto Old Mine Road, Punch's mind was racing. There was nothing on the old dirt road except for dead trees and that old dilapidated mansion.

What the hell?

Figuring that the only place they could possibly be going was the mansion, he stopped the truck and waited at the stop sign for at least ten minutes before following. He didn't want to be detected. There was no way on God's green earth that he was turning back now.

Waiting at the intersection of nowhere and nothing made ten minutes seem like ten hours. The clouds thickened and the skies grew dark and threatening. The dust that had been kicked up from the dirt road danced in the wind.

Punch crinkled his nose—that crud was going to form a thick paste on his shiny red truck when it mixed with the impending rain. In need of a distraction, he checked his cell phone for messages. There were none. For that matter, there wasn't any service either.

It was a dead zone—in more ways than he cared to think about.

Finally, with Lugowski's vehicle out of sight, Punch turned on his parking lights and proceeded through the stop sign onto Old Mine Road. The desolate road was dusty and winding and bumpy. The dead stubby trees yawned toward the sky like tormented twisted hostages pleading for mercy in the birth of the storm.

With the dimness of the thunderheads casting dark shadows, he almost missed the white SUV parked alongside the road in the brush. Thinking he had probably been made, he stopped. Then, he realized that the vehicle was abandoned. Quickly, he parked the pickup next to the SUV.

While rifling through the glove box for a flashlight agitation rolled through him when the injured arm in the sling hindered his movements. It was time to ditch the sling. He yanked it over his head and tossed it to the floor before hopping from the cab to climb into the bed of the truck to search the long silver tool box.

He stopped mid-motion.

The sound of water slapping over rocks caught his attention. He listened. *Reardon's Run.* The right side of his lip lifted at the memory of the winding creek that ran along the outskirts of the strip mines.

He and the West boys used to swim in the lower portion of Reardon's Run that spilled into the creeks at Westwood. That ended when the water became murky and rusty from the waste that the mining company pumped into the creek. After the mining company went belly-up, the water had been cleared, but life's commitments didn't leave much time for taking a cool dip in a boyhood swimming hole.

Popping open the lid to the tool box, he turned on the flashlight while looking for anything that might be of assistance in a bad situation: hammers, pliers, screwdrivers, and duct tape. *Duct tape, now there's a handy dandy item that has so many uses.*

Shoving the duct tape into his back pocket, he jumped from the truck bed and began the trek toward the old mansion. Since he hadn't been out in this area in many years, he wasn't exactly sure how far he would have to go to catch up.

Silhouetted against the stormy skies, the once gracious hacienda rose above the stucco walls that corralled it. All appeared quiet and deserted.

Lugowski and Kate crept along the walls until they came to a gap where the stucco coated bricks had collapsed, or something had rammed through it. Lugowski put his fingers to his lips to hush any sound that Kate may make and gestured for her to stay put.

She nodded in agreement.

Drawing his Glock from its holster, he slipped through the opening. Immediately, he spotted the Impala parked behind the mansion. Ducking low, he jogged across the dense lawn, and sneaked along the car until he reached the driver's side. He eased the door open to crawl into the driver's seat.

The car smelled like a stale cigarette and booze. The bench seat was torn and stained. The dashboard was coated with a thick layer of dust. The leather laced steering wheel cover was dry-rotted, torn, and peeling off. Hollow caucuses of dead wasps and flies rested in peace in the crevice between the dash and the windshield.

Lugowski leaned over the seat to dig through the glove box. After rummaging through the mounds of papers, he found an out-of-date owner's card: Carlos Rivera.

After stuffing the card back into the glove box, he took advantage of his hiding place to check out any movement in or around the house. Nothing was moving, there were no lights of any kind, the only sound was that of the crickets, the wind, and the thunder. He eased out of the car and made his way back to Kate as a smatter of rain kissed his face. *Yep we're gonna get wet.* He slipped behind the wall to look into her anticipating expression. "I found an owner's card in the car—Carlos Rivera, familiar?"

"Carlos Rivera is one of our stable hands," Kate whispered, "he didn't show up for work this morning. I guess I know why."

"We don't know that for sure, Kate."

"Did you see anyone around?"

"No, but that doesn't mean they're not inside somewhere. We're going to enter through that open metal gate to the right of the house, and see if anyone's home." Glancing back at her determined expression, he yanked his cell phone from his jacket. "But I seriously think we should wait for backup."

Kate folded her arms under her breasts and leaned against the wall with an arched look, while Lugowski's eyes grew wide. "Awe c'mon. No service?"

"No service," she said, "I tried to call my dad while you were looking through the car. C'mon, Carl, we can make it to the gate."

He shot her a stern look, but it was too late. She scurried through the crumbling wall, bent low to take the same path that he had taken to the Impala, and ducked down behind it.

Lugowski groaned. There was just no stopping her. He fell in line to chase after her while taking in the view of her delicious derriere. He slipped in behind the car next to her. He tried to grab her arm, but she wasn't going to give him a chance to stop her. She dashed from their hiding place toward the metal gate and plastered herself against the wall while waiting for him to catch up.

Not this time, babe.

When Lugowski arrived at the gate, he pinned her to the wall so she wouldn't escape again. He planted his hands on each side of her shoulders. Standing very close, the adrenaline rushed through his body while he looked into her eyes.

He could feel her breath feathering his face. He breathed in her sensual flowery scent. Being this close to her, he wasn't sure if in fact it was adrenaline, or the unbridled feelings that he had for this woman pulsing through him.

"I'm assuming that you've got a plan," Kate whispered between heavy breaths.

"Yeah, don't run ahead of me again, or I'll tackle your ass and haul it right outta here."

That earned him a snarky smirk. "Okay, let's call that Plan B. Somehow, I'm thinking that you've got something more solid?"

Standing this close, feeling the heat permeating from her body was making Plan B look like the option he'd most enjoy.

Focus, Lugowski.

He dragged his gaze from hers to peer through the gate into what looked like a courtyard. The sudden burst of lightening illuminated a fountain surrounded by scrub grass. He leaned in closer to scan the corridors of the house flanking the courtyard. There was no sign of movement, sound, or light. The estate was ghostly quiet. The breeze whirled dust and papers about the fountain like a tiny tornado.

Lugowski drew his gun and held it close to his chest. "Stick like glue, *capiche?*"

"Capiche."

They crept along the wall to the wrought iron trellis until they came to the first turret. As they climbed the wobbly staircase, Lugowski winced at the sound of their echoing footsteps on the creaking wooden stairs.

Upon reaching the top, he gently pushed Kate against the wall while hushing her once again with his fingers to his lips. "Stay here, I'm going to check out these rooms. If anything happens, you high-tail it out of here for my car, you got that?"

Hesitantly, she nodded.

He wasn't convinced. "*Promise me,* Kate,"

She swallowed hard. "Promise."

With no choice but to trust her, he inched his way into the first room. Stepping through the threshold of the battered living room, his eyes were drawn to the great pool of blood staining the warped floor. Dropping the Glock to his side, he knelt to the floor to examine the puddle.

Shit, I hope that isn't Shane West's blood. It's time to stop playing games. It's time for back up.

Drawing in a braced breath, he prepared to play it cool in front of Kate. He had to get help before it was too late, if it wasn't already.

Displaying a cool front, he holstered the Glock and walked back into the hallway. "If they were here, they're gone now. Let's go." Feeling badly at the look of loss in her beautiful eyes, he palmed her elbow to guide her toward the stairs.

Worry scraped through her. She didn't know what had become of her entire family, and he wasn't so sure either. They made their way back down through the tower and through the doorway.

Thunder bellowed and lightening clashed illuminating the fountain once more. Gasping, Kate jerked her arm from his grasp.

"Oh my God!"

He followed her gaze through the trellis where the wind swept the disheveled dirt at the base of the fountain. The shovel fell. They hadn't noticed it upon entering the mansion because the huge fountain blocked the view from the gate in which they entered.

"Shit." Lugowski made a mad dash for the courtyard. Sliding to a stop beside the shallow grave, he knew exactly what they had found, and was terrified for Kate's sake who they would find in the hole.

Kate was breathless, her voice quivered with fret. "Oh my God," she repeated, "Carl, what if—"

"Don't go there, Kate." He picked up the shovel, and, with a troubled sigh, stabbed it into the dirt. The deafening sound of dozens of powerful engines roaring against the thunder interrupted the dig, Lugowski's head jerked up and his breathing stopped.

The windows in the old mansion rattled and the ground beneath him vibrated.

Christ Jesus, not now!

❧　❧　❧　❧

The black Harley Sportster came to a stop at the gate of the mansion. Gunner whipped his dark glasses from his scowling, pocked face when he laid eyes on Vic's Ford Ranger parked in front of the old house. He scratched his long dark beard and jutted out his lip, while listening to the bikes lining up behind him like iron horse warriors revving their engines.

Someone was in their mansion and that someone was going to get a good ass kicking—or worse.

He twisted the accelerator on the Harley's handle to rev the engine before reaching into his saddlebag to pull out an Uzi. He hoisted it over his head for his gang to follow suit. Pushing forward, he drove through the gate and up the driveway while shooting rounds into the air.

Whoops and hoots from the other bikers echoed through the compound as they pulled out their guns and raised them up to fill the violent dark skies with war zone gunfire. The bikes raced around the side of the mansion to discover the old Impala. Shooting and wailing like coyotes into the wind as they circled the crumbling estate.

Smashing it into pieces, Gunner and several others burst through the gate into the courtyard. The tires of the motorcycles dug up the ground in the courtyard. They fired their weapons into the air to shatter more of the windows above.

Jack Haliday was pulling up the rear, to be greeted by the explosion of gunfire. He took note of the Ford Ranger in the driveway.

Shit.

∽ ∾ ∽ ∾

Lugowski wasted no time. The moment he heard the engines, he grabbed Kate's hand to drag her at a full run into the mansion, into the tower, and up the staircase. The gunfire ignited when they reached the top.

Tossing Kate to the floor, he covered her with his body while glass from the shattering windows rained down around them. Hooting and screaming, the bikers surrounded the rattling quaking house. He had to get her the hell out of there, or they were both as good as dead.

~ FOURTEEN ~

Thank God for small miracles. Scratch that, thank God for huge enormous miracles.

Jen Fleming steered her car through the stone entrance of Westwood Thoroughbred Farm.

The wind tossed the tangle of branches draped over the winding driveway leading to the Victorian farmhouse. The storm clouds had blocked out the sun's rays to make it as dark as night. When Jen pulled up and parked she noticed that the only light in the house was from the electric candles burning in the tall deeply set windows.

Kate still wasn't home.

Eric had called Jen asking if she had heard or had seen Kate, but she hadn't. He was calling from Rosemount Memorial Hospital while he and Mike waited for the doctors to sew a few stitches above Shane's eye, and for the police to finish their interviews.

After asking about Kate, he relayed the events of the past day. Horrifying. She could hear the disillusionment in Eric's voice while he reiterated Vic Deveaux's scheme, betrayal, and his arrest. Exhaustion clung to his words, as well as relief and thankfulness that Shane was a bit abused, but overall, okay.

Now he was worried about his daughter.

Jen decided to stop at the grocery store, drive to the farm to see what was going on, and welcome the West men home with a nice hot meal on the table. Maybe Kate would arrive home to spend some time in the kitchen with her and enjoy the meal with her father and brothers.

Hopefully.

The darkening skies cued the solar lanterns to glimmer amid the bright pink and white blooms of impatiens bordering the sidewalk when she made her way toward the rear of the house. The wind danced across the pond beyond the quaint back porch. At the far end of the water, a weeping willow swayed in the breeze to dip its wispy branches into the gentle lap of the water.

Jen took a moment to breathe in the beauty. Taking in the spectacular view, she was having no problem understanding why Eric loved his bucolic haven so much; she was like a lovely lady dressed for a romance.

A half-smile crept across her lips. In time she could picture herself as the mistress of Westwood Thoroughbred Farm. It was a muse that she allowed herself to carefully fantasize about every once-in-a-while. With one last glance, she set the daydream aside while shifting the groceries into a more manageable position in her arms. She was most thankful that she would get into the house before the storm took hold.

It only took an instant to find the back door key under a cushion on the wicker loveseat. Eric had shared the secret location of the key with her several weeks ago. "*In case of an emergency ...* " he had told her.

Supposing that this definitely qualified, she snatched the key from its hiding place and let herself in. After searching the cabinets for cookware, she began preparing the pork roast with apple chutney dressing that she was famous for. At least her ex-husband Clay loved it. So did her son, Brandon. She was most certain that Eric and his sons would devour it, especially after the brutal day they just had.

The apples sent a warm and pleasing waft throughout the old house. After folding up a map and placing it on the china closet, Jen hummed while setting the dining room table. Noticing a large X on the map, she made sure to place it on the top—in case it was an important notation.

Finding a lovely Chardonnay in the wine cabinet, she pulled the cork and set it on the table to breathe.

She had tried Kate's cell phone several times with no luck, and had left several messages on her voice mail. While pressing the STOP button on her phone, she realized that she may know where Kate was. A svelte smile crept across her lips as a feeling of relief fell over her.

Jen sank into the sofa in the study. She had been alone in the house for several hours when she realized that she had never been upstairs.

Wondering why Eric had never invited her, she imagined that perhaps he had pictures of his late wife, Barbara, on his dresser, on the nightstand, or maybe he kept one under his pillow for all she knew. Barbara was no threat to her, she had been gone for quite some time, and Jen wasn't going to waste any sweat on silly feelings of jealousy over a dead woman. Eric would ask her into his bedroom and his bed when he was good and ready. They spent quiet evenings in the study in front of the fireplace watching TV, playing *Scrabble,* drinking wine, and for the first time Friday night, they made love.

Although she flirted with him shamelessly, it was still an unexpected event, and they ended up in the throes of passion on the fluffy sheepskin rug. Staring at the rug, her lips curled at the sultry secret that it held. Actually, it had been sexier than a bed, so there. It was a lovely momentary thought.

The front door opened and Eric, Mike, and Shane stepped into the foyer.

Shane breathed in the apple cinnamon scent that greeted him, and thought of Kate. She always had some candle burning, and he was feeling welcomed by the homey smells surrounding him. He had waited for this moment. Not at all sure that he was going to make it out of that hell hole, he had prayed for this moment. By the grace of God, he did. He felt his father's hand clap on his shoulder.

"You should take a quick shower, and maybe get out of those clothes. I feel like you're going to arrest me at any moment." Eric smirked while gesturing to the navy blue police jumpsuit that Shane was wearing. The police had confiscated his clothes as evidence. Not a problem, they were a daunting reminder of Rivera's cold death. With a somber nod, he trotted up the stairs. He was going to shower in the hottest water possible. He wanted to wash away the filth, the blood, and the degradation that Krebs wielded. He wished he could wash away the memory of Rivera's death and of that damned dungeon as well. The water could never get hot enough. Most certainly, the recall would hang on for a very long time.

Jen came in from the study. Her face was bright, lovely, and welcoming, "Hi, supper should be ready soon. I'm just waiting on the rolls."

"Smells good," Mike said

Eric wrapped his arms around Jen's waist and squeezed. "You didn't have to make dinner."

"I wanted to," she reached up and gave him a quick kiss, "but I still haven't heard from Kate. Have you?"

Concern washed over Eric's face. "No. Where the hell could she be?"

Holy Shit! Punch hit the ground hard when the gunfire exploded along with the mighty roar of motorcycle engines beyond the mansion's walls. Crawling on his belly, he fought the pain shooting through his injured arm when he crawled through the wiry scrub brush. Finally, he made his way to the wall and peered through the huge hole in the barrier to watch in shock as the bikers circled the house while shooting semi-automatic guns into the air. He strained to see through the smoke, but didn't spot Kate or Lugowski. They had to be in there, somewhere.

Sucking his body tightly against the wall, he waited. He didn't know exactly what he was waiting for, but he knew that sooner or later the gunfire would die down, and he could get a better handle on the situation.

Lightning split the sky and the rain poured down to pound the earth.

Awakened by the exploding guns, Luzetta jerked from her pillow. *They're here!* Drained from the terrible ordeal that had played out in her mansion earlier, she had slept through the motorcycles approach. Panic shot through her, they had never entered the property shooting their guns with such fury. Fear and desperation heightened her senses.

Lifting her tired, bony body from the bed, she padded across her room in bare feet. Grabbing a lantern, she slipped through the hidden hallway to see what was going on that had them in such lather, and who was on the receiving end of their rage.

Furtively, she slid the secret door open only a bit to peek through the crack into the long corridor. Glass spattered down over a man lying on top of a blonde woman. When the guns halted, there was a terrifying silence.

The thunder growled as a gruff voice echoed through the compound like that of Lucifer's. "Who's here?" The man lifted his body from the woman's and shook the broken glass from his clothing while offering his hand to her.

"Are you all right?" he whispered while pulling her to her feet. "Careful of the glass," he warned. Blood dripped down his neck. His eyes scanned the corridor in search of a place to hide.

"You're cut," she whispered back while touching his neck, tugging a sharp piece of glass from his skin. He cringed at the pricking.

"You got three seconds to show yourselves," the steel toned voice barked, "one... two... "

Luzetta pushed the door open. "This way. Come." She waved to the woman and the man.

For a second, they stood frozen while exchanging indecisive glances.

"*Three! S*earch every inch of the house! No one fucks with the Nomad's territory!" Gunner yelled. With that the sound of swift heavy footsteps clambered into the lower corridors, into both turrets stomping fiercely up the stairwells mixing violently with the thunder and rain beating on the roof.

"Hurry! They're going to find you," Luzetta implored.

Lugowski grabbed Kate's hand and followed the old woman through the slit into the dark hallway. She led them hurriedly to her humble quarters with the dimly lit lantern. Through the walls, they could hear the hasty stomping of footsteps searching for the unidentified intruders, and the cursing grumbles of the agitated bikers.

"You're safe here." Luzetta gestured for them to sit on her bed. "I don't know why you've come here, it wasn't wise. My mansion has been very busy lately, I'm afraid." Transfixed by the sight of Lugowski's collar saturated with blood, she threw a rag into the old red cooler filled with pop and beer and icy water. After wringing it out, she handed it to Kate.

With her heart still pounding in her chest, Kate gently loosened Lugowski's tie with quivering fingers and slipped it from his shirt. It dripped with blood. She helped him out of his suit jacket, laid it on the bed, and then unbuttoned several buttons of his shirt to expose his taut chest.

His breath caught mesmerized by the way her gentle hands tentatively opened his shirt to access the wound.

Gently tilting his head forward with her fingers, she gingerly dabbed the cut. "You could use a few stitches." She tried not to stare at his muscled chest and abs.

"I'll be okay," Lugowski managed in a raspy voice. He was terrified that she could sense his pulse racing, and an erection starting to swell. God help him. Abruptly, he grabbed her wrist to take the rag from her hand, he held it against his neck for himself.

Trying not to think about the way she touched him and how moments ago he'd been lying on top of her, he fixed his eyes on the old woman while trying like hell not to think about what deep shit they were in.

He turned to Luzetta. "I'm Lieutenant Carl Lugowski of the Rosemount Police Department, and this is Kate West. You are ..."

"My name is Luzetta Valentine." Her gaze dragged to Kate. "Your name is West? There was a young man here named Shane West, do you know him?"

Kate's eyes widened with anticipation. "He's my brother. He was here?"

"Yes," the old woman confirmed, "a tall man had him chained to the wall downstairs, but they have since left, I don't know where."

"Was there anyone else?" Lugowski asked.

"Yes, there were two older men and a Mexican man, but the tall man killed the Mexican man." Rubbing her hands up and down her arms, she shuddered. "He made your brother bury him in the courtyard. It was just … ghastly."

Lugowski looked to Kate.

"It must be Rivera in the grave." Kate let go of the air she'd been holding in her lungs since they had found the shallow grave.

"Who would the tall man be?" he asked Kate.

"I don't know. Vic didn't mention the names of his partners."

He glanced down at his watch. "We've got to get out of here. We've got to get to that old car."

The short moment of bereft that her brother was still alive and that they were safe was now gone. Tension washed across Kate's face. Lugowski continued to think out loud. "We'll wait until the Nomads bed down for the night, and then we'll make our move."

⚮ ⚭ ⚮ ⚭

Soaked and agitated, Punch waited and watched from behind the crumbling exterior wall. Stabbing at the buttons on his cell phone, he was irritated as hell that he couldn't get any service—there were no damned bars. He couldn't call Eric or Mike, if they were even available. He couldn't call Kate to alert her to his presence, and perhaps map out a plan with Lugowski.

The rain had subsided, but the darkness loomed in the sky, the thunder groaned like a scorned lover threatening to wield another round.

The Nomads planted torches in the ground and broke out the booze and marijuana, while a small group gathered at the far corner of the estate to indulge in heroin. The women moved from man to man to seduce them into remote areas of the mansion for pleasure. Some performed sexual favors right out in the open.

Relieved, Punch surmised that they had given up the search for Kate and Lugowski—for the moment anyway. He prayed that they had found a good hiding place, and stayed there.

He was startled by the rustle of weeds a few yards away. Sucking tightly against the wall, he saw a stocky biker with an AK slung on his shoulder urinating in the brush. A quick surge of lightning lit up his back. Alone, the biker was staggering drunk.

Punch crept along the wall until he was directly behind him. Briskly, he grabbed the man in a sleeper hold until he fell limp to the ground. Snatching the AK, Punch slung it over his shoulder. Ignoring the throbbing in his arm, he dragged the man to the wall, and then bound his hands, feet, and mouth with duct tape.

One down, two thousand to go.

So it seemed, but at least he now had some fire power of his own.

With his new friend bound, gagged, and still taking a snooze, Punch decided it was a good time to disable the bikes. Creeping along the wall, he made his way to the corner of the wall to peer along the long length to the front. Staying low and cringing every time his foot stomped on a twig, he finally reached the half-way point. He came upon another section of the wall crumbling down. He peered through the gap to see a dilapidated statue of three cupids dancing in a circle near the house. A leather jacket dangled from the broken arm of one of the merry pixies.

Pausing, he listened intently for movement, and he found it. Groaning and heavy breathes and raspy whispers.

Punch's gaze lugged to the opposite side of the pathetic statue where a topless dark-haired woman straddled a man wearing nothing but his do-rag. Madly, she pumped and ground her hips. Her skin was pallid against her long dark strands and her huge breasts sagged almost to her navel. Tattoos swept across her breasts, shoulders, and down her arms in undistinguishable patterns.

Wincing and cringing, Punch continued toward the front of the house. The Spanish thistles were thick, and clung like tiny hitch-hikers to his wet jeans.

Finally reaching the corner, he made a dash for the front of the mansion to crouch beneath one of the mighty lions. He peered through the gates.

The motorcycles were arranged in a nice neat line along the driveway. Ahhh, they were a glorious sight, indeed. Their chrome gleamed in the bright frequent surges of lightning; their handlebars were all turned to the right, as synchronized as the freaking New York City Rockettes, only prettier. He hated to do what he was about to do, but hey, it had to be done. The magnificent motorcycles would have to take one for the team ... their team.

Scanning the front lawn, his eyes fell upon Vic's Ford Ranger. He couldn't figure what Vic's truck was doing at the mansion. Was he in the house with Kate and Lugowski? *Is he the "friend" that Kate was talking about?* He thought, as he scurried to the old overgrown rhododendron bush in the middle of the yard, and then darted behind the truck. Briefly, he peeked into the cab. Vic's riding helmet and crop lie on the floor. *Yep, it's Deveaux's truck. What the hell?*

Listening for movement, looking for shadows, he waited. Yanking his pen knife from his hip pocket he stealthily traveled to each bike and cut the fuel line. The cloying stench of gasoline was overwhelming, and he had to fight fiercely not to cough out loud.

When he returned to his post, he found his captive awake and attempting to crawl toward the hole in the wall. Grabbing him by his feet, Punch dragged him to the far end of the wall. His arm protested with pain as the man's body bumped over the weeds and wads of wet dirt. When the biker twisted and bucked in dissent, Punch shoved the man against the wall and pointed his own gun into his muddy twisted face.

"Two choices, bro. Sit tight and be cool, or I'll smack you with the butt of this gun so hard that you'll sleep for a month. You got that?" Punch whispered. The biker glared at him but soon nodded at the enormous black man hovering over him. Punch patted the biker's shoulder and then returned to his post to wait and watch, for God only knew what.

Shane let the hot water wash over him. The steam rippled above the shower stall, and then billowed throughout the small bathroom to fog the oval mirror above the sink. When the water ran cold, he turned it off and grabbed a towel from the rack on the wall. He dried off, pulled on a pair of boxer briefs, and then with the towel draped over his damp shoulders, he closed the toilet lid and sat down. Dropping his elbows onto his knees, he stared at the floor between his feet without really seeing it.

The police had scoured the entire area around the wreck and had come up with nothing.

Where the hell is Krebs? The thought that the man who had tortured him and killed his partner so easily was not dead, but instead was still on the loose, was tormenting him. Krebs was a smart, cunning, and a malicious rat-bastard. Shane couldn't figure why Krebs didn't kill them while they were unconscious. He had the money, maybe he would disappear forever, or maybe the bastard would surface later for some sick revenge. He shuddered, and then he got mad. *What hell's the matter with you? You're letting him do exactly what he wanted to do—get inside your head. C'mon, he's got what he wanted. He's gone. Let it go, asshole.*

No matter how he tried, the feeling that he hadn't seen or felt the last of Martin Krebs' wrath stabbed him all the way to his soul. He wasn't so much worried that Krebs would come after him; he was more concerned that he may attack members of his family instead. That ripped at him like a two-edged sword.

When he finally made his way downstairs to the dining room, Jen was placing a basket of piping hot dinner rolls on the table. His father and Mike looked whipped, but hungry, and the delectable smells that were wafting through the house were making his stomach scream for sustenance. The rain rapping against the window drew his attention. He couldn't help but hope that wherever he was, Krebs was getting soaked to the skin.

"Everything looks great," Mike noted.

The four of them bowed their heads and gave thanks, for the dinner and for Shane's safe return. When grace was through, Eric drew a long weary breath.

Jen pinched her bottom lip between her teeth in concern. "Ya know, I was thinking, maybe Kate is with Dr. Reese. She's still seeing him, isn't she?"

This brought Eric to attention.

"She may have needed a little moral support, Eric," Jen said. "Perhaps her cell phone died, and she just hasn't realized it."

"I've been thinking the same thing," Mike put in. "It would be like Kate to find something to occupy her mind rather than sit around here worrying half to death."

"It makes sense to me," Shane added.

"Maybe." Eric forked a piece of pork onto his plate, and then passed it on to Mike. "After dinner we'll drive to his apartment and see if she's with him."

"Good, I'll drive," Jen stated.

"Not necessary, I'll drive," Eric replied.

"Eric, you look like you've been run over by a truck. You're exhausted. *I'll* drive."

Stuffing a forkful of the scrumptious pork into his mouth, he shrugged. "If you insist."

Mike and Shane exchanged speaking glances that seemed to say, Could it be? Had their father had just been "handled"? They hadn't seen anyone, much less a woman handle Eric West in well, in ten years, since their mother, Barbara, used to handle him. They snickered under their breath. Evidently, Jen Fleming was one hell of a woman. Eric West may have just met his match. It was about time.

The storm had quieted by the time the dinner dishes had been cleared. Jen and Eric left for Rosewood Commons hoping that they would find Kate with Holden. The young veterinarian had been looking for an assistant, so Eric was working hard on convincing himself that perhaps she had been helping him at the track in an attempt to keep her mind off the kidnapping. Jen could see his exhaustion and his anxiety spread not only over his face but his body as well. She was terrified what his reaction would be if they did not find Kate with Dr. Reese.

Mike was hoping for the same. On his way to the kitchen for another cup of coffee, he noticed the map lying on the China closet. Picking it up to put it in the drawer, he found the large black X marked on Old Mine Road. His eyes narrowed and his head tilted. He didn't remember his father marking the road when they were studying the map. A bad feeling rattled through his gut. He meandered into the study where he found Shane lounging on the sofa, lost in thought, while staring into the tiny crackling flames in the fireplace. His eyes were molested with dark blue smudges of fatigue. The kid was beyond exhausted. Mike could see that a bad feeling was haunting him to make it impossible to close his weary eyes and rest. Oh yeah, Martin Krebs was screwing with his head.

He could identify with that. Krebs was among the bad feelings that he had of his own.

"You don't think Kate would have gone out to Old Mine Road, would you?" Mike asked.

Shane's hollow eyes fluttered open. He pushed his sore body up. "I hope not."

"Why?" Mike asked with a lift to his shoulders. "No one should be out there. Maybe the police."

Suddenly awake, Shane jerked to his feet while wincing at the pain in his legs and ribs, "The police didn't seem in any hurry to go to the mansion, and that old lady who lives there said that a biker gang sometimes hung out at the mansion. She was expecting them to visit at anytime." He made haste for the foyer. "We better get out there."

Mike ran to his father's desk, yanked open the middle drawer, retrieving the Glock that he had just put away. Shoving it into his jeans, he followed his younger brother out the front door.

∾ ∾ ∾ ∾

The torch lights flickered over the courtyard. Gunner watched the bikers slowly emerge from the mansion while shaking their heads. They had searched for hours without a trace of anyone. The huge man crossed his massive tattooed arms over his broad chest. His bald head shone in the sputter of light from the torches, and his long sleeveless black leather duster floated on the breeze. Someone was in his mansion. He could feel it. When he found them, they would pay dearly for their infringement. But, right now, his focus was on the short mound of loose dirt under the fountain, and the shovel lying on top.

Carrying the black case filled with the weapons that he had retrieved on Gunners behalf at the old warehouse, Jack made his way through the crowd of bikers. Scrubbing his large hand over the beard that partially hid his pocked face, Gunner measured him as he approached. The newest member of his gang had come through. He promised high quality cocaine for the final payment for the guns, and he managed to retrieve the guns as well. *The cocaine must have been up to standard or that sonofabitch, Duly, wouldn't have accepted the final payment, and this poor sonofabitch would be dead right now.*

"Things must've gone good." Gunner took the case from Jack's hand.

"Good enough," Jack said, "no one found anything or anyone inside, I assume."

Gunner looked at him askance. "Not yet ... dig." He shoved the shovel into Jack's chest. Immediately, he noticed the shallow grave at the base of the fountain. Not good.

Knowing that it was in his best interest to be a team player, Jack stabbed the shovel into the dirt. A group of bikers crowded around. Only a few scoops later, a man's swollen discolored hand came to the surface. The bikers stepped back. Jack winced. Now was a good time to stop digging. Now was a good time to get the hell out of there, or his entire operation was gonna go FUBAR, fast.

He was well aware why the police hadn't already ascended upon the mansion to claim the body—if they knew about the body. Captain Lutz was keeping them at bay to give him time to run some damage control. They were so close to cracking this gang wide open. A SWAT team coming down on them right now would blow the whole operation to smithereens.

"I'm thinking we'd better get out of here real quick," Jack firmly suggested to Gunner. "My guess is those two vehicles have been abandoned, and it won't be long before the cops show up." A rumble rose from the crowd surrounding the fountain.

Gunner's face twisted fiercely. "We'll go when I say!"

"What about the cops?" Jack cautiously inquired.

"My customers want these guns, and they pay good. If the cops show up, they'll be sorry."

The cool evening air whipped through the window to toss Mike's hair. He drove his dually pickup truck along the back roads toward the strip mined area, and the Valentine mansion. He glanced across the cab.

Shane looked exhausted, battered, and worried as hell about their sister.

Surely, the police would be there to collect Rivera's body. Except, when Mike thought back on Shane's interview with Captain Lutz, the police didn't seem in a big hurry to check out the mansion. In fact, he seemed down-right hesitant about sending any teams out there at all.

If they arrived at the mansion to face a gang of bikers, they would need help. As much as Mike hated the thought, he seriously considered calling Lugowski. Yep that's right, he needed help from the guy that was sleeping with his ex-wife. *Shit.* Hey, this was Kate. Mike was willing to do whatever was necessary to keep her safe. If that meant asking for help from that asshole, then... so be it.

Begrudgingly, he pulled his cell phone from his pocket. Under Shane's watchful eye, he dialed the dreaded number. It went straight to voice mail. *Shit.* He had been under the impression that cops kept their cell phones active at all times, evidently not. Letting out a long breath, he dialed the other dreaded number—Ava.

Surprisingly, she answered on the second ring. "What's up, Michael?"

He cleared his throat. "Hey, Ava, I was wondering if Lugowski was there?" *Smooth, real smooth.* He could picture her rolling her naked body over to nudge Lugowski from his sated sleep to give him the phone. Not exactly a pleasant vision.

Instead, she cleared her throat and spoke tersely. "He's not here. He left earlier today after getting a call from some woman." She paused for a moment. He could almost feel her brows furrow through the phone and her brain click into high gear. "Why are *you* calling for Carl?"

"What woman? Was it Kate?"

Bingo. She thought the voice sounded familiar. "Why the hell would Kate be calling Carl? Don't play games with me, Michael, what's going on?" she snapped.

"I'm not sure, thanks anyway, Ava." Quickly, he hung up.

He could feel that woman's wrath rising like a mushroom cloud, and he was grateful as hell that he was miles away from the explosion.

"Someone's gonna pay big for that phone conversation," Shane muttered. He was right. Mike was just hoping it wasn't him. At this point, Lugowski was down for the count. They had to hope that there were no bikers at the mansion. If there weren't, then they had a whole new set of worries.

As if they didn't have enough.

~ FIFTEEN ~

Ava was furious.

After taking a shower and refreshing her make-up, she slid into her Crossfire, and was now whipping along the winding roads out of Lanzville. Eyes narrowed, the throb in her brain felt like it was going to burst.

What the hell was Kate thinking? Did she actually think she could compete with the likes of Ava Marie West? The little trollop isn't in my league. Hell, she isn't even in my galaxy.

Angrily, she pressed down on the clutch hard, shifting not only the sports car into high gear, but her adrenaline as well. *Since when does Carl leave my bed to take a booty call from ... Kate West? Really? Seriously? Ahhh, c'mon!*

She blew out a disgusted breath. Her frustration was in overdrive. *Michael is well aware of my temper, evidently it has eluded my ex-sister-in-law. Has the man never warned her? Too late now, bitch. They say that you learn something new everyday, and today Kate will be learning something she'll never forget. I'll deal with her in a way that she will totally understand. She'll never mess with any of Ava West's men again, guaranteed. And Carl? Well, let's just say that he'll be sorry for the day he ever spoke to Michael's little sister.*

She rolled the Crossfire to a stop at a red light. Her eyes rotated to the apartment complex across the intersection, Rosewood Commons. She was quite certain that Dr. Holden Reese would be home from the track by now. She checked her lips in the rear view mirror just before the light turned green, and then she made the left turn into the complex to cruise along the line of apartments in search of his vet truck.

Not even half way through the first row of apartments she spotted the white vet truck with red letters on the doors: Reese Veterinary Services. The truck was parked in front of apartment number thirteen, Kate's lucky number. It was proving to be lucky indeed—for Ava anyway.

There was a light on in the living room. Through the window she could see Holden, shirtless, holding a remote in his hand while standing in front of the TV. His tiny driveway only had room for his truck and the street had many cars parked along the sidewalk, so she parked several apartments down. She ran her fingers through her auburn hair to fluff it.

She glanced down to the passenger's seat where a paper sign lay: WANTED: VET ASSISTANT, APPLY WITHIN. She had seen the sign hanging on Dr. Reese's office door at the track earlier that day and thinking that the young handsome doctor would be so much nicer to work for than that old crusty coot, Spears, had snatched it. At the time, she was merely considering applying for the job. Why wouldn't Kate want to work with her boyfriend? No problem, Ava was more than willing to 'apply within' right now.

Clutching the sign in her hand, she walked to the door and rang the bell.

A moment later, the door jerked open and there Holden stood, still shimmying a white t-shirt over his firm abs. His hair was slightly damp, and he smelled fresh of sandalwood, like he'd just got out of the shower. The shirt clung tautly to accentuate his sculpted chest, and his jeans clung to his lean hips. There was a rip in the right knee of the faded jeans, and he was bare footed. He flashed his white teeth at her, but his gorgeous brown eyes were filled with befuddlement.

Easily, she could read his mind. It was most obvious that he was asking himself, *why is Ava West on my doorstep?* He was about to find out. Oh yeah, he was going to find out in a very big way.

Holden looked past her to search up and down the block. "Is everything okay? Did you break down or something?"

Lifting the sign in front of her chest, she smiled as innocently as a child on Santa's lap. "I'm sorry about the late hour, Dr. Reese, but I was visiting with a friend a few doors down, and saw that your lights were on. And ... I was so hoping that this position hadn't been filled yet."

Staring at the sign that he had made and hung on his office door, he was no longer befuddled, but rather taken aback. "Well, no, but couldn't you wait until tomorrow to see me?" He wondered if she was drunk.

She sniffed. "No, I really can't. I can't stand the thought of working for that tyrant for one more day." Her eyes watered convincingly. She batted a tear away. "Please, Dr. Reese, could I come in to go over my qualifications? I'm sure you'll find my credentials quite impressive."

He didn't know what to say. The poor woman was falling apart on his doorstep. Kate and many others at the track were always telling him what a crotchety coot Dr. Spears was. He had experienced his cantankerous demeanor himself on several occasions, but Kate had a fierce loyalty to the man, and a great amount of respect as well. She said that she would not leave Dr. Spears to work for him, unless their relationship grew to a very serious level—whatever that meant. However, Ava seemed undone by the old vet's sour disposition, and he couldn't see any harm in hearing what she had to say, so he stepped aside to allow her entrance.

Ava perused Holden's apartment.

The living room was small with a sectional sofa and a large flat screen TV that sat on a dark smoky glass television stand. It was clearly a bachelor pad. There was a cheap black coffee table that had no other purpose than to prop his feet up while watching TV, and eating a microwave meal.

Of course his wallet, keys, and cell phone were tossed carelessly on the smudged table. Ava had no doubt that he probably spent several minutes each morning searching for them before he trotted out the door for his morning rounds at the racetrack.

The galley kitchen provided apartment size appliances, several dishes in the small sink, a coffee maker, and a tiny microwave on the counter. Between the living room and the kitchen was a short hallway that led to the bathroom and a bedroom. There were no pictures on the walls. It was null and void of any decorations at all, including pictures of Kate.

Swiping the remote from the sofa, Holden gestured for Ava to have a seat. She slowly lowered into the comfy cushions. He turned the TV off and took a seat at the far end of the sofa. He seemed nervous, and his eyes twitched like someone trying to find a polite way out of a sticky situation. Luckily, there was also a measure of concern in his gaze. Concern ... always a good man-lever.

"Can I get you something to drink?" he asked.

"Oh no, I never drink during a job interview," she teased while allowing a coquettish smile to crawl across her full glossy lips.

He chuckled. "I don't know if we could call this a formal *job interview*, but—"

"Oh, I understand. You probably aren't interested in me because I'm Kate's ex-sister-in-law." She sniffed and a crocodile tear rolled down her cheek.

"No, no ... I just meant that—"

"The ex-wife always gets a bad rap, you know. I did everything that I could to keep Michael happy. He was so overbearing and demanding—" She was interrupted by a knock at the door.

Holden was relieved, yet amazed at the number of visitors that he was getting all at one time. A second rap on the door caused him to flinch. Ava cupped her hand over her mouth.

"Holden, its Eric West ..."

Ava's eyes widened. She lurched forward to grab his wrist. "You do *not* want him to find me here, Dr. Reese," she whispered.

"Why? We're not doing anything wrong."

"That's not what Eric will think, believe me. I need to hide. Where's your bedroom?"

Holden's befuddlement had returned in a big way. He knew that Mike was divorced from Ava, and he knew that she was not well liked by the Wests', however he and Kate had never really discussed what happened, or why. Feeling that her advice may be in his best interest, he pointed down the hallway.

Quickly, she trotted in that direction and closed the bedroom door behind her. Once Ava was securely hidden away, he padded across the floor to open the door. Eric's noticeable fatigued expression and angst greeted him.

"Mr. West ... is everything okay?"

"Is Kate here?"

His brows pinched together. "No sir, I haven't heard from Kate all day. What's going on?"

His last hope dashed, Eric's shoulders dropped, he sighed. "We can't find her anywhere, and she's not answering her cell phone." He ran his fingers through his hair, and down the nape of his neck.

"I'll get my shoes—"

"No, I'm going to go home. If you hear from her, will you call me?"

"Absolutely, and if she's home will you have her call me? Is there anything I can do?"

Eric wished there was something anyone could do. He was beginning to think that the only thing left to do was wait until someone contacted them. If he could, he'd go down to that jail and beat the information out of Vic.

Whip lashed, he shook his head. "Stay close to the phone. Maybe she'll call." He turned toward his vehicle, where Jen was waiting.

Holden watched them drive away before he closed the door. Leaning against the door, worry washed over him.

"Don't be terribly concerned, Holden," Ava stated from the threshold of the bedroom.

He looked up.

Ava staggered forward but managed to cling to the wall. Her eyes were suddenly half lidded, and her lips quivering in distress.

Holden darted down the hallway to catch her in his arms as she fell to her knees. "Ava, are you all right—"

"I know exactly where Kate is," she said in a breathy whisper. Tears rolled down her cheeks over her plump lips. "She's not going to surface until she's good and ready."

He lifted her up and carried her to the edge of his bed. Setting her down gently, he knelt down in front of her. "Calm down, Ava. What are you talking about?"

She traced his jaw line with her finger. "I need comforted, Holden, and you're going to need comforted too, when I tell you how we've been played for fools."

He blinked back hard.

"It breaks my heart to have to fill you in." She wiped the tears from her face with the palm of her hand. "I'll take that drink now."

~ SIXTEEN ~

Time dragged by. Lugowski retired to the floor to sit with his back against the wall and his legs stretched out in front of him and crossed at the ankles. It was a wise decision to get as far away from Kate as possible. The emergency pack of cigarettes in the breast pocket of his shirt whispered his name. *A freaking nicotine fix would be a life saver right about now.*

Yeah, that wasn't going to happen, so he had to find ways to keep his mind off the way Kate's soft hand brushed against his jaw when she tended to the cut on his neck that burned like hellfire. Now the burning had settled into a dull, simmering ache, but the way his brain smoldered over Kate West never seemed to cool.

Talking for hours, Luzetta and Kate sat on the bed. The old woman spun yarns of the movies that had been filmed in this very mansion. She wove a web of fascinating stories about the actors and actresses that had been part of the filming and how her father, Salvador Valentine, threw lavish parties after a movie had been completed. She went on to explain how the mansion had fallen into ruin, and how she had taken refuge in the secret rooms that her father had built within the walls to protect them if the Russians invaded the United States.

Kate was completely awe struck by her stories. She found them compelling and fascinating. *Fascinating and creepy, wrapped up into one*, if you asked him, which no one did.

Luzetta ran out of steam, and Kate's adrenalin rush took a nose dive around eleven. They were both asleep on the bed.

Lugowski checked his watch. It was twelve-thirty. The laughter and yelling beyond the walls had silenced. It was time to check out an escape route. Slowly, he pushed his stiff body from the hard floor. Yawning and stretching his arms over his head, his gaze fell upon the lovely blonde fast asleep across the bed.

Unable to resist, he gently brushed a wisp of hair from her cheek and ran his finger along her soft jaw line. Expelling a thin sigh, she stirred. He imagined how she would feel in his arms as she slept soft, warm, and inviting. His lips tightened. Oh yeah, the girl was so inviting, so tempting, and so damned out of the question.

Quickly, he shook the thought from his mind, and then quietly made his way down the dark hallway to slide open the concealed door, peer out, and then slip into the open corridor. The shards of glass from the shattered windows twinkled in the moonlight. Furtively, he slunk along the wall toward a long dark pass that led to the east turret.

His plan was to find a clear cut way to get to the Impala, hot wire it, and then drive like hell through the opening in the crumbled wall. First, he had to survey the area to see where the bikers were sleeping and how accessible the car would be. Then, he would go back for Kate and the old woman.

❧ ❧ ❧ ❧

Mike's eyes narrowed and Shane sat straight up in his seat, when the truck's headlights fell upon Lugowski's SUV and Punch's pickup parked side-by-side in the tall brush.

"What the hell is going on?" Mike parked his truck next to Punch's and then glanced across the cab at his brother. "I think we've hit the jackpot."

"Okay, so did they walk to the house from here, I'm guessing?" Shane searched the darkness.

Mike opened the door and slid from the seat, "That's what I'm thinking. And that's what we're gonna do." He walked to the other side of the truck to look for a small puddle from the storm. Kneeling down, he swirled his fingers through the mud and wiped it on his face, and then motioned for Shane to squat down next to him.

"Seriously?" Shane moaned.

Mike held a blop of mud on his fingers. "Don't be a wuss."

Kate rolled over on the lumpy musty mattress. Slowly, her eyes slugged open. Immediately, they focused on the cracked and water stained ceiling. The memory of where she was and the events of the day before came rushing to her consciousness. *Was it yesterday or just hours ago? How long have I been sleeping?*

There was no natural light filtering into the room through a window. She had lost all track of time and the fret of where Martin Krebs and Vic had taken Shane, and where her father and Mike could be, bled like a crimson river back into her mind. Thankfully, she had the relief of know-ing that Shane's body wasn't lying in that shallow grave in the court-yard. She could only hope and pray that Vic still possessed some shred of loyalty to her father, and didn't allow his partners to harm Shane. Still Rivera was dead and that meant that something went terribly awry among them. *Maybe the partners were having a melt-down, and that can't be good, or could it?*

Cupping her hand on her forehead, she tried not to obsess over the scenarios. She rolled over to search the room for Lugowski. He had been sitting on the floor in the corner listening to Luzetta's stories about her father's movies, and the amazing history of the Valentine mansion. The stories were mesmerizing, and a pleasant diversion from her worries. The most interesting diversion, through her peripheral vision, was how sexy Lugowski looked with his hair askew, his tie discarded, and the buttons of his once pristine shirt, dangling open. Yeah, his disheveled look wasn't lost on her. Even the blood that had absorbed into the collar of his shirt from the deep cut on his neck, gave him a Rambo quality. *Hokay, maybe that's a bit of an exaggeration, but still ...*

She could always tell that the man was in prime condition, but when she opened his shirt to tend to his cut, her breath caught at the sight of his flawlessly defined, supple pecks.

Why should I be surprised? Ava would have nothing less than a well-built, muscled specimen in her bed. Once again she asked herself, *What the hell is Carl Lugowski doing with Ava? The woman is a royal manipulative bitch. Well, she is a royal, gorgeous, manipulative bitch.* That was the crux of her allure. Ava was gorgeous.

Letting out a resigned sigh, she lifted herself to one elbow for a better view of the small room. Her eyes darted around the room like she was watching an intense ping-pong match when she realized that Lugowski was gone. Dragging her fingers through her hair, a surge of panic caught in her throat.

How long has he been gone? She pushed herself up to a sitting position. *Has he been caught?*

There were no windows, no cracks or slits for her to peer through to see what was happening on the other side of the walls. She looked down. Luzetta was still fast asleep. The woman had hid in this room for years. She was safe here. Kate slid from the bed and, with measured steps, made her way down the dark hidden passageway to the secret door.

Punch's popularity was growing by leaps and bounds. He had a small but notable entourage bundled in duct tape, lined against the stucco wall. His little arsenal was becoming quite impressive as well, two Uzis, one Beretta-45, and an AK-47. After rifling through his new friends' pockets he came up with quite a few extra magazines. Not bad.

Sweet Jesus, these bikers play with some serious freaking toys. There was still no sign of Lugowski or Kate. He wasn't sure if that was a blessing or a curse. The activity behind the mansion's walls had died down. Most of the bikers had passed out. He was most impressed with how early they were beginning to crash. With the amount of drugs and alcohol that was being passed around he supposed that he shouldn't be. Punch would've liked to get some sleep as well, but he was most vigilant on collecting bikers that wandered beyond the walls to seek a private place to relieve themselves.

He had detained six to be exact, when the tall weeds rustled once more.

Punch's eyes scanned beyond the wall. These two brainiacs were approaching crawling on their bellies. Perhaps they were wondering about their buddies. Perhaps they were starting to suspect that something was amiss. A cock-eyed smile slithered across his lips. Grabbing one of the Uzis, just because he thought they were cool, he made his way carefully around circling behind them.

"Hey, boys, wanna join my party?" Punch stood over them, legs spread wide with the Uzi pointed at the back of their heads. "Drop your gun and roll over nice and easy with your hands behind your head."

After a loud groan, they complied.

"Punch!" Mike exclaimed in a loud whisper of relief.

In disbelief, Punch stared at the West brothers lying amongst the bristly weeds. The mud they had smudged over their faces made them look like deranged Indians on the war path. *White people.*

"What the hell are you doing here?" Shane asked while trying to catch his breath.

"I followed Kate and Lugowski out here. They're in the mansion somewhere with all those bikers. I haven't seen hide nor hair of them, so I'm guessing they found a good hiding place."

"Luzetta." Shane remembered the old woman that lived covertly in the mansion, who had brought him a drink and a doughnut to help him through his dark hours in the dungeon. He told Captain Lutz about her. He couldn't figure out why the police weren't searching the mansion. Hopefully, Kate and Lugowski had bumped into her, and she had them safely hidden away.

Punch stuffed the Uzi into his pants and extended his hands out to hoist them to their feet. Stealthily, they followed him back to his secure location behind the wall. Mike's eyes widened and his mouth opened at the sight of the six men along the wall, bound in duct tape.

"Meet the X-men." Punch gestured to his unhappy guests.

"Wow, you've been busy," Mike snorted in amazement, "remind me to keep the duct tape hidden at all times at the farm."

"Do you mind telling me what the hell is going on? Why did Kate call Lugowski, and why did they come here?"

Raking his fingers through his hair, Mike proceeded to brief him on the events of the last twenty-four hours. Punch was just as shocked as they were at Vic Deveaux's treachery. Planting his hands on his hips and bowing his head, he listened intently to the details of Shane's imprisonment in the dungeon, and the horrible account of Rivera's death and Krebs' disappearance. Lastly, they informed him that Rivera's body was buried in the courtyard.

The dramatic tale didn't end there. Mike continued by explaining that they couldn't get a hold of Kate, and they thought that somehow she had figured out that Shane was being held at the mansion, which confirmed Punch's notion that one of the Wests was in deep do-do, when he decided to tail Kate.

Mike and Shane were thankful that he did.

"So what's the plan?" Shane did not enjoy the trip down morbid memory lane.

"We have to wait until we see Kate or Lugowski. We're greatly outnumbered, but with surprise on our side, we can do some real damage at the right moment." Punch nodded toward the M-16 and the AK-47.

A shudder of angst skittered down Shane's spine at the thought of more death, more graves, and more blood. He would do what he had to do for his sister, without hesitation, no questions asked.

"I'd love to call the police, but I can't get any cell service. How about you?" Punch said.

Mike and Shane pulled their cell phones from their pockets and thumbed the buttons before blowing out disgusted breaths. "Shane could go back to the truck and drive into town for help," Mike suggested.

"No freakin' way," Shane bit out, "I could get to the truck, and then all hell breaks loose. Then it's just the two of you against all of them."

He had a point. Mike scrubbed his hand across his unshaven exhausted and muddy face. "I don't get it. The police know about Rivera's body. Why aren't they coming to claim it?"

Quiet blanketed the mansion. Jack sat sedately on the last three steps in the east turret. He preferred the privacy and the darkness of the tower while trying to figure why there would be two abandoned vehicles and where the owners were.

He could understand one, but why would they murder a man, bury him, and then leave two vehicles behind? One of the vehicles belonged to the corpse, no doubt, so who owned the Ford Ranger, and did they plan to come back for it?

Man, I hope not.

He yanked the do-rag from his head dragging his fingers through his hair. He couldn't wait for this op to be over. He couldn't wait to get home to Laura, and he wanted a haircut and a shave, bad. He leaned against the wall, closed his eyes, and let the cool hush of the night draw him within a whisper of sleep, when he was jarred by a *thud* above him.

Lugowski snaked his way past the broken window encasements, where the moonlight lit his path until he reached the section of the corridor that was draped in total darkness. Running his hands along the wall to help guide him closer to the turret, he was almost to the doorway when his feet became entangled with a pair of legs. He lurched forward to land face down on the floor in front of the doorway with a *thud*. A thin gasp filled his ears just as a beam of light flashed in his face and then whipped across the wall to pin Kate. The hefty biker held his gun solid, and a wicked yellow-toothed grin crept across his gruff bearded face.

Kate squinted while trying to block the harsh beam from her eyes.

Licking his lips at her smooth delicious curves, he moved the light up and down her body before jerking the gun at Lugowski.

"Get up," he growled, "keep your hands where I can see 'em."

Slowly, Lugowski pulled himself up, and then made his way near Kate. Protectively, he stepped in front of her. He could see the look in the biker's eyes. He knew what he was thinking, and it wasn't happening.

"Where you guys been all this time?" His eyes focused on her breasts to make her feel defiled without him even touching her. "Gunner's gonna like your bitch, dude."

Lugowski's gut twisted. He tucked Kate farther behind him when the biker yanked Lugowski's Glock from his shoulder holster.

"What's going on, Buck?" a voice quietly called from the entrance of the turret.

"This guy tripped over my feet. I was sleeping against that wall there."

Jack stepped into the light to pitch Lugowski a steely glance. Roughly, he grabbed Kate by the arm to pull her into the light. Gauging her up and down with wanton in his eyes, he smiled and licked his lips.

Looking to Lugowski for reassurance, Kate swallowed hard.

Lugowski's jaw was clenched. The skin rippled over his jaw bone and his stare was turgid.

Jack ran his fingers through her hair, she stiffened, and then he ran his thumb across her cheek.

"She's a nice piece of tail. I'll take her to Gunner." He drew his gun with one hand while grabbing Kate's arm by the other. Lugowski stepped forward to be greeted by Jack's Glock. "Don't worry we won't leave you out. You can watch."

Lugowski's eyes narrowed, his nostrils flared, his jaw became so sharp that you could have cut a 2x4 with it.

"Wait a goddamned minute," Buck protested, "I found her and I'm gonna take her. He might let me have her when he's done."

"And he might sell her to his customers that come for the guns tomorrow. Look at her, she's prime, man." He ran the back of his fingers over her shoulder, across her breast and down her arm. She jerked her head away while trying to free her arm. "Feisty too," he chuckled. "She'll bring a damned good price."

Kate was fighting the nausea that was swelling in her throat. His grip tightened around her arm fiercely and jerked her hard toward the turret. He stabbed Lugowski in the shoulder hard with his gun. "Walk, asshole," he harshly instructed.

Buck was pissed as hell at having his find taken away from him, but this guy was Gunner's golden boy, so he tromped along behind them.

The sound of their feet clomping down through the turret echoed. The tower was dark. Lugowski could see the moonlight yawning through the trellis illuminating the bottom of the stairs. If they made it to Gunner he was a dead man, and Kate would be somebody's sex slave. Not on his watch. He slowed his cadence as they approached the bottom of the stairs. Curling his right hand into a fist, he let the biker get closer to him.

Lugowski stepped off the stairs onto the main floor while waiting for the biker and Kate to do the same, and then he slammed his right hand up smacking the biker in the face. Jack flung backward with blood spewing from his nose. His body sprawling into Buck, he let go of Kate's arm while making sure he didn't squeeze the trigger of his gun. That plan was futile. Buck pressed the trigger of his semi-automatic, to let the bullets rip from the barrel and rattle piercingly throughout the turret bouncing off the walls over their heads.

Lugowski grabbed Kate's hand, to haul ass for the broken wrought iron gate leading outside. Every biker in the joint had just been alerted to some breach in security. They burst through the smashed gateway spilling into the moonlit side yard.

The gunfire in the east turret continued to explode. Buck screamed warnings and cursing.

The adrenaline surging through him, Lugowski glanced right and then left. Bikers were sprawled all over the ground, slugging awake, searching for the threat, and grappling for their weapons. There was no other way. He squeezed Kate's hand tight and focused on the Impala. They had to go straight through them.

Damned to hell.

~ Seventeen ~

Eric slammed the door behind them when he and Jen returned home. No, they had not found Kate with Holden, and much to Eric's alarm, Holden had not seen or heard from her all day. The only thing they had accomplished was clenching Holden in the tight grip of worry that was spreading through the family like a Texas wildfire.

They had spent several hours driving around the town of Rosemount to see if they would spot her vehicle.

Eric's head was spinning. He felt like a dog chasing his tail. His mind was traveling in a bad direction. *Were there more partners involved in Vic's kidnapping scheme that had not been apprehended? If so, did they come to the farm and grab Kate?*

His mind twisted to the more ghastly scenario, *Shit! Is it possible that Krebs escaped the crash with help from those partners and now he has Kate?*

He couldn't stomach the thought.

"Eric, you really need to calm down—" Jen followed closely behind him into the foyer.

"How can I calm down, Jen? My daughter is missing. Where the hell are the boys?" He was exhausted, and terrified that Krebs failed at killing Shane, but he'd just scored a second chance with Kate.

Jen wrung her hands with worry.

"Maybe Mike went home to catch some sleep." Eric marched back into the foyer. "Shane!" He bellowed up the staircase. No response. "Shane!" He dashed to the large window in the study, tossed back the curtains, and looked across the farm.

Mike's house was dark and his truck wasn't in the driveway.

Eric quickly made his way across the study to his desk, when he noticed the map and the large black X marking Old Mine Road. His tired mind was racing, and his eyes bruised by fatigue, burned while yearning to close. The map hadn't been on his desk earlier that evening. Mike must have spotted the X while he and Jen were out. *Surely Kate wouldn't have gone out there alone.*

He picked up the phone on the desk to dial Mike's cell. It went straight to voice mail. Damn, his gut was telling him exactly what that meant. He didn't want to believe it. "I think they're at the mansion on Old Mine Road," he told Jen while punching a different set of numbers out.

"Why would they go there?"

"I've got a feeling, but I'm hoping that I'm wrong."

Pressing the HOLD button, Detective Larson let out a long breath and jogged through the squad room to Captain Lutz's office. He tapped on the door frame. Lutz looked up from his pile of paperwork and frowned.

"You'd better take this call on line four, Captain. I'm not liking the sound of this. Something might be going down at the Valentine mansion," Larson said.

Lutz swiftly swiped the phone from its cradle, "Captain Lutz..." He listened intently to Eric explaining about his missing daughter, and his fears that the kidnapping situation may have taken on another theme. Then he revealed his suspicions that his sons may have gone to the mansion looking for their sister.

"Shit!" Lutz slammed down the receiver. "Larson, get a team pulled together quick. Haliday's in trouble."

Dangerous Deception

Eric shoved the phone onto its cradle while pulling open his desk drawer to seize the Glock, and shove it into his pants.

Jen grabbed his arm, "Please Eric, let the police do their jobs."

He turned to look into her pleading fright-filled eyes. He ran the back of his fingers gently over her cheek. "I have every intention of letting them do their jobs, but there's no way I can just sit here and wait. Everything will be okay." Kissing her on the forehead, and tossing her a comforting wink, he darted out of the house.

Through the window she watched the headlights of Eric's Denali slice the darkness and disappear through the stone entrance, and then onto the road. With a deep, fretful sigh she sank into the sofa, and rubbed her hands up and down her arms while praying that they all would return home safely.

Weak and exhausted and staggering on legs so wobbly that it was a wonder that he had made it this far, Krebs dragged his body through the scrub brush. The briefcase felt like it weighed eighty pounds. His right arm dangled at his side and eyes were so swollen that it was like looking through narrowly slatted Venetian blinds. His mouth was dry and his hair was matted to his head with globs of blood mixed with dirt from the roots of the tree where he had hid.

He stopped to rest along the way. Time was like a long strip of road that had no end and no destination. He would make it to the mansion. Vic's truck was still there. He'll drive it to a hotel, get some food, get some rest, and plan some deaths.

The bitter drip of anger in his gut rolled like thunderheads to surge him forward. Killing Shane wouldn't be enough after the amount of suffering he was enduring. Oh no, he wanted them all to die. The entire West family—he would execute them all—only Shane would be last. The sweet thoughts of revenge kept him focused on his task to give him the will to take the next step—the step that would get him closer to his objective.

Krebs had just walked over the crest of the hill when his eyes fell upon three vehicles parked alongside Old Mine Road in the tall weeds. He hobbled to the trunk of a hollowed-out tree and collapsed to his knees behind it. Clinging to the trunk to stay upright, he peered down on the vehicles. His vision was blurred and his eyes burned like blazes, but there didn't seem to be anyone around. Bracing against the briefcase with his left hand and leaning against the trunk with his right shoulder, he struggled against the pain to hoist himself back to his feet. He tottered down the hill toward the vehicles—two trucks and an SUV.

He buckled against the red pickup. Sweat poured down his face to saturate his ripped, dirty, and bloodied shirt that limply hung open. His head throbbed and his body screamed with pain and stiffness. A wave of nausea washed over him and he had to fight back the fierce urge to wretch. He yanked on the handle, but the truck was locked. Wiping the sweat from his brow with his left forearm, he groped along his waistband, pulled his out gun, and smashed the driver's side window with the butt of the gun. He reached in and unlocked the door, and then he pulled the door open. Barely able to stay upright and conscious, he clung to the door.

His heavy breathes boomed inside his head, as he lifted the ten-ton briefcase to the seat. His swollen eyes fell upon a bottle of water in the cup holder. Enticement raced through him. It took every bit of his might and constitution, but he crawled into the driver's seat and snatched the bottle from the holder. His right arm was useless. Clamping down on the lid between his teeth, he twisted the bottle open with his left hand, and spat the lid across the cab. His hand shook uncontrollably when he lifted the bottle to his quivering lips and gulped it dry. Closing his sore eyes, he let his head fall against the headrest. His shoulders slumped, and his head rolled to the side.

Mike's Glock lay on the ground between Shane's feet, as he sat leaning against the wall. It took every ounce of Shane's constitution to fight back sleep. The gentle breeze rustling the tall weeds, and the cool night air was lulling him to the hush of sweet slumber. His body was so exhausted that every muscle ached and his head still throbbed. Only one day ago he was playing pool at Barney's with his buddies, and hooking-up with that pretty little sable-haired jockey, Ginger LaFond. Now he was sitting in the middle of ever lovin' nowhere while keeping his gun within quick reach, and praying that they would be able to get Kate safely out of that damned mansion.

He hadn't prayed in a very long time, but he was praying now that she and Lugowski weren't being held in that ghastly dungeon. Then there was the other worry on his mind—Martin freaking Krebs. Not knowing where he was or what he would do next, was almost as bad as the torture that sonofabitch wielded upon him in the dungeon.

His head nodded forward. He was losing the battle against an unforgiving Sandman. His eyelids dipped lower. He shook his head. *Stay awake, asshole!* He realized that the only way that he was going to be able to stay conscious was to stand up. Laboriously, he pushed himself to a standing position.

Then, all hell broke loose.

~ EIGHTEEN ~

Guns exploded. Yelling and cursing sliced the quiet of the night.
"Holy shit!" Shane peered through the hole in the wall.
Punch and Mike gathered around him.

Grabbing guns and ammo, bikers were running in all directions—
not knowing which direction to shoot, or from which direction to be on
the defensive.

Just then Shane pointed to the side yard. Jumping over bikers in a
desperate frantic attempt to get to the Impala parked near the back of
the house, Lugowski and Kate were running full force.

Punch grabbed the AK and tossed Mike the M-16. "This is it! Give
them some cover. Buy them some time!" The three men took position in
the crumpled section of the wall spraying gunfire over the biker's heads.

"Where are we going?" Kate screamed above the chaos.

"To the car!" Lugowski yelled back

"You've got the keys?"

"I'm improvising." He tried to gulp some air into his lungs. *Damned
cigarettes.* "Hot wire!" was all he could manage. Not sure where the gunfire was coming from, or how precise the aim, they kept low as they ran.

They were fifty feet from the car when a lone biker came up from
the ground wide awake and ready. His six-foot-two physique stood firm

with his feet spread apart, his fists in tight balls, and his mighty broad chest burst from his black leather duster. His chest pounded up and down with each angry threatening breath, his bearded pocked face wore a scowl, and he gritted his teeth.

There was no way around the massive brut that had more resemblance to a Cyclops than a human. His gun lay at his feet. He thought that he had no need for it, and Lugowski was worried that he might be correct.

"Keep going!" Lugowski shoved Kate farther to the left in hopes that she would be able to scoot past the man that he had no choice but to face.

She stumbled but regained her footing quickly. Knowing the plan, she made haste for the Impala while muttering a prayer that Lugowski would soon be right behind her. The gunfire continued to spew above her head.

Gunner made no move to grab Kate. He had his sights firmly on the man he was about to pulverize, and then he would make him watch as he ravaged his pretty blonde bitch. He swung his right fist making hard contact with Lugowski's jaw to knock him backward. Lugowski stumbled a few steps but managed to stay on his feet, and then he decided that his best defense was to rush the huge man. He tucked his head and ran straight for the Gunner's torso and wrapped his arms tautly around him.

Out of breath, Kate made it to the old car. She fumbled with the door latch, and then finally yanked the door open. Throwing herself to her knees behind the door, she squeezed her body under the steering column. Sweat trickled down her temples, her heart pounded madly in her chest as if it would burst through her skin, and her damp hair clung to her cheeks. Her trembling fingers clawed at the plastic panels under the steering wheel until she finally tugged it open to let the tangle of wires drop from the encasement. Her eyes narrowed. Struggling to make out the difference between the wires in the dim light, she bit down on her lip. Locating the correct wires, she peeled the plastic cover away to identify the power wires. Quickly, she twisted them together while praying that the car would start when she touched the wires together, and fully aware that the other option was getting her the shock of her life.

Gunner punched Lugowski in the neck. Blood began to disgorge from the gash he had suffered earlier. It burned like hell fire, but he kept his tight grip. Grunting like a professional wrestler, the biker kneed him in the gut hard to force him to let go and hurled him to the ground. Gunner loomed over him and brought his booted foot up to kick him. Lugowski grabbed his boot, twisted his ankle and flipped the enraged biker to the ground. Without hesitation, Lugowski punched him hard in a pressure point area behind the knee. Gunner shrieked and grabbed his leg paralyzed by pain.

Lugowski scrambled to his feet. A wall of angry Nomads rounded the corner of the mansion and was coming at him fast. He needed to get to that freaking car.

"You're mine, bastard!" Gunner screamed while clawing at the ground. "And you're little bitch will be mine too!" He grappled for his gun lying on the ground. He would shoot the sonofabitch in the leg and then the party would really begin.

Kate touched the starter wire to the power wire and the old Impala's engine choked and sputtered. Panicked, she peered over her shoulder. Soon she would be discovered. She squeezed her eyes closed and tightly to touch the wires together again, while whispering a desperate prayer. The car's engine ground and sputtered and then it roared to life. She breathed a sigh of relief and turned to look for Lugowski.

Her eyes widened and her chest tightened in terror while she watched Lugowski charge the car. Just beyond him she saw the enormous man aiming his gun at Lugowski, while yet another biker came from behind. Gun drawn, aiming, a rush of now organized, cognizant, and armed Nomads followed behind and were approaching fast.

She jumped into the driver's seat, swung her legs across the tattered bench seat, and kicked frantically at the passenger's door until it popped open.

Gunner trained his gun on Lugowski's leg. *Easy, don't kill him, just mess him up so I can enjoy killing him slowly after we have our fun with the blonde.* With Lugowski dead in his sight, he pulled the trigger. Suddenly, he lurched forward with a mean scorching burn in his shoulder that forced him to drop the gun. He cupped his hand onto his shoulder to come up with a blood soaked hand. Grunting in pain and fury, he looked up to see Lugowski fall to the ground while grabbing his leg and struggling to get up.

Jack Haliday dashed past Gunner to grab Lugowski by the shoulder. "C'mon Lugowski, move your ass!"

Lugowski threw his arm around Jack's shoulder and the two of them hobbled quickly to the car.

Jack shoved him through the passenger door, hopped in and slammed it shut. "Well, honey, you got it started. Now let's see if you can drive it. Go!" he commanded.

She was shocked to have the Nomad that had grabbed her and forced her down through the tower now sitting in the car, but she didn't have time to analyze it. Through the windshield she gauged how far she would have to drive to reach the opening in the wall. Shoving the car into DRIVE, she pressed the accelerator down hard. Spinning wheels, and spitting dirt through the air, the Impala sped forward toward the wall. Bullets pinged off the metal, and the back window shattered. Flinching in terror, Kate's fingers held a white knuckle grip on the steering wheel, while trying not to think about the gunfire. Instead she tried like hell to concentrate on getting through that wall.

Wincing in pain, while blood seeped through his pant leg, and oozed between his fingers, Lugowski grabbed her thigh with his clean hand to give her a reassuring squeeze and nod.

They were running out of ammo quick, and it was only a matter of moments until the Nomads would realize that there were only three men holding them down. Kneeling to reload, Mike scanned the perimeter of the wall. He was expecting groups of them to surge around the sides at any second to surround them and take them prisoners and then ... who the hell knew. The six captive Nomads huddled together in an attempt to steer clear of the gunfire. They shot him steely glares as if to say, *"You've got five minutes to live, make the most of it, assholes!"* Mike preferred not to think about that right now.

"Hot damn! Here comes the car!" Shane shouted.

"Get ready! We've gotta get in that car or we're toast!" Punch slammed his last magazine into the AK.

❦ ❧ ❦ ❧

Jack let down his window to rest his Uzi on the frame. "You hot wired this thing? Pretty damned impressive, sweetheart!" He let several rounds rip to ward off any advancements.

"Hey, I earned my fair share of girl scout badges, *love drop,*" she retorted. Jack chuckled. Lugowski smirked while puffing out a quiet laugh. *Note to self: Kate doesn't care to be patronized with silly terms of endearment.* Why would that surprise him? *Geesh, she's such a West.*

Without warning a body slammed across the hood of the car. The ugly biker's mug pressed against the windshield as he clung to it. The human hood ornament shoved his gun against the glass to point it at Kate. She couldn't help it. It was a natural reaction. She screamed and swerved. Clutching, the rider struggled and lost his aim, but managed to hang on tight.

"We've got a hitchhiker." Jack handed the Uzi off to Lugowski. Holding on to the roof, he pulled his torso through the window. Kate couldn't see past the uninvited passenger, so she held her breath while holding the steering wheel steady and hoped that she was going in the right direction.

Jack grabbed the man's ankle to slide him hard across the hood toward him, and then he grabbed his belt and hurled him off the car onto the ground with a thud with a few random shots in the air and a very loud grunt. He climbed back into the car and claimed his gun back from a pallid Lugowski. "You look like shit, Lugowski. You gonna be okay?"

"Yeah," he bit out, "I think he just grazed me, but it's bleeding like a sonofabitch."

No kidding, Kate was trying like hell not to look at the blood soaking into his slacks and dripping down the seat. His bloodied hand pressed hard to keep compression on the wound, not to mention the fresh blood on his collar and neck.

"Look!" Kate cried out.

Jack and Lugowski's attention jerked toward her pointing finger, to see a large black man with an AK waving at them between shots from the wall. "It's Punch!" She wailed with tears streaming down her cheeks. She gunned the gas pedal to blowing through the hole in the wall, and then slammed on the brake which sent the car into a sideways slide to an abrupt stop.

Mike, Shane, and Punch made haste for the car. Jerking the back doors open, they jumped in as a group of Nomads, firing recklessly at the car, came around the side of the wall.

Kate watched them pile into the backseat through the rear view mirror. Shane was squished in the middle between Mike and Punch. Before the doors were closed she pressed the gas hard to pull away fast, while fish tailing and spitting mud into the air.

Jack engaged the Uzi from his window, while Mike let his Glock rip through the back. The broken glass jabbed through his jeans into his knees. In the distance, he could see the bikers running for their motorcycles. "We're gonna have a whole lotta company real soon." Mike lifted his legs one at a time to escape the sharp jags slicing into his knees.

The car sputtered once. Kate glanced down at the fuel gauge, *Oh shit!* "We're almost out of gas! I hope we make it to the vehicles!" Her tone was laced with strain.

"Eh, sit back and enjoy the ride. They aren't coming for us any time soon." Punch swiped glass off the seat, and settled into a comfortable position.

Mike looked at him. "You wanna share?"

Punch snorted. "I cut the fuel lines on the motorcycles. They're gonna be pissed as hell."

Mike lowered his gun and eased himself into the seat, "Dang, you *were* busy."

"All in a day's work, bro." Punch and Mike bumped fists across Shane.

Pulling his Uzi away from the window, Jack turned to Lugowski. "Mind if I ask who these guys are?"

"Whoa, biker boy, I think the better question is who the hell are you?" Kate insisted.

Smiling, Shane couldn't help but think, and chuckle to himself, just how much she could take on the Eric West "tone" as convincingly as her brothers. He was so glad to see his big sister.

"This is Kate West," Lugowski said, "and the guys in the back seat are evidently the freaking *Justice League*, Mike and Shane West. The big ugly one is Punch McMinn."

Punch flipped him off.

Lugowski snorted, "Everyone, this is Jack Haliday. I didn't recognize him until we started running for the car, he's on the gang squad, but I'm thinking his cover has been blown to smithereens." The boys shook Jack's hand over the car seat.

"Ya think?" Jack wryly retorted, as he tossed Kate a playful salute, accompanied with a cocky grin.

She wasn't sure how she felt about Jack, after all he'd man-handled her and touched her boobs when they came upon him and Buck near the turret. Relief overtook those feelings, and she let out a long breath that felt stale in her lungs from holding it in for so long.

She slowed the car, "I never thought I'd be so happy to see your SUV Carl, but she's a beautiful sight." She steered the Impala toward the parked vehicles among the deadwood. Suddenly, her spine stiffened and her hand cupped her mouth with a gasp. "Luzetta!" She turned to Lugowski. "We forgot all about that poor old woman, she's still back there, Carl!"

He squeezed her hand in his. "She's been hiding in those secret passageways for years, Kate. I'm sure she's just fine," he said in a weary, comforting voice.

Suddenly the moonlit sky wasn't so ominous. The dark clouds gave way sending short spikes of beams through the sinewy remnants of the trees. Kate let her shoulders droop and her hands loosen from their severe hold on the steering wheel.

Relief, they had made it. They could get in the vehicles and go home. She took in a deep cleansing breath.

In the next nanosecond, *BAM!* The front fender of the Impala crunched, as the vehicle slid violently sideways. Kate let out a scream while grabbing the steering wheel tightly in an attempt to counter steer.

The red Dodge Ram pickup truck slammed into the old car and was pushing it hard. The force of the impact knocked Jack's Uzi out the passenger window.

Bracing hard in the backseat, the boy's bodies smashed against one and others. Their heads jerked toward the truck. "That's my freaking truck!" Punch roared.

"Shit!" Shane yelled, "That's Krebs in the driver's seat!"

Fueled by sheer malevolence and adrenaline, and after pushing the car fifteen feet, Krebs slammed on the brake. Ignoring the pain, he reached across his body with his good arm to throw the gear shift into reverse, and then pressed the accelerator down hard.

Kate's eyes widened. There was no question in her mind what he planned to do next. She pressed down on the gas to get the Impala out of the line of fire, but when she depressed the pedal there was no response. The car had died. Her eyes darted to the fuel gauge. Tauntingly, the little red arrow pointed at E.

They were like metal ducks in a sideshow at the fair, swimming across the stage, waiting to be plucked off by an over-achieving redneck armed with a cheap plastic gun.

Krebs would have smiled if it didn't hurt so much. He could see Kate and Mike in the car. He couldn't make out any of the faces of the other passengers, it didn't make much difference who they were—they were collateral damage. A good feeling bubbled up inside him that Shane was most likely amongst the group, *three Wests for the price of one—not a bad day at the office.*

Dirt and rocks and weeds spit into the air as the truck's tires spun, digging in deep, and then bolting forward at the crippled Impala.

"Brace yourselves!" Jack cried out. "Here he comes for more!"

"Shit!" Punch complained, "I just had that truck detailed!"

Kate squeezed her eyes closed. She didn't realize it, but she was screaming. Lugowski grabbed her and tucked her into his chest. "Hold on, baby," he muttered into her hair.

The truck made hard contact to the same fender, sending the car into a spin. The brutal whirl came to an abrupt stop against a large hollow trunk that broke-off and was projected into the air.

Dust engulfed the car to billow into the cab. The car rocked slightly onto its side and then fell back onto its tires, hard, as Krebs backed the truck farther away this time. They coughed and choked and batted at the cloud of dust, while trying to crawl back into seated positions to get a handle on where the truck was. The sound of the engine revving cued them that another collision was imminent.

The sound of water slapping over rocks pulled Punch's gaze to his window. The sound confirmed what he suspected. "I don't want to alarm anyone, but ten more feet and I believe we're heading over this embankment into the creek bed."

Everyone sat straight up and stretched to look out the passenger's side of the car. Indeed, Krebs had pushed the car very close to the edge of a rocky embankment, and thirty feet below ran the wide fast creek, Reardon's Run. Krebs revved the truck's engine again. He allowed the truck to lurch forward and then slammed the brake, revved the engine, and then lurched again. He was toying with them.

Shane's blood was boiling. Krebs had toyed with him in the dungeon and now he was playing his cat and mouse bullshit game with all of them. He was at the end of his rope with this sonofabitch! It was time to pull the thorn out of his side and toss his cross to bear to the ground. He wanted to charge the truck and kill the bastard with his bare hands.

Feverishly, he tried to climb over Mike to get to the door. "What're we gonna do?" he shrieked, "Sit here like a bunch of wussies, and let him run us down? No way!"

Mike grabbed him by the shoulders and struggled hard to push him back. Finally, Punch clenched his torso pulling him against his chest.

"Somebody, give me a freaking gun," Jack said.

Punch yanked the AK from the floor. "I don't know what's left in the magazine, if anything." he told the ex-Navy SEAL.

"It's all we've got." Jack lifted his body through the window and sat down on the window frame.

The truck lurched forward again, only this time it didn't retreat. Spinning wheels and dust blooming in its wake, the Dodge charged forward—straight for them. Jack perched motionless with the AK trained over the roof of the Impala for the truck. Slowing his breathing, steadying his thoughts, and carefully concentrating on his target rather than the dire situation, he took slow mechanical aim. The AK was not a sniper's rifle, and Jack was not a sniper. It was what it was, improvising at best, and this was the shot. If he couldn't stop the truck, it would ram the car over the embankment and six people would lose their lives.

Not today, dickhead.

Lugowski tightened his hold on Kate. Clutching a handful of his shirt, she closed her eyes against his chest.

Punch, Mike, and Shane weren't sure what to brace for—the exploding sound of the AK or the impending impact. Sweat dribbled down Jack's temple and his finger twitched on the AK's trigger. The truck bolted forward like an angry bull charging a matador.

Krebs was ready for any retaliation that they could muster-up, he turned on the high beams blinding the asshole with the gun.

Jack's face jerked back. His eyes squinted at the sudden burst of light. He couldn't make out the truck—he had lost his aim! *Shit!* He took a deep disgusted breath, *here goes a helluvalotta nothing!*

He pulled the trigger, the AK spit—nothing came out! "Shit!" Jack cursed, "No ammo!"

Shane lunged from Punch's hold snatching the gun lying between Mike's legs. He lay across his brother and took quick aim at the truck's windshield. It was time for Krebs to receive the retribution that he deserved. Praying for one round—just one precious round, he pressed the trigger. The windshield shattered, bobbles of glass bounced and danced over the hood, and the horn blew relentlessly. Krebs' dead body pressed the horn, and still the truck rolled forward.

"Get out!" Jack screamed. Bolting from their ducked-down positions, everyone scrambled and fumbled with door handles, until they all jumped from the Impala, as the truck gained momentum, while rolling toward them. Jack tossed his legs over the door to leap onto his stomach clear of the car, but the loop in his cargo-style jeans caught on the lock latch of the door. Jack struggled to free himself from the latch to escape the car before the assault. The truck made sharp contact with the car pushing it over the edge of the embankment. The sound of crunching metal against rocks, breaking glass, and the vehicles slamming against each other as they plunged into the creek was deafening.

Lugowski lifted his face from the dirt that he was eating. Removing his arm from Kate, he looked around to take a quick head count: Mike and Punch and Shane were struggling to their feet, Kate was pushing herself up onto her knees next to him, and Jack... *where the hell is Jack?*

~ Nineteen ~

Panic ripped through him. "Jack!" Lugowski cried out.

Fighting the gripping pain in his leg, he scrambled to his feet to hobble toward the rim of the embankment. Mike, Punch, Shane, and Kate's eyes scanned the area, and when they didn't come up with the biker-in-disguise they dashed to the cliff, passing Lugowski, to peer over the ledge. Punch's truck and the Impala lay in the creek bed below in a tangle of metal. Smoke billowed up from the engines of the wreckage.

Kate cupped her hand over her mouth. Tears streamed down her cheeks, and the men allowed their shoulders to droop, and their faces to fall to their chests. The water slapping over the rocks and the cool early morning breeze lent a somber funeral anthem feeding the overwhelming sense of loss and defeat. *Krebs got was he deserved, and yet he still won.* Shane couldn't fight back the bitter biting thought.

"What the hell are you assholes doing? Get a fucking rope!"

Their heads popped up, their eyes widened and rotated to the far right of the cliff. The moon barely provided enough light to see him. Kate gasped, "Oh my God!"

Jack clung to a small branch of a tree root growing out from the embankment, and it was giving out fast.

"My tool box!" Mike exclaimed, "I've got rope and a winch!" He and Punch spun on their heels into a sprint toward the pickup across the field of dead trees and bristly weeds. Mike vaulted into the bed of the pickup to yank the silver tool box lid open. Tossing hammers, wrenches, and screwdrivers over his shoulder, he rifled through the contents. Finally, he found the long loop of rope tied up with baler twine, and a winch lying in the bottom of the long box. He tossed the rope and winch to Punch, and then they took off at a dead run toward the embankment.

Shane waved his arms over his head. "Here! This is the biggest and strongest tree trunk of the bunch," he proclaimed. Quickly, Punch wrapped the rope around the trunk. Mike hooked the winch to the rope, and then Punch unwound the loop of rope. He hustled toward Lugowski, who was lying on his stomach to peer over the rim above Jack.

The tree root jerked and slipped away from the embankment. Dirt and rubble fell from the roots smacking Jack in the face and into his eyes.

Nimbly, Lugowski let the rope over the embankment. "Jesus, Jack, I hope you can grab hold," he said with a raspy stressed voice.

Barely able to watch, Kate knelt next to him.

"Just get the rope down here, I'll climb up. I'm a SEAL, remember?" Jack watched the rope dangle and sway as it slowly descended toward him.

"I hope you're part freaking mountain goat," Lugowski said.

Mike manned the winch, while Punch and Shane held the rope. They waited for Jack's weight to bear-down on them. Finally, the rope came within reach. It had a large metal hook on the end. Jack took several deep gulps of air. He had to let go of the branch with one hand to grasp the rope. He was a strong man. A work-out fanatic, but his arms were tiring from supporting his one-hundred-ninety-five pounds for the last six to seven minutes. He could make the climb. He had to make the climb, if he wanted to see Laura and be there for their new baby.

The rope was right there within reach. Letting go of the branch, a plug of dirt fell from the hillside and hit him square in the eye. Burning and watering, his eye couldn't focus. He couldn't see the rope. He grabbed the branch again with both hands. The branch slipped lower on the hillside and more stony rubble molested him. The branch was barely secured in by less and less of the root.

Jack's tears finally cleared the dirt enough that he could see the rope again above his head, except it was now out of his reach.

"More rope, Lugowski!" he called up the hillside.

Lugowski turned to Punch. "More rope,"

Punch shook his head. "That's all we've got, bro."

Lugowski swallowed hard, *Jesus,* "That's it, Jack. Can you climb the hill a bit to reach the hook?"

The roots were giving, the soil was tumbling, and he could barely see the rope. It was go time. *This is for Laura and my baby!* Jack used the brittle branch as a catapult to lift himself to the hook. He would only have one chance. His weight would rip the roots right out the hillside to fall into the long rocky distance into the creek. Stretching his arms beyond their limits toward the hook until his hand wrapped around it, he jerked his body upward. The hook dug into his palm. Ignoring the stab, he grabbed the rope with his other hand and secured his feet against the hillside. The roots holding the scrawny branch gave way to take a gulp of the hillside with it. It tumbled down into the creek bed below.

"C'mon, Jack!" Lugowski desperately urged, "C'mon!"

Biting down hard on her lip, Kate laced the fingers from both hands into her hair. Punch and Shane felt the tug at the rope. They waited tentatively for Lugowski's signal.

One foot at a time, and hand over hand, Jack made his way up the hillside. The rope burned into his hands. A bead of blood surged and then a steady trickle began to drip down his wrists toward his elbows. The dirty sweat from his brow dribbled into his eyes to cause a salty burn, and blur his vision. He blinked to clear his eyes to no avail.

Lugowski turned toward the boys. "Slowly now ... nice and easy."

Punch and Shane gently pulled the rope, while Mike twisted the winch with kid-glove-care. Closer and closer to the top he emerged. Lugowski stretched his arms out to Jack over the ledge.

Suddenly, the soil and stones on the hillside beneath his feet gave way.

Jack's boots rolled with the rolling rubble, and his legs fell out from underneath him. He held on with every bit of constitution he had, while he dangled.

"Oh, God!" Kate covered her eyes.

Shit! Lugowski needed big help so he turned to a big man. "McMinn! Grab my feet!" Shane stopped pulling. Mike hesitated. Punch dropped the rope and ran forward to take hold of Lugowski's feet. Digging into the ground, Punch braced himself with his heels. He held, Lugowski by his legs.

Reaching, stretching, Jack locked his bloodied wrists with Lugowski. With fiery pain screaming fiercely through his wounded leg Lugowski pulled with all his might, until Jack hiked up over the ledge to fall to the ground on his stomach. Kate dropped to her knees next to Lugowski and Jack. Half laughing, half crying, she said, "Oh, thank God, biker boy, you made it."

Huffing and puffing and happy as hell to be on solid ground, Jack looked up at the relieved group hovering over him. "I can't believe you guys had rope," he said around his gasps for breath.

"Dude, we're farmers." Mike snorted in relief.

"Shit, you're lethal rednecks, is what you are," Jack happily and thankfully said.

"Oh yeah, then there's that too," Mike laughed.

The scream of sirens sliced through their reprieve. "It sounds like the Calvary is coming, although I don't know how." Lugowski struggled to get up. Jack and Punch reached to help him off the ground, and lend a helping hand to Kate, as well.

"Oh, I'll bet I do." Shane was reassured to know that his father had their backs.

The police cars whizzed by.

Captain Lutz's cruiser pulled in next to Lugowski's SUV. Sliding from the seat, he slammed the door and marched toward Jack and Punch, who was helping Lugowski hobble toward his vehicle. "Haliday..." His eyes fell upon someone that he didn't expect, "*Lugowski?* What the hell is going on?"

"A shitload, sir." Jack said, "Over that embankment you've got two wrecked vehicles with the body of man inside the red truck." He scratched his dusty head. "I'm not exactly sure what his motives were but he wanted us all dead, real bad." he gestured over his shoulders with a nod, "Down the road about a half mile, you've got a gang of bikers trespassing on private property with drugs and illegal arms, sir. They also tried to kill a police officer, and you're probably looking at some casualties." Jack quickly summed up the situation knowing that it wasn't going to cut the mustard, but hey, he had to give it a try.

"The dead body in the truck is Martin Krebs," Lugowski added, "I believe he's one of the kidnappers you're looking for."

Lutz took in Lugowski's bloody pant leg, and collar, and his general battered appearance. He studied the West brother's muddy faces, and Kate's wide eyed pallid expression. Lastly he measured the huge black man that Lugowski was leaning against, and Jack's filthy exhausted face. It was a motley crew, indeed. Jutting out his lower lip, he crossed his arms over his chest.

"And the necessary information?" he directed at Jack on a terse breath.

"Negative, sir." Jack solemnly replied.

He let out a frustrated sigh, and then nodded toward Lugowski, "Get his ass to a hospital. I want a full report from both of you on my desk by noon. You got that?"

"Yes sir," Jack and Lugowski responded sounding like a small tone-deaf boy's choir.

His steely gaze fell upon the Wests and Punch, "As for the rest of you, stay close to home. We'll be talking, very soon." Lutz yanked his cell phone from his jacket while pitching them one more abrasive glare. Marching back to his cruiser, he paused, "Haliday..." Jack lifted his chin, "go see your wife, for Christ's sake."

"Yes sir."

Jack and Punch hoisted Lugowski into the SUV. Jack nodded thanks to Punch and then jogged to the driver's side, where he was met by Kate.

"He's going to be okay, right?" she asked with concern bleeding like a sieve through her tone.

"He'll be fine." Jack clapped his hand on her shoulder. He climbed into the driver's seat.

"Can you hold up a minute?" She asked.

Smiling, he nodded. She hurried to the passenger's side window. The right side of Lugowski's lip curled when she reached through the window to affectionately squeeze his shoulder. Her beautiful blue eyes were filled with gratitude and compassion.

Lifting her shoulder, she breathed in deep. "I don't know what to say, except thank you, Carl." Pressing up on tip-toes, she stretched through the window to kiss him gently on the cheek.

Lugowski smiled into his chest. "You can hot wire a freaking car. Who knew?" They shared a tender chuckle. Her hand slipped away from his shoulder as Jack eased the vehicle forward, bumping through the rough dry grasses onto the road.

A black Denali crested the hill and slowed, pulling in where the SUV had been parked. The door flung open. Eric jumped out. Fatigued relief bathed his face at the sight of his three children safe. Kate rushed to her father. He swallowed her into his chest and kissed the top of her head.

"If you weren't a full grown woman, I'd ground you for six months," he muttered into her hair.

Hugging him fiercely, she chortled into the loving security of his shoulder. "Actually that doesn't sound all that bad. Although I think Doc Spears would complain—very loudly."

Eric noticed Captain Lutz sitting in his cruiser on his cell phone. His eyes narrowed in concern. Punch patted his shoulder. "We'll fill you in on the way home. I'm just hoping that my insurance guy is super under-standing, cuz I've got one helluva tall tale to tell him."

"Okay, is everyone accounted for now?" Mike raked his fingers wearily through his dark locks. "Because I'm ready to go home, and sleep for as long as I damned well please."

Chuckling, Eric cupped his hand on his eldest son's shoulder. "That goes for me too. I think someone else might be a bit tired-out as well..." He nodded toward Shane, who was leaning against Mike's truck, his head hung low, his eyes closed. He was snoring.

~ TWENTY ~

When the small caravan pulled through the stone entrance of Westwood Farm, Kate was asleep on her father's shoulder. Mike steered his dually pickup down the driveway toward his bungalow across the way. He was looking forward to a hot shower, and a long nap. Shane was passed-out in the back seat against the passenger's door. Punch was comfortably slouched on the other side of the seat. Mike had offered for Punch to ride with him, but he figured the Denali was a more comfortable, roomy ride. As promised, Punch briefed Eric on all the details of the early morning, Lugowski and Kate escaping the mansion with the bikers at their heels, Krebs' assault on the old Impala which sent both vehicles over the cliff, and finally the rescue of one ex-Navy SEAL disguised as a Nomad. The story was quite a cliffhanger ... literally.

The entire debacle infuriated Eric. What a sadly ridiculous way for two people to lose their lives, one man facing a certain prison term, and for a long-time friendship to be completely shattered. If Vic had just given him a chance to offer him the job of the breeding manager instead of getting involved in the kidnapping scheme, none of the events of the past two days would've occurred. *Ridiculous.*

Eric's eyes were bruised and burned from sleep deprivation, nevertheless his lips curled at the sight of Jen's car still parked in front of the house. Probably not so patiently, she awaited their return. Actually, he wasn't one bit surprised to find her still there. Immediately he noticed another vehicle sitting in the driveway as well. Gently, he nudged his sleeping daughter. Her eyes slowly fluttered open. He nodded toward the windshield at the white vet truck parked next to Jen's car... Holden's.

Kate's face brightened. Quickly, she pushed upward to the rearview mirror to adjust it so she could see her face. Wincing at her tattered appearance, she ran her fingers through her hair to fluff it. Licking her finger, she wiped the thin smear of mascara from under her eyes. Reaching into the hip pocket of her jeans, she retrieved a tube of lip gloss, and quickly smoothed it over her lips. Even though Eric was completely done in, he found this female ritual quite impressive. He allowed himself a quiet snicker as he slid from the vehicle.

Motivated to move a bit faster than her father, Kate beat Eric to the porch just as Jen yanked the front door open. Looking washed out but relieved, she grabbed Kate to hug her tightly.

"Thank God," she whispered, "I was frantic with worry." Eric shuffled up the steps. She scolded, "Oh Eric, you look terrible. C'mon, I've made some fresh biscuits, and then it's straight to bed with you."

An ornery grin snaked across his face, as he pulled her into his arms, "Jen... not in front of the children."

"Ooh, you." Giggling, she tugged him by the arm through the front door. On his way past, he nodded at Holden, who was standing in the doorway while waiting for his chance to talk to Kate. The moment Eric and Jen were in the foyer on their way to the kitchen, he swept her into his arms to cover her lips with his. His kiss was filled with possessive passion. Kate circled his neck with her arms to take in every lush second.

He was awakened in the middle of the night to his cell phone ringing and vibrating and tinkling against the empty wine glasses that clinked against the two empty wine bottles on the nightstand. Jen had called to inform him that Kate had been found, and what had taken place. He already had the dull thump of a headache going on when he opened his eyes, but after she told him the story, it grew into a healthy, full-blown throb.

A flood of anger rolled through him. He felt foolish when he glanced at the redhead sleeping next to him. Ava had manipulated him. The lies tumbled from her lips as easily as rain drops tumble from the sky. *She was so damned believable, the little bitch. And I was so damned gullible. What a freaking idiot!*

He had even agreed to give her the position of his assistant. As she gathered her clothing from the floor, Ava not-so-subtly hinted that if he reneged, she would update Kate of their roll in the sheets.

Christ, I really like Kate. No, it's way past the like stage. I don't want to screw this up. But it was looking as though he already had. Voila! Holden had been acrimoniously enlightened as to why the West family held Ava in such contempt.

Kate was taken aback by the quiver in his lips. For her the loving message was most clear, he had been worried, and he was so very glad to have her in his arms, as she was so very glad to be there. When he pulled away he brushed her cheek gently with the pad of his thumb. There was a placid curve to his lips, while he searched her eyes with concern. "Are you okay?"

"A little tired, but I'm fine," she softly replied.

He brushed a frock of her hair from her eyes. He needed to be near her to make up for the doubt that had been planted in his mind— for what he had permitted to happen. God, he hated himself for allowing Ava to suck him in so easily, "You want to rest at my place?"

"I could use a shower."

"Yeah, I was counting on that," he said with a lift to his lips.

Looking into his deep brown eyes, she couldn't help but smile. Oh yeah, a hot shower with Dr. Holden Reese was just what said doctor ordered. She loved showering with him. It was always an exercise in Oh-la-la. After the shower and some sexy love-making, her rest would be a deep sated sleep, snuggled against his chest letting his fresh clean scent lull her into dreamland.

"What are we waiting for?" Her eyes were gleaming.

Grinning, he lifted her hand to his lips to kiss her fingers, and then he led her down the porch steps.

Punch was peering into the Denali. Scrubbing his hand over his chin, he wasn't exactly sure what to do about the youngest West who was now sprawled across the seat, dead to the world, snoring light and steady.

"Aren't you gonna wake him?" Holden asked.

Scratching his head, Punch shrugged. "I dunno. He seems pretty comfortable. I think we should just leave him there," he nodded toward the barn, "I'm gonna go check on Cody, and then crash on Mike's couch for a couple hours."

Hugging him with all her might, Kate wrapped her arms around Punch's torso. This urged a loving smile from the big man. He hugged her back. "Thank you," she muttered into his chest.

He lifted her chin with his hand. "Hey, what are *friends* for?"

~ EPILOGUE ~

Four months later...

It was time. Punch had given Cody all the time that Dr. Spears recommended, but the old gelding just wasn't coming around. The puffiness in his ankle never dissipated. The old boy limped severely. Yes, it was tough to admit, tough to face, but it was time.

Punch patted the old Quarter Horse gelding's neck, he loved that horse. He was just a yearling when Eric gave him to Punch as a birthday present. Cody was all legs and eyes and full of piss and vinegar. That was seventeen years ago. Until most recently Cody still had plenty of that piss and vinegar in reserve when galloping after runaway Thoroughbreds on the training track. Unfortunately, it had become his demise the morning they ran down Vic Deveaux on that lanky sorrel mare.

Punch's arm had healed, but Cody's ankle would not.

It was time. Bitter sweet, Punch led Cody to the gate while pulling an apple from his jacket. His ears perked, he chomped the apple from Punch's palm, which urged a smile from the huge gentle black man. Hey, it wouldn't be all that bad, he was being released into the vast, lush, broodmare pasture. He'd have all those women fussing over him ... not that he could act upon any of the fussing, but they were women none-the-less—beautiful women to boot—Thoroughbreds, it just doesn't get any prettier than that.

"You take care of yourself now, ya hear me?" Punch muttered. "And don't let them nag you too much." He chuckled. "No pun intended."

He led him through the gate, removed his halter smacking him on the rump. Limping, Cody loped away through the grassy pasture. Punch watched until his old friend was out of sight.

"Grudges are like hand grenades. It is better to throw it away before it destroys you." Yeah, Eric was thinking that might be easier said than done. He waited for the heavy metal bars to slide open with a loud clang. A visitors badge dangled from the clip attached to his collar. A large surly-faced guard flanked his side.

Vic had set disastrous repercussions in motion the moment he walked into the study demanding the money in the safe. He almost lost Shane. Kate came damned close as well.

This was one grenade that could possibly go boom. Jerking Eric from his thoughts, the prison guard escorted him down a long hallway with gray walls and shiny gray floors brightly lit by florescent lighting along the ceiling. Their footsteps echoed in a hollow rhythmic cadence through the corridor. The guard opened a metal door and gestured for Eric to enter the large room. Metal folding chairs were pressed close to tiny desks with metal divides. Clearly, they weren't interested in the comfort of the visitors or the inmates. He made his way past several women and one old man visiting with prisoners on the other side of the plate glass windows. They all seemed to be balancing their hand grenades at the tips of their unsteady fingers.

Eric was directed to sit in a chair. For several moments, he listened to the low murmur of voices of the other visitors asking about the food, or their activities on the "inside". Finally a guard led Vic through a metal door on the other side of the enclosure and directed him to a seat at the tiny desk on his side of the window. Vic looked pallid and embarrassed of his prison attire. He took a moment to cautiously eye-up the other inmates sitting at the visitor stations.

The two old ex-friends stared at each other through the thick glass, until Vic finally picked up the phone receiver on his side to place it tentatively to his ear. Hesitating for a moment to release a deep sigh, Eric picked up the receiver on his end.

"Good to see ya, Eric," Vic began.

"Shane convinced me to come," he replied, succinct.

"He's a good kid. If it weren't for his and Jose's testimony, they'd let me rot in here." He met Eric's steely gaze square on. "What I did was wrong, dead wrong."

"Damned straight," Eric flatly agreed.

Struggling for words, Vic breathed in deep. "I've got ten months left in this shit hole. I gotta know how to make this up to you, Eric. How to get your forgiveness?"

Eric studied him for a long moment. Memories of glorious Winners' Circle victories, Steelers' games on a Monday night in the study, and many evening deliberations by the fire planning the training schedules for young up-and-coming Thoroughbreds raced through his mind. A grand friendship destroyed. The shame of it all bit ferociously like a rabid dog.

"Friendship is given, Vic, forgiveness is earned. We'll see how you do when you get back to Westwood."

The tender sound of his baby daughter's breathing as she slept in his arms gave Jack Haliday a feeling he had never in his life experienced, pure contentment. The sheer perfection of her tiny features never failed to overwhelm him, as he rocked her gently back and forth in the rocker. Laura quietly came to him lifting her from his arms.

"She needs to go to her bassinette, Jack, or she'll expect us to hold her all the time while she sleeps," Laura said. That was fine by him. He could hold that little bundle and never let go, but Laura had rules.

Sure he was used to rules. When you're a SEAL there are always plenty of rules, and he had to admit, when it came to the baby, Laura was the more vigilant than any drill sergeant he'd ever faced.

He loved Laura. Now he had a baby girl to love, and to protect.

Protect, that was something that was heavy on his mind of late. Four months ago his cover as a Nomad had been blown, when the team moved in on the Valentine mansion, they managed to round-up most of the bikers and confiscate the guns and the drugs.

But they did not apprehend Gunner. He had escaped. He was still out there. Jack spent a lot of time wondering if he would come looking for the man who had penetrated his group, betrayed him, and shot him. He wasn't worried for himself. He could handle pretty much anything that was thrown at him. He feared for Laura, for his daughter. Guys like Gunner didn't think twice about harming women and children. In fact they enjoyed making examples of them to instill fear and insure loyalty from the members of their group.

Maybe it's time for a change of scenery for my family's safety ... protection.

Lugowski pulled into the drive-through at McDonald's to order up two coffees, one for him and one for Kate West. He hadn't seen her since their run-in with the bikers. She had called several times to see how his leg and his neck were healing; they spoke for only a few moments. At the time it seemed like it was best. Except try as he might, he couldn't unravel the knot that she tied in his chest. She monopolized his dreams. When he made love to Ava, somehow Kate made her way into the bed. How he felt about Kate West was undeniable. It was time to face his feelings. It was time to talk to Kate.

To hell with the fact that she is Mike West's little sister, and Ava's ex-sister-in-law. I need to know if, by any chance, she thinks of me the way I think of her. Is that even possible? And if so, where does that leave Ava? Who am I kidding? I'm pretty damned sure of the answer.

He had spend the better part of the last months making up to Ava, doting over her, spending every extra moment he had with her, it was penance for leaving her bed to go to Kate's abet. Funny thing was that even after all his pampering, Ava was holding something back. She had a new job with a different veterinarian at the racetrack—that much he knew. Problem was, she acting strangely covert about the new position. Hell, he didn't even know the new boss's name. *What's the hitch?*

"Sir..."

He was jerked from his deliberations by the drive-through attendant. He smiled at the tiny teenage girl, collected the coffees, carefully placed them into the cup holders, and then he pulled out of the McDonald's lot on his way to the Valentine mansion.

Over the months he had been keeping track of the newspaper articles about the renovations that had been taking place at the mansion. Kate had contacted the Rosemount Historical Society to inform them of the rich and unique history that the mansion held, within its crumbling walls. She had helped organize many fundraisers for the renovations. He had heard through the grapevine that a group was gathering at the mansion this afternoon to replace many of the broken windows. There was little doubt in his mind that Kate would miss the event.

After the fifty minute drive to Old Mine Road, Lugowski was a little concerned that Kate's coffee would be lukewarm, at best. *It's the thought that counts, right?*

The stone lions still kept a vigilant guard over the mansion from their perches. He noticed that the wrought iron gates were missing. Scaffolding cloaked the front of the mansion and around the east turret. The grounds were bustling with volunteers carrying ladders and paint cans and tool boxes. He parked the SUV among the many vehicles in the driveway, and made his way to the opening that led into the courtyard. Immediately, he spotted Kate kneeling next to the fountain. She was working it over vigorously with a wire brush. Her blonde mane was twisted into a pile on top of her head held by a clip. One wavy wisp dangled over her cheek, she brushed it away with the back of her hand. Lordy she was a sight. He had to fight the urge to walk right over there, take her in his arms, and kiss her long and hard. No warning, no explanation, just the release of his primal need to taste her.

"Hey..." Lugowski hoarsely chirped while keeping that primal need in check.

Looking up, she noticed the McDonald's cup in his hand. She smiled when he took her hand to hoist her to her feet. "Is that coffee for me?"

"Cream and a half a packet of sweetener." He handed her the cup.

Kate always enjoyed the view of that boyish smirk that Lugowski often displayed. She was quite sure that he was totally unaware of it, which made it all that more appealing. Taking a sip of the coffee, while peering at him over the cup, she wondered if Ava ever noticed how sexy the man really was. She seriously doubted it. *Ya know if he didn't belong to that manipulative bitch... Hokay, I really shouldn't go there...*

"So, what brings you all the way out here? You need a car hot wired?" She playfully inquired.

Snarky and sexy and the prettiest blue eyes he'd ever gazed into, yeah, keeping his feelings and his primal need in check was not longer an option. They needed to talk, and after the talk he had every intention of taking her to his apartment and giving in to his primal need—in every way.

"I came to see what kind of progress you were making. Looks like things are starting to really come together." He thought that it would be a good start, anyway.

"Yeah, when it's all finished they are going to offer tours of the mansion. Luzetta is going to be the tour guide. She's very excited, as am I," she said.

"I'm glad. Kate, I wanted to t—"

"Kate!"

She turned. Lugowski's gaze shot to a tall, handsome, broad shouldered man approaching them. "Kate, Luzetta is looking for you." The man ran his hands affectionately up and down her spine.

"Oh, I'll be right there." Slipping her arm around the man's waist with a smitten curl to her lips, she turned back to Lugowski. "Carl, this is Dr. Holden Reese. Holden, this is Lieutenant Carl Lugowski of the Rosemount Police Department."

He hesitated at first, and then Holden extended his hand. "Good to meet you, lieutenant. Kate has told me all about you. She holds you in very high regard."

He's got a good handshake, confident and firm. Of course it is, stupid. Kate would never be involved with a wimp. This is a solid man, and I'm happy for her, right?

Much to Kate's disgust, Ava had been Holden's new assistant for four months now. Regardless, she would've thought Carl had met Ava's new employer by now, right? How could he possibly not know Holden?

"Carl, I would've thought that you'd met—"

"Luzetta really needs you, Kate," Holden quickly interjected.

"No, no, you're busy, I understand." Lugowski cleared his throat. "I'm going to walk around and see what you've been up to. Good to meet you, Dr. Reese." Holden nodded at him before quickly whisking Kate around toward the other end of the courtyard, where he noticed Luzetta giving Shane a big hug. Beyond them Mike and Punch were holding an arched window in place, while Eric tightened the screws into the encasement.

Luzetta looked great. Her long white hair was swept up in a bun at the nape of her neck. She was wearing a pair of capris and a pristine pink shirt. She looked well rested and well fed. The haggard appearance she once wore was gone. Lugowski was sure that Kate was tending to her well being. The woman never failed to amaze or to stir him.

Thankful that he hadn't made a total fool of himself, Lugowski shuffled toward the gate. He was close to telling her how he felt, when tall dark and doctor showed up. *Eh, she's better off with him. He's a safer choice than a freaking cop, and being a doctor, he makes a hell of a lot more money, that's for damned sure.*

Hey, he had the woman of his dreams, remember? Ava was right where he always wanted her to be, in his life and in his bed.

"Carl," Kate called out.

He turned to see her jogging toward him. She was smiling, not just with her full inviting lips, but with those dazzling baby blues of hers. When she reached him, she squeezed his arm. "Next time we have coffee, don't let me talk you into anything crazy, *capiche?*"

He urged a gentle smile. Kate West was what Lugowski would define as a "keeper". Regretfully she was someone else's "keeper". He cupped her chin in his hand. Smoothing his thumb over her cheek, he took in every detail of those crystal blue eyes. Primal.

"Capiche," he murmured.

The End...for now

A note from author, Cindy McDonald...

Thank you for reading **Dangerous Deception**, I hope you enjoyed it. I would like to invite you to read an excerpt from the next book of The Unbridled Series...

AGAINST THE ROPES

Available in 2013

Gravel spit from the tires of Punch McMinn's red Dodge Ram pickup truck, as it rambled along the desolate dusty road. A dirty haze levitated on the horizon in the intense August heat and the leaves on the maple trees turned upward to the heavens begging for a drink. The sky was crystal clear not showing any prayer for storm clouds to rumble through. It had been a damned dry summer.

Glancing at the rear view mirror, Punch could see the pallet of blocks in the bed of his truck. He had gone into Rosemount early this morning to pickup the blocks for the wall that was being re-built in the old brood mare shed on the far side of Westwood Thoroughbred Farm where he'd been the farm manager for many years. He promised Eric West that he would get the wall re-built before the leaves started to turn shades of gold and amber and the autumn chill would set forth a welcome relief. When you made a promise to the patriarch of the West family, you kept it. Disappointing that man was never an option. Eric had practically raised

Punch. When his father left his mother with no warning and children to feed, it was Eric that took Punch under his wing. He gave him jobs at the farm to earn a paycheck, and he saw to it that Punch continued playing high school football with his eldest son, Mike. He grew up at Westwood with the West kids Mike, Kate, and Shane. They cleaned stalls side-by-side, lugged heavy water buckets, and groomed the Thoroughbreds to a laser sheen before they entered the paddock for a race. A game of hide-n-seek or a pickup football game always filled their spare time—what little of that they could scrounge. And Sunday or Monday night football with the Steelers on the TV in the West's study was a favorite back then, and still remained a weekly ritual to this day. The Wests were his second family and his loyalty to Eric and the clan ran as deep as Reardon's Run. They always had each others back—because that's what families are made of.

Trying to beat the heat, he went to Miller Block and Brick early. The brickyard was located smack-dab in the middle of downtown Rosemount. The chain-link fence surrounding the huge yard was rather out of place, as were the piles and piles of cement blocks and bricks that lined the perimeter. Miller Block and Brick had set up business in the small dusty town of Rosemount in 1917 before it had become a bustling busy city with tall buildings, fast-food restaurants, theaters, and a four lane running through the center of downtown. The brickyard was a staple as was the Miller family.

Harris Miller was the fourth generation to operate the business and his daughter, Zoe, would take over the reins when Harris retired. Well into his seventies, Harris was not even beginning to entertain the thought of sitting on the front porch in a rocking chair. The very notion made him queasy, so he showed up to open the business every morning by six a.m.

Yep, Punch was trying to beat the heat, and if the truth were being told, he was also trying to avoid Zoe Miller with his early morning errand. He was unsuccessful at both tasks. The sun came up with a golden fury to scorch the morning as it had done the day before, and when he walked through the door of the brickyard sales office, there stood Zoe, waiting for him at the counter with a grin that stretched all the way through the blush of her cheeks to her bright sapphire eyes.

Suspicion ripped through him. If he didn't know better, he would've sworn that one of his loyal "family" members called to alert her of his impending arrival. That's another thing family does—meddle. He couldn't decide which West would be that spry so early in the morning, Shane? Hmmm, it certainly fit his MO, but Punch seriously doubted it. Shane had trouble rolling out of bed in the morning. *I won't bust his balls...yet.*

Maybe Kate was the culprit. He loved the slender blonde-haired blue-eyed woman of Westwood. She knew what was best for her West men—and Punch. Last week she sat him down on a bale of straw and had a little "talk" with him about the virtues of one, Miss Zoe Miller. Kate could be quite convincing and when necessary, quite conniving. Except he was having his doubts about the shrewd little matchmaker, for the past several months she'd been very preoccupied with Dr. Holden Reese. Kate had been dating the newest and very handsome veterinarian at Keystone Downs. *Naw...not Kate, not this time, anyway.*

But Mike...oh yeah, he was a morning person. Always bright and alert and ready to roll, he was good at playing the innocent one—steering clear of other people's business. *Yeah, he's as innocent as a fox in a chicken coop.* Punch was having no trouble picturing him dialing his cell phone with an ornery grin on his lips the minute he pulled out of the driveway. *Payback's gonna be a bitch, buddy.*

Twinkling coaxing eyes greeted him, as Zoe looped her arm through his to escort him through the brickyard, where her father was starting up the forklift. She was an attractive woman, with full lips, pretty blue eyes, and dark blonde hair that drifted over her shoulders. She was a full-figured gal, an armful, and if he let her drag him into the relationship that she obviously desired, he was most certain that she would be a handful. Truth be told, Punch felt a tug of attraction to Zoe, but even though he was thirty-three, he wasn't ready for that heavy relationship stuff...nosiree.

It took some finagling, and some smooth talking, but he managed to escape the brickyard without a lifetime commitment, or bruising Zoe's feelings. Punch was a huge black man, broad shoulders, expansive chest, and arms that bulked out of the sleeves of his T-shirt. His sheer size was daunting, but he was nothing more than a tender-hearted, softy. And hurting Zoe's feelings was not Punch McMinn's style. It just wasn't in him— okay, especially with Zoe.

Sweat dribbled down his temples. Removing his Steelers ball cap, he swiped the sweat from his brow with his forearm, and then plopped the cap back on his head—crooked. The right side of his mouth sucked in with frustration, as he tapped the button for the air conditioning unit, but warm air poured from the vents. Damn, he meant to have that fixed last spring, but time got away from him, and now the blazing heat of summer was punishing him for his procrastination. B.O.B. was rapping on the radio that he could use a wish right now, and Punch was wishing that some damned cool air would miraculously blow through those freaking vents. Not happening.

The truck bumped and rattled over the old abandoned railroad tracks. No trains had traveled the tracks in over twenty years, but they remained as an annoying hump in the road that everyone forgot to slow down for until they found themselves bouncing on their seats, with their brain clattering inside their skull, while swearing at their car's suspension system. The tracks disappeared into the tall weeds and then over a rusted-out, boarded-up bridge that spanned the wide white water section of Reardon's Run.

Except the bumping and bouncing in the cab of his truck, and the slight rock of the heavy pallet piled with cement blocks was not his focus at the moment. The dysfunctional air conditioning unit, and Zoe Miller was all but forgotten when his gaze fell upon an older Honda Civic smashed against a tree. Ashen steam billowed out from under the hood that was curled almost to the cracked windshield, and the driver's side door hung open. Eyes narrowed and his brows pinched together, Punch slowed the truck to a stop and slid from the seat, measuring the wreck with caution.

As he slowly approached the vehicle, his eyes scanned the area. The dirt road wound into the hazy distance. The locust and maple trees spread their branches overhead, and the sun beat down on the brittle and singed tall grasses alongside the road. The air was tight and still in the cloying heat. The only sound was that of the car hissing, as the steam slithered like a phantom serpent into the air.

Punch peered into the car. The airbag slumped from the steering wheel. The interior was pristine, without any personal belongings lying on the seats or on the floor. He straightened with his hands on his hips, pushing his ball cap above his forehead.

"Hey!" Punch called out. Surely whoever wrecked the vehicle couldn't be very far. And then his gaze fell upon the tall bristly weeds across the roadway. They fell away as if someone had just tromped through toward the old bridge. Taking a braced breath, he followed the newly beaten trail. He could see the bridge in the short distance, and could hear the water running fast; slapping over the rocks in Reardon's Run.

Emerging from the brush he came to a dead stop, as if someone had splashed him in the face with a bucket of ice water. Narrowing his eyes, he slowly inched his way to the broken and rotted boards that blocked the entrance to the abandoned dilapidated bridge, where a hulk of a man stood on the other side of the rusted railing, with his eyes fixated on the rushing water far below. His huge wide hands clenched the rickety railing, sweat rippled down his reddened face. He seemed frozen, almost in shock, but he didn't look injured. Punch had to assume that he belonged to the wrecked Honda. He looked fraught and flushed and filled with angst.

Tentatively Punch climbed over the boards and quietly made his way toward the man desperately clinging to the railing on the very edge of the bridge. Punch wrinkled his nose and then he said, "Whatcha gonna do?"

Startled, the man's head jerked toward him. His eyes were as big as dinner plates, and the skin on his knuckles was so stretched that it looked like they could burst through at any second. Dripping sweat, his brows pinched in sudden irritation. "What's it look like?" He growled at the uninvited black man.

Pursing his lips, Punch raised his eyebrows at the man, and then he peered over the railing at the rushing white water, and the jagged rocks in the fast creek bed. Cocking his head, he expelled a long downward whistle. "It's a long way down there," he began. The man dared a glance at the water, and then thought better of it, rotating his eyes back toward Punch. "Ya know if you hit those rocks…it's gonna hurt like hell…while you're drowning, dude."

The man's mouth dropped open a bit, and then his brows formed a disparaging V between his eyes, "Good thing you're not a counselor, cuz you suck at this."

"At what?"

"At talking someone out of suicide." The man said.

"Ooh, you want me to talk you out of it?" Punch lifted a beefy shoulder, "I dunno, seems like you've got you're mind made up, right?" He said, as he leaned against a rusted flaking bracket, folding his arms over his wide chest.

The man took in a deep disgusted breath. He managed another peek at the water thrashing over the rocks. He groaned. "Why don't you leave me be?" He expelled a hopeless sigh, "I can't do anything right. I thought if I slammed my car hard enough into that tree—"

"Damned air bags." Punch interjected.

"Yeah…I tried to shoot myself yesterday, but I flinched." He turned his head so Punch could view a burned graze across his temple. Punch winced. The man expelled a miserable sigh. "So I figured I'd jump, and as you pointed out, either the rocks kill me or I'll drown."

"Well, it sounds like a plan." Punch said, slapping the man on the shoulder, hard. The man flinched, grasping the railing more tightly. Punch took several steps, and then hesitated, turning back toward him. "Is there anybody you'd like me to call? Family? Friends?" He asked.

The man sighed again, sadly shaking his head. "No…there's nobody."

Punch stepped toward him to extend his hand out to him, "My name's Punch McMinn. And you are?" The man looked at Punch as if his nose had just grown ten inches out of his face, and then he looked at his big hand. Punch shrugged, "I mean, I gotta know. So I can tell the police whose floating in the creek."

Apprehensively he let go of the railing, and extended his hand to him, "Earl…Earl Strom."

Punch half-smiled, "Nice knowing ya, Earl." And with that Punch grabbed the large man's hand and yanked him toward the inside of the railing. But Earl wasn't having it. He was big and he was strong. Wrestling against Punch's grip, he pulled him closer to the edge. The old railing groaned in distress, and the bolts that still barely held it in place jerked. Punch managed to wrap his arms around Earl's waist and heave him over the railing. The two enormous men crashed onto the floor of the bridge, but the boards that Punch fell against gave way and he fell through the rotted splintering wood.

CATCH UP WITH
CINDY McDONALD
AND
EVERYTHING UNBRIDLED AT:

www.cindymcwriter.com

**HEY,
YOU CAN VIEW BOOK TRAILERS
AT THE WEBSITE TOO!**

ABOUT THE AUTHOR

For twenty-six years my life whirled around a song and a dance: I was a professional dancer/choreographer for most of my adult life and never gave much thought to a writing career until 2005. Don't ask me what happened, but suddenly I felt drawn to my computer to write about things I have experienced (greatly exaggerated upon of course) with my husband's Thoroughbreds and the happenings at the racetrack.

Surprised? Why didn't I write about my experiences with dance? Eh, believe it or not life at the racetrack is more…racy. The drama is outrageous—not that dancers don't know how to create drama, believe me, they do but race trackers just seem to get more down and dirty with it which makes great story telling—great fiction.

I didn't start out writing books, The Unbridled Series started out as a TV drama, and the Hollywood readers loved the show. The problem was we just couldn't sell it. So one of the readers said to me, "Cindy, don't be stupid. Turn your scripts into a book series." and so I did!

In May of 2011 I took the big leap and exchanged my dancin' shoes for a lap top—I retired from dance. It was a scary proposition, I was terrified, but I had the full support of my husband, Saint Bill. It has been a huge change for me. I went from dancing hard five hours a night to sitting in front of a computer. I still work-out and I take my dog, Harvey, for a daily run. I have to or I'd be as big as a house. Do I miss dance? Sometimes I do. I miss my students. I miss choreographing musicals, but I love my books and I love sharing them with you.

To read excerpts from future books, view book trailers, and keep up with everything that is Unbridled, please visit Cindy's website at: www.cindymcwriter.com

Make a note: never agitate a madman. Successful Thoroughbred trainer Mike West just made that mistake, and he's gonna pay—more than he ever realized. But it's all in the family; his sister, Kate, has been the object of the madman's desire on the social network site "My Town". Her constant rejections have infuriated him. People who seem to be in his way start turning up dead, and he's got Kate and Mike next on his list! In the first book of The Unbridled Series Cindy McDonald introduces you to the world of Thoroughbred racing, while taking her cast of characters for a wild ride through a maniac's mind.

Here's what reviewers have been saying:

Collection of Thrills and Chills

What makes the person that everyone identifies as 'creep' burn forward? "Deadly.com" is a collection of stories, focusing on George Smuts, a man who everyone avoids in his strong presence at the local horse racing track. Lurching out using his own social networking site, he begins to make connections he and the women he lusts after may regret. With more stories surrounding the track, "Deadly.com" is a collection of thriller short stories compiled into one gripping narrative.

Reviewer: Midwest Book Reviews

A TOUCH OF EVIL

George is an absolutely horrible person. I hated him from the get go and, as I read, hungrily awaited his demise—he is the epitome of evil. I don't care if he is a little bit psycho or if his mother made him this way—EVIL. It amazes me that McDonald was able to evoke such strong, passionate feelings of abhorrence from me over a fictional character, but it is a testament of McDonald's writing ability! I liked the pacing of the story, especially as the action picks up almost as soon as the story begins. It was very well done.

Reviewer: A Book Vacation

YOU DON'T WANT TO MISS HOT COCO!!

HOT: Coco Beardmore.

NOT: Coco's calamities.

HOT: Mike's fantasies.

NOT: Mike's reality.

Let's face it, everyone knows a beautiful woman who can't walk through a room without tripping over the coffee table, or turning every situation into a total debacle. Trainers at Keystone Downs have been dumping Coco Beardmore and she's landed in Mike West's lap. The problem is that Coco is a complete klutz! Her driving skills are a real bang—into Mike's horse trailer. Her sultry seduction will set the room on fire—the kitchen that is.

What's more are her Thoroughbreds: one flips while being saddled, one sits down like a dog in the starting gate, and then there's the one that's an escape artist. It's enough to drive a normally calm and collected Mike West to the very edge.

Mike's not the only one having problems with women. His father Eric has taken on more than he can chew, and he's about to get spit out by two women: One that he's in love with and one that thinks he's in love with her.

Oh yeah, things are hot around Westwood Thoroughbred Farm… and someone's about to get burned!

FUNNY AND HEART WARMING

Hot Coco is not just a steamy romance novel - but is funny, and heart warming, and really touches the heart. I love that this story takes place on a Thoroughbred farm. I love horses! I love Cindy McDonald's writing style which is fast, easy, and keeps you turning the pages to find out what happens next. The characters are believable and totally relatable. This book is the second book in the series. I haven't read the first book, but Hot Coco was good as a stand-alone. I plan to down load the first book in the series - and anything else Cindy McDonald puts out.

Reviewer: Jennifer Golub
Waiting for Sunday to Drown

UNEXPECTEDLY INSIGHTFUL

The book is fun, quirky, unexpectedly insightful (especially when you consider how Margie is treated because of her looks), funny (the bits with Coco are very funny), and warm. A truly good read, I give this book 4 out of 5 clouds.

Reviewer: Mindy Wall
Books, Books, and More Books